The Three Lives of Cate Kay

THE THREE LIVES OF CATE KAY

KATE FAGAN

THORNDIKE PRESS
A part of Gale, a Cengage Company

Copyright © 2025 by Kate Fagan.
Thorndike Press, a part of Gale, a Cengage Company.

ALL RIGHTS RESERVED

This book is a work of fiction. Any references to historical events, real people, or real places are used fictitiously. Other names, characters, places, and events are products of the author's imagination, and any resemblance to actual events or places or persons, living or dead, is entirely coincidental.

Thorndike Press® Large Print Top Shelf.
The text of this Large Print edition is unabridged.
Other aspects of the book may vary from the original edition.
Set in 16 pt. Plantin.

> **LIBRARY OF CONGRESS CIP DATA ON FILE.**
> **CATALOGUING IN PUBLICATION FOR THIS BOOK**
> **IS AVAILABLE FROM THE LIBRARY OF CONGRESS.**
>
> ISBN-13: 978-1-4205-2060-6 (hardcover alk. paper)

Published in 2025 by arrangement with Atria Books, a division of Simon & Schuster, Inc.

For Kathryn

For Kathryn

FOREWORD

February 27, 2014
Charleston, SC

About a year ago, a FedEx package landed on the porch of my home in Charleston, South Carolina. I don't get much personal mail, a consequence of multiple name changes, I guess.

A saga, actually — my name. I've had too many. I was born Anne Marie Callahan, but growing up, my best friend called me Annie. A few years later, I legally changed it to Cass Ford. Then, I published under the pseudonym Cate Kay. I wish it was simpler. Trust me, I do. Creating a new life (or lives) takes a devastating amount of energy, of imagination. And I've missed hearing my real name.

So, this FedEx box was an anomaly in my world. I glanced at the return address: Mason, Cowell & Collins, the law firm of Sidney Collins. Not only was Sidney the architect of my literary empire — manager of all things Cate Kay — she was also my ex-girlfriend.

I carefully opened the box. Inside was a stack of blue binders and sitting atop was a handwritten note from Sidney. She explained that by sending over all this paperwork, she was relinquishing control of my Cate Kay business dealings and righting past wrongs. (One of them, anyway.) What she couldn't have known was that this package, and her letter, set in motion a series of events that would forever alter the trajectory of my life.

She signed it: *I'll think of you — fondly. xo, Sidney.*

I was glad her tone was conciliatory. Sidney is not someone I want as an enemy. Or, really, as a friend. No relationship at all was my preference. We hadn't spoken in seven years — not since the long-ago night when I'd frantically taken a red-eye from Los Angeles to the apartment the two of us shared in Harlem.

But let's not get started down that path; let's stick with the binders.

Before I closed the last one, I caught sight of a second handwritten note on crisp stationery. The letterhead belonged to my literary agent, Melody Huber. The note was addressed to me, dated four years prior. I read Melody's words with great curiosity. She gently invited me to come out of hiding. Her idea: a memoir. She'd suggested this previously, no doubt, but the message never reached me. The success was mine, she wrote, even if the name was not.

I looked at her words. A memoir? I liked the thought of it — of freeing myself. But I knew it couldn't happen. A book would require me to confront my past, which I was committed to not doing. Maybe someday I would feel differently, but not anytime soon.

Then, a week later, everything changed. And Melody's words had stayed with me:

You could tell everyone the full story, every little detail.

My mind kept catching on that last clause: *every little detail*. I remembered so many. They flooded my mind, a kaleidoscope — of sunbeams, of brown hair tossed, us blowing into our hands for warmth. Maybe Melody was right? Maybe it was time. I called her office and for the first time ever, heard the voice of the woman who had plucked my manuscript from the slush pile all those years ago.

I told Melody on that first phone call that I couldn't be the only one to tell this story.

I'd lived inside it for far too long. Better to throw open the windows and tell it from every angle, for better or worse. Within these pages, you will read about what happened from my perspective, as well as from those whose stories collided with my own.

And that is how we got here, to this book you now hold in your hands. My memoir, but more than that — it is a monument. Carved from a mass of bad decisions and selfishness and, it pains me to admit, cruelty. And yet, I want you to love me anyway. No use pretending otherwise. I'm done hiding who I am. My mind's long been divided on the question of my goodness — and now here you are, the deciding vote.

I ask only that you read with an open heart.

Annie Callahan
aka Cass Ford
aka Cate Kay

CHAPTER 1

ANNE MARIE CALLAHAN

1991
Bolton Landing

My earliest memory is wearing my favorite shirt for an entire month of summer without my mom noticing. I was going into fourth grade and my mom figured since I was now in the public school system, she could leave me alone if needed. There was even a socially acceptable term for it — a latchkey kid.

We lived in an apartment building that was once a motel. The kitchen consisted of a toaster oven and microwave, and Mom worked cleaning rooms at the Chateau, this fancy resort on the shore of Lake George. This was upstate New York, very upstate, with a complicated mix of blue-collar locals and vacationing urban elite. My mom and I, as you've probably guessed, were the former.

My mom had lots of formers. Former jobs, former friends, former boyfriends, a former husband, who was also my dad but had never been anything of the kind. Apparently, he'd wanted to make her an honest woman (eye roll), but then a few months after I was born decided he didn't want honesty *that bad.*

The shirt, my *Tom and Jerry* shirt, was white with a cartoon graphic on the front. I loved it. It fit so perfectly that I forgot I was wearing it, which was all I wanted from clothing — for it to disappear. When I wore other shirts, I was always tugging and rearranging, but not this one. Plus, I was wearing it the day this story started — the day I caught the sickness of wanting to eat the world.

It was a summer day, so hot, humid. I was bored, and movement combated the languor of those endless afternoons, so I flipped the kickstand on my bike and pedaled to town, which was overrun with vacationers, as I knew it would be. Even as a kid I could spot city money. It was the way they held their car keys, like they were a sexy prop, and how they tenderly touched the edges of their sunglasses. I'd sit on the bench outside the ice cream shop and watch.

That afternoon, the sky was mostly a crisp blue with an occasional fluffy white cloud. Like I imagine wallpaper of the sky would look. I was sitting on my bench when I looked up into an aqua sea. I visualized myself piercing through the blue, then through the ozone into outer space, then I imagined piercing outer space into — what? The thought triggered a moment of pure derealization — that's what I might call it now — and my body filled with this odd sensation of *the universe is all there is; there's nothing outside the universe.* This wasn't a feeling of atheism; it wasn't about heaven; the closest descriptor is uncanny, if uncanny was on steroids.

I sat on the bench, unmoving, until the feeling disappeared, which didn't take long. It's not a feeling you can hold on to, nor one you can forget. When I rode home that afternoon, it felt like I'd swallowed a black hole and it demanded filling, somehow.

My mom came home late that night. I was in my creaky twin bed beneath the window, wide-awake. I'd been listening intently for her while watching the raindrops on the glass; the beads of liquid kept merging before I was prepared to lose them.

I heard shoes on gravel, always the first sound of my mom's return. Then, a few seconds later, her key in the door, a slow turn because she thought I was already asleep — that is, if she was thinking about me at all, which she probably wasn't. As she was hanging her bag, I said, *Hi Mom*. I wanted her to know I was still awake. Maybe she'd consider feeling badly that I'd been alone for so long in the dark, desperately needing a hug.

"Oh, hi, honey," she said sweetly, which is how I knew she'd stopped for many glasses of white wine at the bar on her walk home. Her keys hit the counter, then she came to my bed and kneeled, wrapping her arms around me. I melted, forgetting for a moment the untethering of the day, swimming happily in her warmth. She was beautiful. Light brown hair and a long neck, high cheekbones, her sly smile. People said we looked alike, which thrilled and terrified me; I watched how men looked at her — like they were hungry.

When she hugged me, I forgot everything else and briefly lived in an alternate universe: safety, love, time — so much time together. But most of all, I enjoyed the feeling that I mattered to her, that she'd choose me before anything else.

Abruptly, she pulled back, but kept her hands on my shoulders. She narrowed her eyes, sniffed. "How many days in a row have you been wearing this shirt?" She began aggressively and clumsily tugging the shirt over my head. The warm moment I'd been living inside imploded.

Most of my childhood memories are hazy — the consistency of dreams. Except this one. This one stuns me with its vividness: the colors of my *Tom and Jerry* shirt; the wallpaper sky before the universe rewired my brain; the presence, and sudden withdrawing, of my mom's love. In the many years since, I've thought of this memory as a blueprint that might help explain the life I constructed afterward.

"Goddamnit, Anne Marie," my mom growled. I can still hear the slight slurring as she pulled off my favorite shirt. The fabric left my brown hair frizzy with static.

I never wore the shirt again.

Anne Marie. She always said it like a scold, and I could never hear it as anything else. Not once did it sound like a warm breeze, or an open door — always, it was clipped and fierce as if warning me against another wrong step. I don't know how the name sounds to others who share it; hopefully they wear it well. On me it was a penance, and growing up, I was always thinking of how to rid myself of it.

The first opportunity came later that summer when I noticed a flyer for a free theater camp run by the high school. I told myself it was a sign from the universe. And I was right. That's where I met my best friend,

Amanda, which taught me to always be on the lookout for signs, both tangible and metaphorical.

By high school, I had spent happy months as Scarlett (*Gone with the Wind*), as Rosalind (*As You Like It*), as Blanche (*A Streetcar Named Desire*), but my first gentle step toward a different life came when Amanda started calling me Annie.

CHAPTER 2

ANNIE

1991
Bolton Landing

What you need to know about me and Amanda is that no friendship like ours had ever existed. We basically redefined the medium, elevated it to an art form. Seriously, that's how we felt. We were like all young people in that way, in full belief that we were revolutionizing the human experience. Those older models, all failures; let us show you how real living is done!

I'll set the stage: 1991. Summer in upstate New York. Small-town theater camp, opening morning. I was standing in line for registration. The girl in front of me was wearing jelly sandals. I complimented them. She made eye contact and said, "Thank you for noticing," which awed me — the self-possession of it. We were nine years old.

Amanda Kent, ladies and gentlemen.

Turns out, Amanda's home life was only slightly better than mine. Her mom had died giving birth to her little sister, Kerri, and her dad spent all his waking hours beneath the hoods of cars, running a repair shop in the next town over. Amanda and her dad, they got along fine, but he was more like an uncle than a dad, and so she was especially close with Kerri, who was four years younger. The two were different in almost every way: Kerri had light hair and loved playing with dolls; Amanda was essentially the person Van Morrison is singing about in "Brown Eyed Girl."

One other thing to know about Amanda: She loved clothes. When we were young, she'd want me to come over and play dress-up. Her dad had kept all her mom's old things in a box in the hallway closet — clothes and makeup and other stuff grown-up women cared about, like pantyhose, which seemed to me like a form of medieval torture. Dress-up wasn't really my thing. But I'd bring a book and sit cross-legged on the carpet at the foot of Amanda's bed. She never minded my indifference; she really just wanted an audience.

She would disappear into the hallway bathroom, and I'd read a few pages. Then she'd present herself in the doorway, do a quick spin and a catwalk, strutting in and out of the room. Nothing subtle in her performance. Clothes made sense on her, which one afternoon she explained was the entire point of fashion.

It was seventh grade, I think. I had just reacted to one of her combinations. She'd taken these fake pearls that had seemed so First Lady–ish at Goodwill and paired them with a cheap black leather jacket. The high-low of it was really working.

"That just looks right on you," is what I said.

"Good." She flopped onto the bed. "I was reading the latest issue of *Cosmo* and there was this part about how to understand your style and the advice was basically like 'make your outside match how you feel on the inside' and that makes so much sense to me."

Matching your outside to your insides seemed like no small feat, so I said, "Isn't that, like, asking a lot of clothes?"

Amanda was still flat on the bed; she made a small *huh?* sound. I closed my eyes and tried examining my insides, but could only feel my brain, its whirlpool of thoughts. What type of clothes matched that?

I tried again: "I mean, does anyone even know how they feel on the inside?"

A second later, a pillow came crashing into my head.

"Come on, let's go to Goodwill," she said. "We'll try to match *your* insides to your outside."

She was off the bed already, grabbing for my hand, and her hand was never something I turned down.

After wandering the thrift store for a few minutes, something caught Amanda's eye, and she beelined to the front counter. Behind the cashier were these bags mounted to the wall. Mostly purses. And purses, if you hadn't already guessed, didn't interest me. But then Amanda was pointing at this canvas tote bag with the words THE STRAND NYC: 18 MILES OF BOOKS printed on the front.

"Can we see that one?" she said.

"We get a bunch every summer," the woman said, handing it over. "People from the city bring them up — use 'em to lug stuff up here, then we see 'em in here before they go back."

"Oh yes, this is so you," Amanda was saying, holding it up to my shoulder.

"Why's it me?"

"You're all quick-witted and *rawr*" — here she snarled like a big cat — "like a

New Yorker . . . plus you love books!" She shrugged and added, "Makes perfect sense."

But when she went to hand it to me, I stepped back. "Nah, it's not quite right," I said, even though it was right. She was absolutely right. But I didn't have any money right then — not even the dollar the bag cost.

She looked at me for a moment and said, "Well, okay, I'll buy it." She knew every layer of what had just happened, of why I'd said no. She knew, in that split second, that if she said "Is it about money?" that my next two thoughts would be "I wish my mom remembered my allowance," followed closely by "Why doesn't she love me more?" And that was not a healthy thought train.

Amanda had four quarters in her pocket. She fished out the coins and dropped them into the woman's cupped hand.

On the way out, I walked ahead, bowing my head and digging my hands into my pockets. Amanda caught up and draped her arm around my shoulders. She held the bag out to me, like, *obviously I got this for you,* but I told her it was okay, that she should keep it. She squinted, trying again to read my fine print.

"Okay, Annie-baby," she said after a moment, slinging the bag over her other shoulder. "But know that every time I use it, I'm gonna think of you."

She used that Strand bag so much. Even though the bag was totally Amanda's, I always thought of it as mine. So years later, when I found it in the back of my car, it almost felt right for me to have it.

I have it still.

CHAPTER 3

ANNIE

1995
Bolton Landing

Amanda was seventy-three days older than me. She would hit milestones first, report back from the front lines. I was a professional overthinker, so it was a relief to have her beta-test life, work out the kinks before I arrived. For example, I might have thought turning thirteen was a big deal. We were so excited for that second syllable!

"You don't feel different at all?" I asked. We were in her garage looking for a Nerf football (don't ask). She paused, closed her eyes. An internal scan was being performed. A few seconds later, eyes still closed, she said, "No, not at all. Feels like twelve years old plus a day."

I grabbed her shoulders and groaned, "We're going to be kids forever!"

"For-ev-er," she said like a robot.

Even then we were impatient for the freedoms of adulthood. Then finally, finally, Amanda's sixteenth birthday arrived. We scheduled her driver's test for that same day — no time to waste. It was early spring, the first warm day, and the testing location was down the street from her dad's garage, so he drove us over, kissed her on the forehead and wished her luck, then walked back to work. Once he was gone, she turned to me and made her eyes big, jingled the keys like *it's happening.*

I said, "Oh my god Amanda, nail this thing, okay?"

"Hand-eye coordination, spatial relationships — c'mon, it's a done deal," she said. She was a confident person. But like all confident people, it was only about 87 percent authentic. Doubt just lived on the outskirts of town instead of in the center, like it does for everyone else.

"Amanda Kent?" called a man, clipboard in hand, walking toward us. I mouthed *Good luck* and jogged across the street to wait, impatiently. I hopped onto the low-slung cobblestone wall in front of the Methodist church, my feet skimming the ground. In my pocket were watermelon Jolly Ranchers — the only flavor worth eating — and I popped one in my mouth. I loved using the sticky candy as cement between my upper and lower molars. Sometimes it really felt like my teeth were glued together.

I was still doing this an hour later when Amanda, behind the wheel of her dad's truck, reappeared up the road with the test supervisor in the passenger seat. That faded blue truck. I'd always loved the sight of it, a dopamine release — Amanda, close.

I watched as she came more into focus, then finally I could see her clearly through the windshield. She grinned and waved, and mentally I was telling her to *Please stop;* what if he flunked her now for carelessness?

But he didn't. She parked the car, shook the man's hand — this felt *very* adult — and strode across the street, perched next to me on the wall. She tossed the keys a few inches in the air, caught them. She was really loving this moment. A performance, but also not, which was the best kind.

"Let's go to Tommy's party tonight," she said, eyebrows raised. Amanda knew that Tommy — aka Mr. High School Quarterback — was into her, but she said it was my imagination. I wasn't a fan.

Going to a party was not exactly what I wanted to do with our new freedom, but Amanda's excitement was contagious. I touched my pocket, felt the bulky outline of the mixtape I'd made as a congratulations present. I'd titled it "Merry Go Freedom." I'd even made cover art from construction paper. My plan for the night had been us going for a drive, listening through together. I had wanted to watch her reaction to each song. But I guess we could do that tomorrow.

"I'm in," I said, dropping off the wall and crossing the street. "Chauffeur me."

She jogged to catch up, called out, "Get ready at my place?" I didn't answer. The question was rhetorical: her closet was way better.

We spent most of the party on the deck at Tommy's house, in and out of groups, laughing and talking. Amanda was drinking; I was taking imaginary sips from an empty red Solo cup, really practicing my stagecraft with each movement. At the end of the night, while watching Amanda take shot number I don't know what, I suddenly realized we didn't have a ride home, that she was our driver. I was mad at myself; logistics were usually my specialty. I walked into the kitchen and pulled her into the hallway.

"Hi," I said.

"Hi." She hugged me. "It's a good day."

"It has definitely been a good day," I said. "But we have a problem."

"Rut-ro," she said, frowning. On the scale of one to wasted, she appeared to be about a seven. Right then, Tommy walked past, grabbing my arm and pulling me away, spinning me back into the kitchen where suddenly I was facing a group of classmates. "Truth or dare?" one of them asked, and since I liked an audience, I was instantly invested. "Dare," I said, moving with the crowd back to the deck. I was out there for a few minutes — the dare was embarrassingly lame — before I remembered Amanda and leaned back inside to catch her eye. She was gone.

I was chill about it at first. But when she wasn't in the first-floor bathroom or the living room, a sense of urgency arrived. I darted upstairs, opening each closed door and finding empty, dark rooms, until there was only one left at the end of the hall. I pushed through, stumbling into a bathroom, and there was Amanda, sitting with her back against the tub. She looked at me, shrugged, then leaned over and vomited into the toilet.

I was relieved, actually. I'd expected to find her with Tommy.

"Sorry," she said, spitting into the bowl. "Not very attractive."

I knelt, collected her hair into a ponytail.

"That last shot Tommy gave me," she slurred. "Not a good idea."

"Let's get out of here," I said. "Can you walk?"

She nodded. I gripped her hand as we walked down the stairs and out to the car. I helped her into the passenger seat, then reached across and pulled on her seat belt.

I climbed behind the wheel and grabbed it with both hands, steadied myself. "Okay, yeah, I can do this," I said aloud, looking over at Amanda: her eyes were closed, her head against the doorframe. Maybe she was more of an eight or nine on the wasted scale.

I'd hidden the mixtape in the console for the drive home, and now I retrieved it, popping the cassette into the deck and cranking the volume.

Tommy lived on the opposite side of the lake, so it was a long ride home. I happily discovered that driving wasn't that difficult. Her dad's truck was an automatic, thankfully. I stayed between the lines and went the speed limit and braked fully for every stop sign. The night was unusually bright, with yellow moonlight bouncing off the lake, and I felt like I'd springboarded into adulthood.

And with adult feelings, too, courtesy of my mixtape. For the third song, which is obviously where the best track on a mixtape goes, I'd chosen the newest from Sarah McLachlan. The song churned up everything I felt about Amanda. An ethereal blend of desire and devotion, of joy and melancholy. A nearly lethal cocktail.

When the opening chords began, I reached for the tape deck, almost hit fast-forward — to save me from myself. But I didn't. Instead, I turned up the volume even higher, let the music own me. Let it build and build and build, a symphony of waves crashing inside me, as our goddess Sarah reached the verse that ended with letting yourself believe.

The crazy thing was, I wasn't sure if the song was me speaking to Amanda, or the other way around. Or maybe some combination of both. When the song ended, it felt like the truck was still radiating with its afterglow. It was in this moment that Amanda, face still pressed against the window, mumbled something.

My eyes darted over. "What was that?" I asked. But she just shook her head and burrowed deeper into the door. I reached over and let my fingers rest on her knuckles, left them there for a full count of one, then quickly brought my hand back to the wheel.

For the next seventy-two days, we borrowed that blue truck whenever we could. Then, on the night of my sixteenth birthday, tipsy and without a present, my mom offered up the keys to the 1991 red Honda Civic that my older cousin had rebuilt and left parked at our apartment complex. He'd taken the train down to the city after high school and hadn't come back, not for the car or anything else.

We nicknamed our new ride "Brando" because it had seen better days. Fresh off the lot, it must have been a sexy little thing, but its luster had faded: chipped paint, dented bumper, worn leather. And not an original flaw, but certainly our favorite: a cracked rearview mirror, as if the gods were tired of Amanda seeing her own beauty. Or the cars behind her.

It happened junior year, one brutally cold morning. We dashed out to the car during free period for a quick spin, huddling inside and blowing on our hands. Brando was covered in the thinnest dusting of snow, which I enjoyed — made me feel like we were in a cave.

Amanda loved driving, so she was behind the wheel, and she tried the engine, but it didn't turn over. A few seconds later, she tried again and the car roared to life — she immediately cranked the heat. I was reaching for the vents, ready for their warm air. Then I heard her shriek and my head whipped to the left: she was gripping the rearview mirror, her body lifted slightly to see herself more clearly in the shattered reflection.

"What — the — fuck," she said, drawing out each word.

I gave her an *um, please explain* look, and in response, she slowly turned the mirror toward me, pointing at the crack. A little yelp escaped my lips. A cracked mirror! It felt dramatic and purposeful, like in a movie when someone breaks into a house but takes nothing except a single piece of art.

"Well, the gods have spoken," I said.

"Did someone do this?" She was squinting and looking around, even though the windows were covered with snow.

"Yeah, it was probably Vanessa," I said. "You know how jealous she is of you and how skilled she is at intimate yet profound gestures . . ." I shot her one of my favorite looks — one raised eyebrow, a mock glower — before continuing, "Amanda, some*one* didn't do this, some*thing* did — the cold."

"Annie-baby," she said, her tone pseudo-serious, "you need to stop reading so many books. All that knowledge is making you too smart for me."

"Never." I stretched the word out for a couple extra beats because I wanted to bathe in her compliment. I'd had this idea I was special, destined for big things, and yet a voice in the back of my mind would every so often terrorize me, sending a thought burning through my psyche: *It's all a lie; you're nobody and you'll always be nobody.* Amanda's compliments helped smother those wildfires.

"Just the cold is what you're saying — for sure?"

"Just the cold," I said. "Although, I'm really in love with the idea of someone breaking into Brando and doing no other damage than smashing the rearview mirror to deliver the ultimate mindfuck."

She grinned. "Kinda genius really."

"I'd want to be friends with them," I said.

"But not, like, too good of friends?" Amanda frowned.

"Oh, no, no, no, just casual friends — like maybe every other week for pizza kind of friends?" I liked this repartee of ours, especially when it blended with an acknowledgment of the depth of our relationship. I didn't need other friends like I needed her.

"Or even every third week?"

"Monthly, let's say." I winked at her, hoping the wink was cool and not cheesy, and it must have been because her hand left the mirror and rested on my cheek for a moment. The warmth of it was nice, and we looked at each other for a few seconds before she broke away and said, "Less than two years, then . . ."

"The future." I gestured as if imagining the words on a marquee, blocking them out: *The Future, starring Anne Marie Callahan and Amanda Kent.* We'd talked about it all the time, nonstop, our plan to drive Brando to Los Angeles after graduation. The pitch, in our minds, was unique and unbeatable: We'd be a package deal, Amanda playing the brunette who turns heads but still possesses fantastic comedic timing, me the quirky sidekick who has acting chops and secretly steals all the scenes.

I hadn't mentioned to Amanda that the big black hole inside me ached for more, and that my brain was constantly spinning ideas for satisfying it. Not once had I told her about my disloyal thoughts: that maybe I would need more than best-friend comedies. That maybe I would need a prestigious solo career, then maybe I would write and produce, then direct, then whatever achievement level came after that, no doubt; an endless pursuit of the golden key that would unlock the highest version of life and make me feel whole.

Listening to my brain was exhausting. Only now do I question my brain's wisdom, wonder if it's actually working in my best interest. But back then? A thought was reality. And how do you tell your best friend that your brain imagines outgrowing them — that it's not even a choice; it's a necessity.

CHAPTER 4

KERRI KENT

1999
Bolton Landing

Amanda was my idol. I loved everything about her. Once, as a middle schooler, I was sitting on the sofa in our living room watching her get ready to leave. She bent down to put on her Converse high-tops and she, like, lost her balance. But she did so in a way that was so charming, kind of hopping on her right foot a few times then steadying herself, arms out like wings. Her eyes flew to me, and she made the funniest face.
"How is that possible?" I asked.
"How is what possible?" She was kneeling now, tying her sneaker.
"That, what just happened, this . . . you making everything look so cool?"
She smiled, came over and kissed me hard on the forehead. I mean, picture that. I never stood a chance! I was her little sister,

already predisposed to want her love. Then she made it so easy with the warmth of her.

We went through only one frosty period, and that was after her junior prom. I'd stayed up late and watched from my window as she and Annie arrived home. Some boy dropped them off at the bottom of the driveway. The way they walked up to the house, like they were magnets trying not to merge, it set my brain bouncing. A few minutes later when I heard Annie go into the bathroom, I darted into Amanda's room and closed the door.

"Um, hi?" she said, not unkindly.

"Are you in love with Annie?" I blurted out.

She covered her ears with her hands and yelled, "Ahhhhhh! Why does everyone think that?"

I looked at her, like, *uh, what is happening here?* Maybe I should have thought the whole thing through, but Amanda usually loved my little sisterness, my curiosity, how I demanded answers about the important things like whether to chew gum while kissing. This didn't seem all that different to me.

"No, I'm not," she said. "I mean, yes, of course I love her, but not like you're asking." She paused, slowly tossed her hair to the other side. "That is what you're asking, right?"

I nodded once.

"It's just, no," she said, and it seemed to pain her, the saying of it. "I'm not — it's not like that for me."

"Is it like that for Annie?"

"We're not talking about this," she said, bending over and taking off her heels. "Please, just go back to bed."

CHAPTER 5

ANNIE

1999
Bolton Landing

The night before junior prom, my mom and I were sitting in the green plastic Adirondack chairs that were outside our apartment.

As the seasons changed, I used those chairs to gauge how close we were to warm weather. In the winter, even though they were tucked beneath an overhang, the wind whipped the snow and stacked it high on the seats and armrests. There was always one week when the chairs became wet from pools of melted snow, and each night I'd get impatient and wipe them down with paper towels. I'd just done that and was sitting, tucked into a ball, my oversized gray hoodie stretched over my knees, when I spotted my mom walking down the street. Even in the dark, I knew it was her; I'd know her silhouette anywhere. I'd spent my childhood looking for her.

"Hi," I said softly as she approached.

"Hi, you." She dropped herself into the chair next to me before I could stop her, then she yelped as the cold wetness soaked her jeans. I cursed the water, prayed it wouldn't keep her from staying. "Damn," she said without getting up, and I slowly exhaled.

"How was your day?" I asked, glancing over. Her head was back against the chair, her eyes closed. The light — a soft glow from the main office — was beautiful in that Americana way, glancing just so off her cheekbones. Amanda and I had become obsessed with movies, and sometimes I pretended I was inside one.

Her eyes popped open and mine darted away.

"So," she said. "How old do I look?"

Even then, I knew this question had nothing to do with me. I pinned my chin to my knees and looked out across the wet grass, then the street beyond. The lake was just a football field away, maybe less, and you could always sense it. Ominous, in some ways, mystical, in others, creating miles of open space, the air above the water waiting for me to fill it, but I didn't know how, or with what words.

"I had the craziest day," my mom said eventually. When she didn't continue, I looked at her and she was glaring. "Well, do you care to hear . . . *Anne Marie?*"

My arms tensed around my knees. "Mmhmm," was all I could manage.

"I walked in on these dykes in bed," she said, then shivered dramatically before continuing. "Guess they didn't hear me knocking." A beat later, she added, "It was sickening."

I froze, eyes fixed on the air above the lake. Why had she told me this story? Because Amanda and I were so close? The chemistry between us seemed palpable (to me), so maybe she had sensed something. Then again, I had thought my yearning for my mom's love was unmistakable, yet she'd never seemed to pick up on that.

I didn't respond, and after a minute she stood and said, "I just don't know about you, Anne Marie." I flinched as she went inside, closing the door harder than necessary.

The next night, the high school gymnasium was dripping with yellow streamers. Amanda spent the evening dancing with her date, Ben, who was named prom king, which we laughed about for weeks — the cliché of it all. My date's name was Joe, and that seemed to represent him perfectly.

After the final note of some slow dance

song, Amanda grabbed me by the arm, pausing to look at Joe and asking — the exchange ironic to Amanda, earnest to Joe — "May I borrow your lady for a moment?" Joe stammered out a yeah, and Amanda curtsied before whisking me to the back corner of the gym, an area cast in shadow by the closed bleachers.

"I thought you'd never," I whispered to her, smiling. "Those fucking idiots."

"I'm just imagining we're starring in a movie," she said. "Isn't that what you're doing?"

"Um, yeah, of course," I said. "The kind of blockbuster script that features two hours of awkward shuffling and a cast of boys who can barely communicate. It's a great movie, really."

"Agreed. I mean, maybe we even bring" — she whipped her head back to the dance floor — "Joe? Is it Joe? Maybe we bring him with us to LA."

"I would absolutely *love* a cross-country drive with Joe."

She wrapped me in a hug and squeezed, and I knew exactly why. She was in love with us. With our wit, our back-and-forth, our inside jokes — with everything that made us, us.

I pulled my head away so I could see her fully. "I need to ask you a question."

"Well now's the perfect time, obviously," she said, laughing, her eyes gleaming in that way that makes you know, for sure, that the person in front of you isn't thinking about anything else. Our eyes looked like this a lot when we were talking to each other.

"So, this is a for-real question, okay? Smart comebacks are not needed."

She nodded her head seriously and, unable to help herself, added a salute. I frowned.

"Got it, got it." She took a step back, did a full-body shake, then said, "Okay, I'm ready now," and the crazy thing — I could see she was.

If I'd learned anything from my mom, beyond ordering salad dressing on the side and dipping your fork in it to save calories, it was how to dance around the truth. To be clear, my mom didn't dance; I did. My mom shot words straight like arrows, often pointed at my heart. But me, I buried my feelings alive, just smothered them down. Then came Amanda; she seemed honored when I shared fragments of my inner chaos.

"So, we have our plan to drive to LA after graduation, right? And we're going to audition together and, of course, we're gonna make it big starring in best-friend comedies."

Amanda waited patiently for me to get to my point.

"Okay," I continued. "My question is: Do you ever think about what comes after that?"

Forever practicing her comedic timing, Amanda waited a moment, then said, "You want to know if I think about what comes after graduating high school, driving with my best friend" — she paused and winked at me — "that's *you,* FYI, to Los Angeles, finding a place to live, and making it big in the movie business?"

Okay, when you put it like that, I thought. God, did I have a dysfunctional brain — one that couldn't relax and unspooled miles and miles of scenarios and hopes and dreams, never ending. *Big, juicy thoughts,* Amanda sometimes called them. When my attention drifted away, she'd say, "Are you busy inside that brain of yours, with all those big, juicy thoughts?" I'd picture a fruit snack. Gushers, with a burst of juice inside. Tagline: "Don't let anyone treat you like a regular fruit snack. You are a Gusher."

"Buuuut," she continued, "I'm sensing that what you're really saying is that *you* have a game plan for after ALL OF THAT." Amanda did not seem angered by this; she seemed tickled. She radiated amusement: *Annie being Annie.*

"What's been going on up there?" She tapped her temple.

And there I was again, being the scary version of me. I hadn't achieved anything and already wanted more. What was the word for that? Insatiable, perhaps. But that was so earthly, calling to mind sex, or food. What I craved was cosmic bigness.

Across the gym, the DJ started a new song, and the first beats had sent everyone into a tizzy, the girls grabbing their friends and streaking to the dance floor. But God bless Amanda, she was locked on me. "Tell me about your grand plan for us," she said.

"I've been thinking about after all that — after we leave here and star in movies together, I mean. I've been thinking about how I'll need to break off and do these prestige dramas — I have to win an Oscar — and then maybe write or produce and direct."

Amanda tilted her head, so slightly, and her lips collected at the corners. She gave a little shake, then stopped. A word popped into my mind: *rueful*. Was I using it correctly? Sadness mixed with pity is what I was seeing. I repeated the word to myself, hoping I'd remember it later.

"Are you saying my dreams aren't dreamy enough? Annie Callahan, I've never met anybody who dreams as hard as you do."

What I remember about this moment is

the way she said my name. She said it like it was a small animal she needed to keep safe, and that's how I felt, deep down. Her understanding of me caused a pang, the sudden pounding of a drum, to reverberate once through my chest.

I stepped toward Amanda and grabbed her hand, brought it to my lips, kissed the top of it softly and said, "You know, I really, really love you." My eyes were open containers, and I made room inside them for her to pour herself into. I inhaled deeply, exhaled like *there, the unsaid thing has been said.*

Unmistakably, I was telling her something a little different from anything we'd said before, and she understood because a subtle ripple of dread passed through her eyes.

Then she was tenderly collecting my hands in hers and pressing them against my heart as if to give me back to myself. The gesture was loving and kind and undeniable.

My head dropped and I toed the yellow streamer at my feet and the music came back into surround sound, the opening beats of the next song: "No Scrubs" by TLC — an irresistible bop that Amanda was always losing her mind over, and there she was losing it again, grabbing my hand and dragging me back to the dance floor.

■ ■ ■ ■

A few weeks later Amanda and I were killing time by walking back and forth through town. Suddenly she veered off the main sidewalk toward the lake, calling over her shoulder for me to follow her. Soon we were standing on a spongy dock, which seemed on its way to disintegrating into the water. Amanda spun herself in a full circle, said, "I know it's somewhere around here," then put her hands on her hips and looked at me.

"The boat," she said, "the one I told you about?" This was ringing some faraway bell for me, and I squinted as if maybe that would help me remember.

Amanda and I had never been on the lake. We'd been *in* the lake, of course, but never *on* it. Some of the richer kids at the high school, their families had boats, but even if we sometimes partied with them, we never got invitations to the fancier things. The inevitable clash of class was too anxiety-inducing for the rich kids. Probably even more so for their parents.

"Yeah," I snapped my fingers. "Yeah, yeah, yeah — the one your dad was building or something?"

"Yup," she said, spinning now toward the

thin trees and grass that surrounded the cabins. "I think I see it."

We dragged the boat into the water, and after much debate, Amanda and I sat facing each other, figuring that would keep the boat better balanced. We started rowing but paused every few minutes to acknowledge how awkward we were.

"What are we even doing?" Amanda laughed.

"It's possible, maybe, that boat life isn't our thing," I said, shrugging.

"What would you say is our thing? Other than theater, obviously."

"We have many things," I said. "We have, for example, Sarah McLachlan."

"Ah, yes, good one," she said. "We are definitely Sarah experts. Oh, and, we also have clothes — though that's more my thing, I guess."

"Still counts," I said, feeling generous.

"Hmm, well, we're also into movies." She tilted her head to the sky. A moment later, a thought seemed to tickle her, and she added, "Let's not forget — each other."

"Awww," I said, putting my hand over my heart. "So cute."

"Yes, I am adorable," she said. "And — oh, oh, oh . . . we know pies!"

An unexpected addition to the list, but

accurate. We did consider ourselves pie connoisseurs, specifically of key lime pie, which was Amanda's favorite dessert and my second-favorite. (Team Oatmeal Raisin: the underdog's cookie of choice.) In the land of apples, loving key lime was contrarian, signaling us as independent thinkers. Also, it felt exotic.

After school dances, we'd stop by the local diner to get a slice, then walk with the little Styrofoam box and plastic fork to a bench around the corner. We savored each bite. Whenever either of us showed up holding a fork and pie box, the other was obliged to say, "That better not be some apple bullshit."

That first time being out on the lake was magic. The colors felt make-believe — the blue of the sky, the navy of the water, the green of the trees and mountainside.

Amanda must have been thinking something similar because she said, "I kind of get it now," and when I looked at her for more, she said, leaning her head back, "how obsessed some people are with nature." When her eyes came level, we looked at each other for a few seconds before we both started laughing and couldn't stop until we got hit with some other boat's wake. Startled, we both grabbed for the sides.

We drifted for a while, the sun making its

way toward the horizon. We didn't say much to each other. Just took it all in, letting the day stretch before us. Then the yellow of the sun was colliding with the mountain and the sky was filling with pink and purple. As the colors were spreading, Amanda said, "Wow, this sunset." It was pretty, so I said, "I know."

And a minute or two later, Amanda, who as far as I knew had never watched a sunset in her life, said, "New York doesn't get enough credit for its sunsets," as if she'd spent a lifetime assessing their quality and ranking in the public consciousness.

I giggled and said, "Are you a sunset expert now?"

She shot me a look — *fuck off* — then said, "Kerri goes out to watch the sunset every Sunday night, did you know that? And almost every time she comes back inside and says, 'New York has the best sunsets.' It's like a family joke at this point."

Family. Suddenly I felt like crying but didn't want to ruin the otherwise perfect day.

CHAPTER 6

RYAN CHANNING

October 2006
Los Angeles

I've gotten too comfortable being Ry Channing, the movie star. It's easy to be her. She is confident, poised, on top of the world. When I'm her, I feel those things. But Ry Channing isn't a person; she's a persona. And deep down I know these feelings are fleeting, a little dangerous. They camouflage a truth: that I feel best about myself when pretending to be someone else.

The real me is just a shy girl from Lawrence, Kansas, who loved wandering the museum as a kid. Who still hates reading aloud (but loves reading silently) because the syllables play hopscotch in her mind and messing up is so embarrassing. Who has undiagnosed dyslexia, itself a cruel word. *Dicklexia* is how I can't help but pronounce it. And, particularly relevant to this endeavor, the girl who began mimicking Hemingway's writing after reading *The Sun Also Rises* in high school. Simple sentences comfort me. Apologies in advance. I'll try to break free a few times.

Don't get me wrong, I also love the spotlight.

We contain multitudes.

When "Cate Kay" asked me to do this, I wondered which me to bring to the page. Shiny and glossy me, or braces and lisp me? My manager said she could have someone write my part if I wanted. That I could approve it after. But I found myself rejecting the idea as soon as she was forming the words. If I kept investing in the Ry Channing facade, soon I'd have to live inside it full-time. And that's no place you want to be. Trust me.

So, here we go. No ghostwriter. All me.

I remember the moment it all started. I was in my trailer between scenes, which could sometimes take hours, when my agent called. His name was Matt. He told me he was having a book couriered to me.

"Give it a read," he said. "The writing's solid, but the story's great and apparently the author, Cate Kay, is using a pseudonym and literally nobody knows who she is; it's causing quite the tizzy. Everyone's on fire for it — they're billing it as 'the beach-read version of Cormac McCarthy's *The Road*.' I think you should play Samantha." I told him that tagline was the most Hollywood thing I'd ever heard, but that it sounded fantastic.

A moment later I heard a quick rap on my trailer door. A courier. He was scrawny, wearing an unclipped bike helmet. I glanced past him and around the set — we were in some small town outside Atlanta — and wondered where exactly the set security was. Not protecting me, that much was clear. I was, after all, fifth on the call sheet.

The movie that would change everything, *Beneath the Same Moon,* was three months from release. I was still that actor you had to snap your fingers and think hard to place. *Oh yeah, the best friend from that one TV show.* Then *Same Moon* came out. And after that it was shrieking fans and Oscar parties and endless scripts and me mostly taking refuge inside my Los Feliz bungalow.

But before that, in this small window of time, I was standing in the doorway of my trailer accepting a brown bag. I pulled out a hardcover book. *The Very Last.* That now-iconic cover: half-black, half-tan, the crumbling subway sign. What I liked about the cover is that it was clearly about something loud, but seemed to suggest it was going to tell you this loud story in a tender, nuanced way. And in stark lettering at the bottom, the author's name. Just who was this Cate Kay?

I opened the book, read the jacket copy:

"The world will remember their names."

2000: Samantha Park and Jeremiah Douglas are best friends with a shared dream, to take TV news by storm. They've come to love working the graveyard shift together at American News Corporation. When the city explodes around them in a nuclear blast, they are the station's only survivors. And so it falls to them to broadcast from the rubble, to tell the world the city's story.

2025: Persephone Park never knew her mother. To everyone else Samantha Park is a fallen hero, to Persephone she is a black hole that cannot be filled. When Persephone, lost and drifting despite her inherited fame, hears of The Core she abandons her comfortable life immediately. Drawn to the site of her mother's legend, she will join the group of outcasts seeking to build a life where the city used to stand . . .

I glanced to where the author photo and bio would be. No picture, just one sentence: *This is Cate Kay's debut novel.* I flopped onto my trailer's couch and started reading.

CHAPTER 1

The Big Apple

Samantha Park loved the nooks and crannies of New York, how the city forced you to make yourself small while simultaneously promising grandiosity. In this way, New York was a perfect match for a woman who thought frequently about how humble she would remain once she became great. Fame corrupted people, Samantha knew, but she was going to be different. She would remain kind and generous; she would pause for fans, always, no matter how busy she was. That was the deal she had made with the universe.

On the evening before the world changed, she and Jeremiah were walking the last blocks toward work as daylight escaped the city. Samantha looked up and saw the faded orange of the New York City sunset. Most nights, she was taken aback by the beauty of the city's final hour of daylight. People didn't give Manhattan enough credit for its sunsets, she thought, but didn't say. Just last week, Jeremiah had pointed out that she said this, or something like it, most nights as they walked to work.

"Do I?" she had said, genuinely surprised. But each day since, she had noticed the thought as it crossed her mind.

Jeremiah noticed her small smile; he leaned into her for warmth and said, "What is it?" They were California kids who couldn't get used to the cold weather.

"Nothing," she said.

"Let me guess, the light in New York doesn't get enough credit?"

"But it doesn't!" Samantha hooked her arm through Jeremiah's, shoving him playfully.

"I think you give it plenty of credit," he said. "Every night, really. Endless amounts of credit."

She looked at Jeremiah now, as they waited at a crosswalk. He brought his coffee to his lips and blew into the small opening in the lid, glancing over at her as he did. Then he smiled a big cheesy grin as they walked the final few steps into the ANC studios — a shiny glass building on the bank of the East River . . .

By the time the assistant director called me to my next scene, I'd read two-thirds of

The Very Last. I thought Matt had it wrong: I shouldn't play Samantha Park. I should play Persephone, her daughter. I was intrigued by Samantha, her endless ambition and brave (or reckless) choices in the aftermath of the explosion. But the world Persephone inhabited lit up all my senses. She was such a perfectly drawn character. The mommy issues, the need to prove something to herself, the curiosity and wandering. I'd loved the cartoon *Tom and Jerry* as a kid. And there was Persephone pulling on a well-worn sweatshirt of the animated duo that I could imagine myself having worn. Plus, I was intrigued by the setting of The Core.

I've heard journalists talk about the benefit of assignments in far-flung locales. How the story can write itself because of the unique backdrop. It can be like that for an actor. Find a character set in a distinct, interesting world and you, as an actor, can often find clearer, simpler ways to reflect their humanity. That's how it had been for me, anyway. The reason my performance in *Moon* went to a new level was because of the intensity of the concept. Rogue scientists, far outside the system, testing potential cures on patients. What my role as Patient Zero didn't need was for me to escalate and escalate and turn the thing into a B horror movie. Rather, I needed calm and discipline in the face of madness.

I saw a similar opportunity in *The Very Last*. Seven Oscars and $4 billion in box office later* and I think we can agree I was right about something.

"Persephone," I told Matt, calling on my way to set. "Not Samantha. I want Persephone."

"So, you like the book?" He seemed pleased with himself.

"The Core, it's the richest setting I've read in a while," I said.

"I agree, and it's so visual, too: the rotting wooden boats they take through the water, the contamination zone, and that last subway stop. Damn —"

"Exactly why it needs to be Persephone," I interrupted.

*Note from Cate: I'm feeling squeamish. Boasting (and about money!) is antithetical to my Irish Catholic upbringing — even when it's someone else doing the boasting. But I understand the need to highlight the books and movies, put them in proper context. So I offer here a clinical timeline for *The Very Last* trilogy: Book one was released in 2006, book two in 2009, and book three in 2011. The movies were each a year after: 2007, 2010, and 2012, respectively. Deep breaths. Okay, let us continue.

"But Samantha, she's absolutely the lead in this," he said. I knew he was thinking about how much more money the lead would make and how much bigger his cut would be as a result, but he would pretend it was about *the creative*. "Imagine the set building for her world, traversing a simmering and smoking Manhattan with a camera. I mean, this is a character obviously motivated by ambition but hailed worldwide as a martyr. What a mindfuck. It's so, so . . . allegorical."

He loved using fancy words and acting like a movie's social commentary mattered to him.

"It's certainly parabolic," I said. I wanted him to know I could play ball.

"But . . . ?"

"I want Persephone." To his credit, he didn't hesitate, just said, "On it."

And that was the first conversation I had about *The Very Last*. That one book would become a trilogy of books and a trilogy of films, and would break box-office records. But for me, the legacy of this cultural phenomenon had nothing to do with A-list or popularity or numbers. Whenever this project comes up, I think immediately of one thing. Or, rather, one person: Cass Ford, known to the world as Cate Kay.

And how she broke my heart.

CHAPTER 7

ANNIE

1999
Bolton Landing

The fall of our senior year I went to see Mr. Riley, who ran the theater department. I didn't tell Amanda. His office looked very much like how I imagined a Broadway theater office to be: small, just enough space for a half-sized desk and chair, black walls covered with photographs and theater posters.

"Anne Marie, what a surprise," Mr. Riley said, looking up when I knocked on the black door, which I did even though it was open. He was a burly man with a well-kept salt-and-pepper beard and rarely seen without an ascot.

"I was hoping you'd have a minute to talk," I said, noticing a folded metal chair leaning against the wall. Before he could answer, I was leaning toward it, the movement spurring him to action. "Oh, absolutely," and then he was up and unfolding the chair and making room. "Should I find another chair for Amanda?"

"Just me," I said, and the assumption I'd be with Amanda snipped a loose thread in my mind and I began pulling at it: Did he only think of me in proximity to Amanda? What did he think of me independent of her?

"Of course, of course." He seemed flustered. This must not happen often, a student stopping by, I realized. After the flurry of movement, he landed back in his chair with a quick exhale as if to reset the energy. He slapped his hands on his knees and said, "All right, whatcha got for me?" His casual way of interacting with students, as if we were real people, had made me like him right from the beginning, starting way back at that first summer camp.

"Have you picked the play yet?"

"Nope, not decided," he said, reaching to touch a stack of papers on his desk. "But don't worry, I'm only considering plays with at least two strong lead roles, and who share the stage plenty." He winked at me, adding, "I'm going to play to our strengths."

"That's actually why I'm here," I said. "I was hoping you would consider doing something different this year." My backpack was at my feet, and I unzipped it and pulled out a small paperback. *Twelfth Night.* I'd read it over the summer, and I wanted to play Viola, a young woman who is shipwrecked and disguises herself as a man, Cesario. Back then I told myself that I was just shaking things up. But now I see that I was putting a wedge between me and Amanda while asking the universe a question: Am I good enough?

I believed I was willing to accept the outcome.

Mr. Riley reached for the book. "A classic, and some fantastic roles in this," he said, fanning the pages. He thumped the book once against his open palm. "Can I ask why?" His eyes met mine.

Hmmm, what to say.

"I think it's about my comfort zone," I said, "and wanting to get outside it."

At this he nodded approvingly, as if I'd said something mature, which pleased me because that was my goal. I thought saying the precise truth, *"I want to see who you'll cast as Viola, me or Amanda,"* would not be received as well.

"I think that's really smart," he said. "Thanks for bringing this to me." Then he held up the copy of *Twelfth Night* and said, "Mind if I borrow this and reacquaint myself with the material?"

"No, yeah, keep it," I said.

Our exchange hadn't taken very long, certainly not long enough to warrant unfolding the chair, and so maybe to prolong the meeting and justify us both sitting in his office, Mr. Riley asked, "Have you thought about what you're going to do after graduation? You have a lot of talent, shame to see it go to waste."

That phrase, "go to waste," conjured images of an oozing garbage can. I planned to let nothing I possessed, figuratively or otherwise, go to waste. I planned to maximize every drop.

"Not sure yet," I said. "But once I do, I'll let you know."

This seemed to satisfy his desire to be seen as a mentor, help me *be all I could be,* or whatever, and he slapped his hands on his knees and popped himself to standing, signaling the end of our meeting.

"I know you haven't always had it easy," he said, now hovering in the doorway. I'd grabbed my backpack and had paused outside the office. This was the first time he'd ever, even opaquely, mentioned all the theater trips I couldn't pay for. I gripped my bag tighter and smashed my lips together. Maybe he could read the energy shift; he quickly steered away: "Anyway, just wanted you to know it's been lovely seeing you"

— he opened his palm and gestured from my head to my toes — "come into your own."

I thanked him and was gone.

Mr. Riley picked *Twelfth Night* as the fall play. Amanda was briefly distraught over the selection — *"Now this pits us against each other!"* — and was momentarily confused by my immediate acceptance and calm defense of his choice. *"It'll be good for us, no matter who gets the part of Viola,"* I had said. But it was not good for us.

The afternoon the roles were posted — computer paper thumbtacked to corkboard — I met Amanda and we looked together. Kids were streaming behind us. She ran her pointer finger down the list, taking it all in, pausing first by her name, then by mine. I was leaning in, following with my eyes, but I'd snuck a peek a few minutes earlier, then peeled off to use the restroom and gather myself before meeting Amanda to pretend to look for the first time.

Amanda was cast as Viola/Cesario; I was given Olivia. Both had plenty of stage time. Olivia was just far less interesting of a character to me. Did I think the casting was backward? Yes. Amanda was so what-you-see-is-what-you-get, and I didn't believe her during auditions, dressed up as Cesario, a girl playing a girl playing a boy. She played it sloppy, for the laughs, but after the roles were announced, I realized maybe I'd gone too deep into the role, really embodying this gender switch in a way Viola might not have, and Shakespeare never intended.

Inside that restroom stall, I'd sat on the toilet and controlled the burning behind my eyes, swallowing the tears. I wondered where those tears went. Were they dripping down behind my cheekbones? Tears were meant to drip. I opened my eyes as wide as possible and let them dry out. I felt like my soul had been stabbed: I wasn't as good as I thought, for sure, and maybe I wasn't good at all.

Maybe Amanda had deemed me her sidekick out of pity because that was all she could imagine for me. Thoughts collided and blended, then separated, then blended again until they formed one long string: You're not good, you're a joke, this dream is absurd, you will crash and burn and end up cleaning rooms at the Chateau and living in a dirty one-bedroom and STOP STOP STOP. I'd stood, lifted my chin to the ceiling, and imagined the thoughts spilling out the back of my head along with the tears.

"My Olivia!" Amanda shrieked after she'd

spotted both our names. She wrapped me in a hug. "The dynamic duo does it again."

It struck me that she'd never considered I'd get Viola.

CHAPTER 8

RYAN

December 2006
Los Angeles

I had loved my life in Kansas. I had a brother and sister I adored, and parents who showered us in love. Every year, I would star in the school play with my closest friends. My family would be there smiling and clapping and filling my arms with flowers. And I thought that if I made it in Hollywood, it would be like that except on a grander scale. Bliss, I assumed. More love, more joy, more friends, more warm parties.

When I hit it big, the isolation is what surprised me. Cut off from all the small joys that give a day meaning. The morning hellos at the local coffee shop. The chat with the bartender at your favorite restaurant. Even the perfunctory, but not unkind, midwestern nod while passing someone on the street.

Right after I got the part of Persephone,

which was just two weeks before *Beneath the Same Moon*'s release in theaters, is a time I think back on fondly. My bungalow in Los Feliz was slate gray with red shutters and this cute backyard with a sliver of a pool. I lived three blocks from a coffee shop called Gem. Any morning I wasn't on set, I'd walk down there in my Vans and cutoffs, a Kansas Jayhawks sweatshirt, my hair in a messy bun.

Sarah, the young woman who worked mornings at the shop, had gone to KU for undergrad. We'd talk basketball. She knew more than I did. But I could hang, the broad strokes, Roy Williams, Paul Pierce, the NCAA tournament. My childhood home was literally around the corner from the house of James Naismith, the game's inventor.

But back to Sarah. She had these hazel eyes and strong arms. When I was there, she'd ignore all the other drinks she had to make. Sometimes, another barista would come over and start making them, and she'd just calmly step to the side, still chatting with me.

Talking to Sarah was an interesting experience for me. All my life, I'd been told I was beautiful. Auburn hair, a dusting of freckles, blue eyes that apparently were set just far enough apart to make my face interesting instead of basic. I was also just above average height for a woman: five six. Casting directors loved that I would "fit" with pretty much any male actor. But standing near Sarah, I wondered what she saw. I hoped that whatever look seemed so appealing to men and casting directors was also appealing to her.

Ahead of *Moon*'s release, we had a slew of meetings about the promotional tour. My team had set up as many of them as possible at my place. One morning, midweek, I headed down to Gem before the first of those meetings. I'm not embarrassed to admit I curated my outfit specifically for Sarah. A vintage 1988 NCAA championship tee, black mesh trucker hat worn backward. Today was the day.

Gem was on a little side street with ivy climbing the front. I popped inside and was relieved to see Sarah at the espresso machine, focused on steaming milk. I ordered, then went around to the side of the bar and waited for her attention.

Eventually she looked up, saw me, looked down, then quickly looked back up and smirked. She was wearing a tank top; I admired the smoothness of her tan skin. She finished the drink she was working on, placed it on the counter, turned her body toward me.

"Sarah," I said. I nodded in a mock-official way. My attempt at a suave greeting.

"Why hello, Ryan Channing, how is your morning?" I liked how she said my full name. It reminded me of being a kid, which was all good memories for me. Almost everyone in Hollywood calls me "Ry." And the poster of every movie I did used "Ry Channing" because — and here I'm directly quoting the publicity folks — "Ryan is a boy's name, but Ry is just mysterious enough to be perfect."

"Better, now," I said, then let that hang there. Did I mean seeing her, did I mean the fresh coffee in my hand, or did I mean both? That was for her to decide.

"Same," she said, and winked. She had game. She'd already walked me home once the week before. That day, when we got to my back gate, she had said goodbye, then walked backward for a few steps, holding eye contact. There was no denying her intention. The look said: *Ball's in your court*.

Challenge accepted. I am a woman of action. At least I try to be.

I stepped toward her, took a sip of my coffee, tilted my head just so. Then I said, "What do you think about getting a drink with me next Saturday?"

I was proud of myself for not using any of my crutch words: *maybe, I don't know, so.*

Just straightforward, clear, concise, honest. A good beginning to whatever this might be. I did not possess shame about liking women, but I had negotiated (with myself) a clear boundary: never let it spill over and affect my work. Which made Sarah perfect for me.

"Yes," she said without hesitation. "Anywhere, anytime."

I floated the three blocks back to my house. My mood wasn't even dampened when I saw two cars in the driveway, reminding me of the morning meeting about the impending publicity tour I didn't want to go on. My manager, Janie, had my key, so she and agent-man Matt, along with Maxine, the studio's head of PR, were already in my living room.

My green velvet couch faced two overstuffed chairs, a circular glass coffee table between. I called out a chipper "Hiya folks!" then went to the kitchen for a glass of water. I was thinking about Sarah and how she'd said *anywhere, anytime* with a hint of menace. Like I had challenged her to a fight. But said in such a way that it conveyed desire. I was getting wet replaying the exchange.

Still on my dopamine high, I carried my water to one of the overstuffed chairs. Janie was next to me. Matt and Maxine were across from us on the couch. I remember this meeting vividly; it's when Hollywood took its first chunk out of me. Maxine had a harsh black bob and was wearing a power skirt and white blouse, which seemed an appropriate outfit for someone so disillusioned with humanity. I already expected the worst of Maxine.

"What's the agenda, team?" I asked, optimistic for an efficient meeting. In other words: show me the itinerary, prep me for media, then get the fuck out of here and let me get back to fantasizing about Sarah.

"Really only one item," said Maxine, and that's when I first noticed a little unease. But only from Janie. Maxine, she'd crushed a thousand souls by that point. Matt thought of me as an asset, not a human. Janie, though, she knew how I felt about her. She was ten years older than me (so thirty-five), and we both came from college towns in the Midwest. I thought of her like a big sister and valued her opinion. She was squirmy in her chair.

I leaned forward, offered a drawn out *okaaay*.

"Listen, Ry," said Maxine. Of course it would be Maxine, who knew me the least, who would deliver this news. "We had a big all-hands meeting at the studio yesterday, looking over the projected revenue for *Moon,* and we all feel we need to play one more card, just tip things in our favor that last little bit."

"Big all-hands meeting?" I repeated. Not actually a question. More like a right-click and highlight. So much about this sentence annoyed me. The phrase "all-hands" for starters. The idea that during a week I'd kept clear for meetings, they had the "big" one without me. And finally, just the general fuckery in the movie business about flexing power based on who gets invited to which meetings and who gets iced out and told their fate later.

One thing Hollywood teaches you is how to micromanage everything. Another is how to collect power through small gestures. Such as who makes the call and who receives it. Entire movies have lived and died on such frivolousness. People say power is intoxicating; you say you'll be the first to stay sober. But let me tell you, everyone gets drunk. So, when you wonder about our sanity, way out here in these Hollywood Hills, remember that we've all pretty much lost it.

I glanced at Janie. She held up her hands as if to say she was innocent in the matter. Over to Matt, who gave a head tilt back to Maxine, his gesture urging me to listen to what she was saying. The glass of water was on the arm of the chair. I took a big gulp.

"All right, just hit me with it." I was acting poised and confident, but I was scared to hear what she would say. People pleasing was an affliction I hadn't conquered. (Still haven't.) Whatever she was going to ask, a request handed down by the studio honchos, I could already feel the habitual "Okay, I'll do it" crawling its way up my throat.

"This is a onetime thing, but we think you and Johnny should be seen out together ahead of next Friday's premiere . . ."

Maxine kept talking, explaining the "strategy," which was that I spend a glamorous (read: scandalous) night with my *Moon* costar, Johnny Muir. The goal was to give people the impression that we were more than costars. Not a long-term relationship, she was saying, nothing like that. Just enough to get us the kind of free press that a darker, nuanced movie like *Moon* really needed in this difficult market.

I laughed. I couldn't help it. I was picturing the studio "all-hands" meeting, with all the bigwigs around a conference table, really plumbing creative depths, filling up the whiteboard, no dumb idea here folks, finally, finally landing on the revolutionary idea that I should . . . pretend to fuck my costar.

Maxine looked taken aback at my laughter. Which made sense, as it was also surprising to me. Matt set his jaw and gave me a death stare. Janie reached over and put her hand on my forearm. I flinched.

She knew. Janie knew I didn't want to pretend-date my costars. But also, more intimately, she knew I didn't want to date men at all. Was her tender touch an apology? I slowly removed my arm. She looked hurt. Not my fault, or my problem, I tried telling myself. But a second later, I reached over and squeezed her hand to reassure her.

"One night?" I heard myself saying.

Maxine leaned back on the sofa, crossed her arms, and said, "Absolutely. That's it. Just a little game to get us on the front pages. It's such a beautiful, stunning movie, and I hate that we must do things like this, but sometimes we do."

Make it make sense! I wanted to scream. But Johnny was fine. He was funny and cute in his shaggy, hangdog way. And whatever, it was one night, some stupid headlines.

"We have you booked at U-Turn, Marcelo Gutierrez's new place, and someone from the team is going to call in the tip ahead of time, to give us maximum bang for the buck."

"I've heard good things about U-Turn" is what, Lord help me, I said next.

I looked at Janie and she seemed relieved. She patted my hand and mouthed, *It's going to be fine,* and I figured it probably would.

I'd signed with Janie Johnson after reading an article on her. In it, she talked about bringing her midwestern values to Hollywood. Our first coffee meeting, she ordered a mocha and a croissant, and I wanted to hug her. It was at that same meeting that I told her I dated women, but that nobody else could know. Being the poster child for anything, that couldn't be me.

Standing in my doorway later that morning, Janie said, "You got this, RyRy. When we get the power, we make the rules, okay?"

CHAPTER 9

ANNIE

2000
Bolton Landing

We graduated in June, but Amanda didn't want to leave before Kerri's birthday. Probably the last one she'd get to attend for a long while, she reasoned, and so I agreed. Amanda had told Kerri about our plan to move to Hollywood — she didn't keep secrets from her little sister.* Kerri worshiped Amanda, and only more so after hearing about our big dreams. She said that once we got settled maybe she'd come visit.

So, we waited out the summer, and into

*****Note from Cate:** Amanda and I never said this aloud, but I think we didn't tell anyone else about our plans because we didn't want the added pressure. If, a year later, we came slinking home, we wanted the chance to rewrite the story about where we'd gone, what we'd done, and why we were back.

the fall, before leaving. That last week before, Amanda and I started packing the car for Los Angeles. Just little things we didn't want to forget, like our sleeping bags, some clothes, and favorite books — items impervious to heat or cold — and each time we tucked something away in Brando's trunk, we'd look at each other and smile maniacally. Time moves slowly when you're that age, and it felt like we'd been talking about this for a hundred years. Now, finally, we were doing it.

Although that same awful thing was still happening to me — had been happening, for many months: I had started imagining life without Amanda.

It was one of those things I could never figure out how to talk about, even in an abstract way. But it was always there, in every exchange over the last year when we talked about the drive west, and our future. As we stashed things in Brando's trunk, a thread of panic wrapped around the moment.

(*How, how, how would I ever fall in love with someone else with her around?* was what the voice I tried to mute was wondering inside my head.)

One Saturday afternoon, we each put a few sweaters in the back of the car. The trunk was slowly filling, but you'd be surprised how much room a Civic has. We were standing shoulder to shoulder staring at our growing collection and there it was — this *need* to create distance between us. I said, "Did you ever have a different plan?"

I wanted to introduce the idea of us apart, make her wonder why I was thinking about it. But also, I made my voice as soft and warm as possible, so maybe she'd ignore the depth of the question and accept it at face value. My hands were overhead, gripping the edge of the trunk, leaning into it. She was just a few inches to my right, and she squinted at me, and I could tell she was deciding how to take my question. How did I want her to take it? Maybe I wanted her to storm away with a *fuck you, Annie,* but also, maybe I didn't.

"A different plan?" she said tentatively, like she was wary of what I was getting at. "You know this has always been my plan."

"Okay," I said, injecting my voice with a quality that was meant to convey the opposite. *Yeah, sure,* was my tone. But right after, I regretted it — why was I picking this fight just before we were supposed to leave?

"What's that supposed to mean?" Amanda had, per usual, read me correctly.

"Absolutely nothing," I said, and this time my voice sounded sincere because it was. She still seemed cautious of me and was leaning slightly away when I looked at her, her left eye squinting like, *What are you playing at?* But I plowed through the weird energy I'd created, slamming the lid of the trunk down, and wrapping my arm around her shoulder, pulling her close to me.

"You ready for this adventure?" I thought I was going to say "our" — *our adventure* — but I just couldn't bring the word to my lips.

CHAPTER 10

RYAN

December 2006
Los Angeles

My date with Sarah was the night after U-Turn. I got to the restaurant, Jack's, a little early and snagged two seats at the end of the bar, my favorite place to sit. My back was to the rest of the restaurant, facing the bartender — it was like having your own private show. Sarah seemed like a sit-at-the-bar kind of person. Casual yet intimate. The place had a nice buzz going. Not so loud you couldn't hear each other talk, which I tested when the bartender leaned over and asked me what I'd like. I felt good about the vibe she was walking into.

"I'm actually waiting for —" Damn, what should I say? My mind spun through my options and their consequences for what I hoped was only the briefest of pauses. "Someone," is what I finished with, then wondered if I'd failed a test of my own making. What would Sarah have said if the roles were reversed? I imagined, given my read on her, that she wouldn't care one bit who knew she was going on a date with a woman. I wished I could be that person.

"But I'd love a seltzer with lime for now," I added. The bartender gave a rap of his knuckles on the wood and went to grab a glass, but then some realization seemed to descend on him. He turned back to me and asked, "Are you waiting for Sarah?"

Hearing her name on his lips at first filled me with a feeling of warmth, like we all knew each other and had created this beautiful bubble of intimacy. I think I smiled a little, kind of shyly, which in a second would feel embarrassing. "I *am* waiting for Sarah," I said.

"Then, oh, shit." He did a quick spin like he was trying to remember where he put something, finally landing on the register and a little pile of notes. Mostly receipts tucked to the side. Over his shoulder he said, "She dropped something off earlier and told me to give it to you." Then he shuffled through the small papers, found what he was looking for, and brought it to me.

It was a white envelope. Inside was a folded newspaper clipping. I was bewildered as I pulled it out. My first thought was that I didn't want to get ink all over my fingers. But that disappeared as I realized it was one of the paparazzi photos of me and Johnny from the night before. The caption read: "New It Couple? Ry Channing and Johnny Muir, who star together in the upcoming *Beneath the Same Moon,* seen cozying up at hot spot U-Turn."

Before I noticed the little note written by Sarah in the margin, I had a moment of pure appreciation for how easily the studio, and Maxine, had scored hundreds of thousands in free advertising for the movie. No wonder shit like this was always in the publicity plans. Then I saw it — in pencil — in the right column: *"Ryan — I'm sure there's an interesting story behind all of this, but where I am in my life, I just can't have the drama. Sarah."*

The bartender, mixing someone else's drink, was pretending not to watch me read the note. I quickly folded it back up and stuffed it in my pocket. Suddenly, and irrationally, it felt like everyone at the bar was looking at me.

Maybe I'd dodged a bullet with Sarah, I told myself as I walked the two blocks home. She was probably possessive and controlling and would want me to be out way sooner than I was ready. But there was also this nagging sensation beneath my hurt. That she'd articulated how I felt. Doing that stunt with Johnny was sick on some level. Of course, of course, *of course* she should run far away from the insanity of the business I was in.

But, I guess, when you get abruptly dumped for being an actor willing to do anything for fame, the best thing to do is double down, go further into the belly of the beast. So, I curled up with *The Very Last*. I'd read the book twice and was in the process of going through it again with sticky notes. It was early winter and filming was starting in two months — February, in Charleston. In a town where turning a book into a movie frequently takes a decade (or many decades), this thing had gone from hot property to production in just seven months.

People were obsessed with the futuristic world Cate Kay had imagined. The story had a little bit of everything. A gay female lead, unheard of back then, as well as a Black costar. Bonkers box-office potential plus Oscars equaled studio executives losing their minds. But beyond all that, what really caused unprecedented attention was the author's anonymity. She was nowhere to be found. I'd lost count of the number of newspaper and magazine stories with the headline

WHO IS CATE KAY? above a shadowy illustration. A proper mystery, as the Brits would say. Everyone was stunned. Who, in fame-hungry America, doesn't come drink from the hose when beckoned?

This last part is what I kept coming back to, lying in bed that night. I'd just been rejected for my own shameless pursuit of fame. Before the U-Turn affair, I'd run through all manner of thought experiments. What might I be willing to do for a breakthrough role? Not a whole lot, I surmised. But Hollywood was a sneaky bastard, coming in through the side door and snatching my robe when I least expected it. But this Cate Kay person, she chose to remain fully clothed.

I fanned through the pages, thinking about the story the author had written and wondering what clues existed about who she (or he?) might be. Tough, considering it toggled between two time periods: Manhattan, in the hours before and after a nuclear attack, and 2025, when the island was no longer habitable.

But then I remembered one little scene:

> They met sophomore year of high school, working on the school newspaper. Two years later — Samantha always laughed thinking about this — and Jeremiah still

didn't know she was gay. Samantha didn't know how Jeremiah could not know. She had introduced Jeremiah to her girlfriend at least half a dozen times, always when her girlfriend would stop by with dinner while Samantha and Jeremiah laid out the paper.

One night toward the end of the year, Jeremiah leaned in to kiss Samantha. Their two chairs were nestled into one computer station. All night, Jeremiah had been noticing each time their knees touched, pinned together as Samantha reached to point at an image on the screen. Then she did it once more, crossing into his space to type out a word, and he reached his right hand to her cheek, then slid his hand to her chin. She had kissed him back for a long second. She remembered the moment so clearly: his strong hands on her skin. He was so beautiful and smart and kind.

Safe, that's what she remembered feeling. But then she pulled away and looked at him. He was smiling dreamily, his eyes still closed.

"Wait," she said. "But you've met my girlfriend?"

"Your girlfriend?" His eyes flew open. He seemed genuinely surprised.

"Yes, the girl who has stopped by this

whole year?" Samantha leaned back to fully take in Jeremiah, to see if he was feigning ignorance. He was not.

A second later, he started laughing uncontrollably. When he regained his composure, he explained how growing up he'd spent most afternoons with his grandma, who had her "girlfriends" over every Thursday to play spades. He'd just always assumed "girlfriend" meant "friend who was a girl."

"That is," he said, leaning back, "until this very moment."

They had laughed for a long time that night. And still, years later, if someone used the term "girlfriend" to describe their friend who happened to be a girl, Jeremiah would flash Samantha a look that translated to *See?*

A straight woman did not write that scene. That came from lived experience. I tossed the book onto the bed and grabbed my phone. I had a fleeting pang of guilt about calling in the middle of the night, but not enough to stop myself. It rang five times before Matt answered with a groggy hello.

"Yes, I know what time it is," I jumped in, though I didn't. Late, I was sure, but how late? I craned my neck to look at the clock on my bedside table, was stunned to see it was one forty-five in the morning. Midnight would have been my guess. I continued, "I'm lying here reading *The Very Last* again, and I need you to do something for me, and no it can't wait until the morning."

It absolutely could have waited until the morning. But I'd just possibly located a fellow queer in the wild, and I wanted to bring her in for questioning. Also, I was young and thrilled at my ability to manipulate a (supposedly) powerful man. My ego had been stepped on earlier that evening; it needed rebuilding.

"I want to meet Cate Kay," I said, and it sounded reasonable coming out of my mouth, but the request was met by a long stretch of silence. So long that I asked Matt if he was still there. In response, he sighed.

"What's this about?" he asked.

"It's not about anything. If I'm going to play Persephone properly, I need to meet the author." As I said this, I thought it sounded like solid, professional reasoning. I almost convinced myself that was why I wanted to meet her. Not because I wanted someone gay in my life, a consolation prize for my disappointing evening, certainly not that.

"Ry, nobody knows who she is."

"Come on, Matt, somebody knows who she is."

"Okay, one person knows who she is, but this isn't one of those vanity pseudonym situations where everyone at the publishing house actually knows who the real author is and it's all just a ploy for media attention. Literally everyone, even her editor — even her *agent* — is in the dark."

Matt seemed particularly appalled that the agent — the agent! — would not be in the loop. A level of secrecy he could not fathom. In his world, he was the secret keeper, not the other way around. What I heard, though, was that one person knew who Cate Kay was. As I mentioned earlier, casting directors swooned over my auburn hair and wide-set blue eyes. Imagine how frequently I got what I wanted, how addictive that could become.

"So, talk to the one person who knows her," I said.

"Have you ever considered maybe there's a reason she wants to be anonymous? That she isn't going to come running just because Hollywood is calling?"

What Matt didn't understand was that I had a personal connection to Cate Kay. I could sense it. No doubt Matt, red-blooded Matt from the Upper East Side of Manhattan, graduate of the finest private schools, could not picture a world in which I desired anyone but the finest male specimen. Telling Matt the truth was a nonstarter, which meant I couldn't trust him to approach Cate Kay with the necessary passion. I would need to do that myself.

"I'm going to write a personal letter to Cate Kay," I said. "And you're going to give it to the one person who knows who she is."

"I'll do my best." He sounded done with the conversation, which really irked me. Earlier that week, he had sat in my living room and asked me to do something slimy, not even admitting that it was.

"Did I deliver at U-Turn — for *Moon?*" I asked. But it wasn't a question, and he knew precisely what I was saying.

The reviews for *Moon* were stellar. Words like *moody, unique, must-see, brilliant,* and on and on. It was a strange feeling, the praise, my career on solid footing. I was never sure I'd make it in Hollywood. The absurd confidence I observed in everyone else I rarely found in myself. (I didn't yet understand confidence as performance — red-carpet life.)

That week, as I endured endless photo

shoots and magazine interviews, I imagined Cate Kay by my side. I wondered what she would think of it all. I pictured someone older and wiser, a mentor, but secretly I hoped she was sexy and fun.

I got the call from Matt about a week later. "I don't know what you wrote in that letter, but it's going to happen," he said. "Although you're going to have to sign the most ridiculous NDA I've ever seen."

At the time, I didn't think of this as the coup it would end up being. Cate Kay was in the opening months of her anonymous fame. No one had maintained their privacy in the face of such scrutiny. I figured she'd be stepping into the spotlight within weeks, that I was just getting a sneak peek.

But Matt was right about the NDA. It was absurd. I could tell no one, not even my mom (and we still talked twice a week, at minimum). Plus, I had to guarantee the privacy of my home. When I signed the document, I knew I'd made promises of privacy and security, and secrecy *in perpetuity,* that I couldn't necessarily keep. But it was one of those cross-the-bridge-if-you-get-to-it situations. Half the things in there I wasn't even sure they could hold me accountable for. But what the NDA clearly communicated to me was that I had been wrong, Cate Kay's privacy wasn't a short-term stunt. And that she had a very good lawyer.

I'd just finished three weeks of relentless publicity for *Moon,* and there was a near-certain Oscar nomination coming down the pike. Remember Jennifer Lawrence right after *Winter's Bone*? It was like that. I went from *Who?* to A-list in a month. If you'd asked me, back then, what my dream was, I would have said becoming famous.

And then, suddenly, I was.

Those early weeks, I still tried to live my life. Workouts at the gym in my neighborhood, dinners out, reading a book at a coffee shop. But I was like Pig-Pen, but with a cloud of onlookers always around me. It started to make me feel self-conscious. Like everyone was whispering about how I must crave the attention. Satisfied only by swallowing gallons of public adoration each day. Only now do I understand this is just what happens to young actors oblivious to the life they've said yes to.

Pretty quickly, I missed my anonymity.

Janie started bringing my morning coffee. We'd sit in my backyard on the blue-and-white-striped chairs, sometimes dipping our feet in the sliver of pool. She'd signed the NDA, too. Only three people knew about my impending meeting with Cate Kay: me,

Matt, and Janie. That was as wide as the circle was allowed to get.

"So, we heard from Sidney Collins yesterday," Janie said during one of these mornings in my backyard. I'd just started wondering when we'd get details from this Sidney character, apparently the only person who knew Cate Kay. Shooting for *The Very Last* was starting the following month in Charleston, South Carolina. The director felt the lowcountry could mimic, as well as anywhere else, his vision for the water-logged Core.

I took a small sip of my coffee and grimaced. Each swallow was making me grouchier. I realized that Janie had cut back on the cream and sugar. Did she think I wouldn't notice? She knew I didn't like coffee. I liked cream and I liked sugar, and coffee was their vessel. I lifted my cup toward her and said, "What is happening here?"

To her credit, she didn't feign confusion. She just sighed and explained that the assistant director on *Last* had called and said they needed me down to a size 2, preferably 0, before filming. I rolled my eyes for a dozen reasons. The first being the infantile treatment. The second being some dude talking about my body to other people. The third being Janie believing she could ruin my morning coffee without me noticing. I pointed at her cup, which was sitting between us on the lip of the pool.

"And what's that?" I asked.

"A dirty chai with whole milk," she said and picked it up, jokingly cradling it against her body like a prized possession.

"Give it to me now." I motioned for the cup. "Just one sip before I plunge into the abyss of body neuroses that will perpetuate a shame cycle for every woman on the planet."

Fake-reluctantly, she handed over the drink. The richness of the milk and the sweetness of the chai tasted pillowy in my mouth. I avoided swallowing for as long as I could. The chai was then returned to Janie, and I pretended it didn't exist as I worked on my bitter, bitter coffee. I knew Janie wasn't to blame. Hollywood had been like this since the beginning. At my lowest moments, Janie would look me dead in the eyes and bolster me with our motto: "Our game, our rules — soon."

"Sidney Collins. What's she like and what did she say?" I asked. Janie seemed relieved to have come unscathed out of the sticky diet conversation. She pounced on this change of topic.

"She's so buttoned-up," she said. "One of those hate-to-play-against-them, love-to-have-them-on-your-team kind of people.

She's thought of everything that could go wrong with this. Made it clear she's not a fan of the whole thing. Oh, but one thing to run by you — apparently Cate doesn't want to stay at a hotel, says it's too risky, wants as small a footprint as possible. She insisted she at least first meet you here."

"She can totally stay with me," I said quickly. These days, I wouldn't let a delivery guy through my front gate to set something on the porch, but this was different — Cate was different.

"She's going to be here for a week," Janie said, eyeing me to see if that changed my offer.

"Perfect," I said. If things were weird, which they wouldn't be, I'd tell Janie and she'd fix it. No big deal. "But wait, back up. Did you say she *insisted*?" I added playfully. These were my first weeks of understanding that now I could bend people to my will, and it turned me on, thinking Cate Kay could do the same.

"Apparently, Cate *insisted*." Janie nudged me like we were girlfriends (old-fashioned usage) gossiping in the high school cafeteria. I loved her in those moments. "She also said Cate would come to your house this Friday."

"This Friday, as in two days from now?"

"Yup," Janie said. "I'm not allowed to be here. Matt can't be here either. Nobody can be here but you. Obviously. You've read the NDA."

That Friday, Janie dropped off my coffee, which now had even less sugar and less cream. She told me that Sidney (first-name basis now!) had called and relayed that Cate would be at my place "late afternoon, early evening." Janie wished me luck and left quickly. But not before standing on the threshold of my front door and admitting her wild jealousy. An unfathomable amount of money, she said, is what she'd pay to meet the mysterious Cate Kay.

"And also, RyRy," she whispered, glancing around to make sure no one was walking their dog. "It's taking me a truly shocking amount of willpower to not call *Vanity Fair* with a hot tip. This is like a really big fucking deal."

I rolled my eyes, said, "I absolutely will not let you know how it goes, under penalty of law."

Was it a big fucking deal? I played out the scenario of Janie calling the media and imagined how many cameras would descend on my little bungalow. Hundreds. So, yeah, I guess it was a big deal.

How shall I prepare for my evening with Cate Kay? I wondered as I lowered myself onto the tile surrounding the pool. I swung my feet into the water and considered what I should do about food. Eating it myself was happening less and less these days. But I remained aware, and jealous, that other people did. An author, with no reason to severely restrict her body, would want dinner. These logistical thoughts were helping drown out my growing anxiety about the meetup.

Eight to nine more hours of this kind of ruminating is what I figured I had in front of me. The morning was chilly, and I was wearing a hoodie and Kansas basketball shorts, which made me think of home.

I'd left Lawrence the summer after my freshman year at KU. College just wasn't for me. My dad said I was throwing away my future. My mom said nothing but drove me to Los Angeles, and we listened to Maroon 5 the whole way. This bungalow was the first house we looked at. Over my budget, of course. I only had two commercials booked at that point. But my mom and I walked around and absorbed all its details. The crown molding, built-in bookcases, the Moroccan tile lining the pool. Mom had pulled me aside. We were in the kitchen, away from the real estate agent. She whispered, "I love this place for you."

"Me too, Mom," I'd said.

She grabbed my hands. "I know it's a little expensive for where you are right now, but I could help you with the rent. We'd just have to promise not to tell your dad. You know how he'd be."

I understood. Mom wished she'd had an adventure like moving to Hollywood. Like living alone in a lovely little bungalow. Like chasing her dreams. But her life hadn't gone that way.

Call Mom. I was making a mental note when I heard something at the front of the house. I leaned back and glanced through the sliding glass door. I squinted and held my breath, waiting for another noise. None came. Janie would know to come around the side for whatever she needed.

I leaned onto my elbows and dropped my head back, staring at the cloudless blue sky. Fame had happened quickly, and it was scaring me. The loneliness of it. Not just the frequent physical isolation from daily life, but also the impossibility of communicating how it felt. To anyone, including family. Probably like an astronaut describing floating in outer space. Trying to use these clumsy, everyday words to relay an experience that could only be understood by being felt.*

Suddenly, I heard this soft knock on the side gate to the backyard. I jumped to my feet, knocking over my coffee. *Shit.* I righted it quickly, losing only a small amount. My eyes flew to the fence, which was taller than me and painted a dark gray. The thought that this person could be Cate Kay hadn't even entered my mind. But when I unlatched the gate and opened it halfway, I saw the duffel bag slung over her shoulder.

Half the clauses in the NDA were being jeopardized by her lingering in my side yard. I darted onto the flat stone walkway, grabbed her by the arm, and dragged Cate Kay into my backyard. As I latched the door, I had this flash of realization: Oh, I get it

***Note from Cate:** I once read this book about near-death experiences. In it, people tried to explain what it felt like when their souls left their bodies, and they all seemed frustrated at the inadequacy of language. They all bumped up against its limitations and eventually concluded that this thing they wanted to convey to the reader, that no words could do it justice. These parts of the book made me think of Ryan, which interested me — what did fame have in common with near-death experiences?

now, this woman doesn't just *have* a secret, which until that moment had felt very high school cafeteria to me, very low stakes. No, she *was* a secret.

I stole a glance: She didn't look like someone being hunted — or haunted. But obviously she believed something was chasing her.

CHAPTER 11

ANNIE

2000
Bolton Landing

The day before we were supposed to leave for Los Angeles, Amanda asked me to meet her at the boat. I was at home, staring at an empty sheet of paper, wondering what — if anything — I should write my mom by way of goodbye. It was a cold fall day; the lake wasn't what I had in mind, but Amanda insisted.

Once we pushed away from the shore, she said, "I have something to show you," which piqued my interest. So many years, so small a town — what was left to discover? Then she gunned the motor and for a moment the front of the boat, me inside, lifted high into the air and I thought I would topple onto her. We quickly leveled out and she grinned. She'd been doing that lately, this odd sort of showing off, like she wanted me to pay more attention to her.

Didn't she know how tightly I was held in her orbit? I snuck a glance: she was in profile, hair blowing perfectly in the wind because that's just how the world interacted with Amanda, casting her in its most flattering light.

"It's coming up," Amanda yelled into the wind. We were nearing a series of small islands in the middle of the lake. By now, we'd explored most of them, but it was all just grass and trees. "My cousin took me here last week — it's the one island we didn't go to!"

Amanda cut the engine, and we drifted toward a patch of sandy beach. A second later, she hopped over the side and pulled us onto shore. Her athleticism was impressive. "Look at you," I said, awkwardly stepping out of the boat. "They should give varsity letters for that."

We walked through a line of trees and came to the back side of the island. Up ahead was a dilapidated house — burnt red, peeling wooden slats — with a collapsed barn and unkempt grass, the overgrowth nearly obscuring a rusted grill in the side yard, a half-deflated floatie tucked behind. Each detail compounded until all I saw was the setting for a post-apocalypse movie. This was the place survivors would scavenge and find a single unopened can of dog food.

"You gotta come see this!" Amanda called from the backyard. I walked around, stepping with high knees to avoid ticks.

More apocalypse in the backyard: a zip line that started high in the tree line, passed over an aboveground pool, and ended on a rotten wooden porch. The pool was empty, its blue lining peeling in long strips. The porch was a death trap of nails and sunken planks.

Amanda was walking toward the tree line, and I trailed far behind her.

A few seconds later, she began climbing a tree, and at first, I didn't know how it was happening so fast. Then I spotted the wooden steps affixed to the trunk, leading toward a platform.

Happily abandoning the safety of ground, that was Amanda. Physically adventurous in ways I'd never been. Like onstage when she allowed herself to be attached to a harness and lifted twenty feet in the air during a performance of *Peter Pan,* which nauseated me. The entire production was run by students who had about zero experience in delicately balancing humans in space. Of course, it had gone perfectly, reinforcing Amanda's belief in her invincibility.

I was thinking of this as she reached the

platform and tested a small amount of her weight with one foot, gripping the zip line with her right hand.

"Maybe let's not do this," I called. She pretended not to hear me.

"Amanda!" I yelled, my anxiety rising. But now she was focused on unwrapping a cord attached to what looked like bike handlebars.

I'd once complimented her daring. Is that what this was about? A performance — just for me?

She unwrapped the handlebars and was now putting more of her weight on the platform. I quickly scanned the length of the zip line. It was held taut, everything appeared to be attached.

And yet there was my heart, making its presence felt, as Amanda stepped fully onto the platform. She was gripping the handlebars with both hands. Was she — she was actually doing this?

I cupped my hands over my mouth and yelled for her to get down, then started speed walking toward her. She thought my panic was funny, laughing as she waved me back, "Annie, no, I'll come to you — that's the whole point!"

"How fucking cool is this!" she yelled a second later.

My last thought before Amanda leapt off

the platform was: *Wow, we're actually really different.*

She made a kind of Tarzan yell as she jumped. I was standing between her and the pool, about a quarter way down the zip line. She was wearing a sweater, jeans, and black Converse high-tops, and she looked strong holding herself in midair, the cut of her body surprising. She tucked her knees and looked down at me with wide eyes, her mouth a perfect O, and I realized I was being overly cautious — she wasn't *that* high. She might twist an ankle, get banged up a little, nothing more.

Then she passed over me, and when I glanced up, I saw the bottoms of her sneakers, that trademark brown with a diamond cut.

The beginning of everything came a moment later. The base of the zip line, bolted to the porch however many years ago, broke free. The sound was like a whipping, like in a movie when a storm hits a boat and one of the sails comes untethered in the wind. It's not a good noise; it's terrifying — an undoing.

Amanda was no longer above the laws of physics; she was now at their mercy.

I spun with the sound, facing the pool, which Amanda was about to pass over. I wished I could instantly fill it. She would climb out soaking wet, and we would stumble into a hug, falling down, laughing at our close call. We'd forget it ever happened a week later.

But the only thing inside that pool was dead leaves and muck and, underneath, the hard ground. I looked up at Amanda, but now I could only see her back. I couldn't tell if she knew what was happening.

I screamed her name, feeling the pointlessness, my helplessness. But the energy my body had instantly generated — the pure fear — needed a release.

Amanda contorted herself in the air. For a moment I thought she might be able to glide into the grass like an expert skydiver, but she contracted her body too quickly, and the cord no longer had any tension. She turned herself sideways. As she fell, now nearly parallel to the ground, her left foot caught the lip of the pool, and the impact spun her headfirst at a sickening angle. She disappeared into the pool with a muffled thud, the sound absorbed by the wet leaves.

I didn't move. Around me the day was a cloudless blue and for a moment I tuned in to the sounds of the island, a songbird's melody drifting from the trees, the percussion of a light breeze through leaves. The world was so, so big — endless, really — and then the sensation of it all collapsing into itself and whooshing through a pinprick, leaving me standing a few yards from that terrible pool. No sounds came from inside it. My first thought was that if she wasn't crying, she must be okay. Maybe the wet leaves softened the fall?

"Amanda." My voice was a gasp. I was at the side of the pool, moving slower than I wanted. I imagined if someone was watching they'd be yelling at me to *fucking hurry, go, go go*, but my mind had put my body in slow motion.

The pool was about my height. I pressed my toes into the grass, *one, two, three,* then launched myself upward, straightening my arms on the side and clumsily lifting myself over. My body was coursing with so much fear that I could feel my jaw shivering.

First, I noticed the handlebars and the cord of the zip line, slack, dangling along the far side of the pool like a downed electric line. Then I saw Amanda, on her back near the curved wall, the heel of her left foot perched a few inches up the side, and as I took in all of this, I felt relieved.

She was not mangled, or at some grotesque angle, and I spent a split second thinking maybe she'd just had the wind knocked out of her. The leaves were muddy and layered with God-knows-what, and I thought about how pissed Amanda would be having that slime all over her.

But then I saw her eyes, and that's when the cycle of fear returned, revved up even higher, and I knelt next to her, touched her arm. Her eyes, they were so wide, and there was so much white they looked like cue balls, and she was staring straight up like she'd never seen the world before.

Then she rolled her eyes to the side to look at me, and the way it happened, like they were detached from the rest of her body, caused a wave of nausea so severe that I launched myself up and vomited a few feet away. A moment later, I stumbled back to her.

"Can you hear me?" I grabbed her hand. Her lips were moving, but no words came out. "Can you feel this?" She blinked. I squeezed again. "What about now?" No blink. My mind was scrambling, desperate for a foothold.

"Amanda, what's going on, what happened?" I asked, my voice careening along the edge, desperate. What did the blink mean? What did no blink mean? Did any of it mean anything? I said nothing for what seemed like a long time but was probably only a few seconds, scanning her body for some obvious sign of breaking. I squeezed her leg, just above the knee, said, "Can you feel this?," but she just stared at the sky. That endless blue above us. I saw a tear collect at the corner of her eye and slowly roll across her temple, disappearing into her hair.

"I'll be right back," I said, then darted over to the ladder, climbed up and out, then sprinted back to the boat.

For a short stretch of time, everything I did was exactly what needed to be done. I dragged the boat into the water, I gunned it back to the dock, I ran to the closest motel office and told the manager to call 911, which he did, handing the phone to me once he had someone on the line. I told them everything I knew: the small island, the red house, the broken zip line, the pool, Amanda motionless and blinking, please hurry as fast as you can.

The operator assured me emergency services were on their way, and I ran back down to the boat and I swear to God I had every intention of going back to Amanda. I even dragged the boat into the water. Then my mind started spinning everything forward. Suddenly I was gulping air, but still couldn't get enough into my lungs. I abandoned the boat, left it half in the water, and walked the mile to where Brando was parked, ducking off the road whenever a car passed, like I was some kind of fugitive. Gradually, my breathing calmed, then I was climbing into the driver's side of the car. I grabbed the rearview mirror to look at my broken reflection, stunned that I'd forgotten the glass was cracked. What else could I forget without even trying?

Turns out the last meaningful words I said to Amanda were "Can you feel this?" And the answer was no, no she couldn't.

CHAPTER 12

MR. RILEY

1999
Bolton Landing

I remember one night, about an hour before opening curtain for *Twelfth Night,* I was looking for Annie and Amanda because one of their costumes needed a last-minute alteration. I was walking backstage when I heard whispering to my left. I paused, stayed quiet, realized the voices were coming from inside a tangle of curtain — thick navy blue, dropping from ceiling to stage. I looked down and saw two pairs of feet and recognized the girls by their shoes.

Gently, so gently, I took a step forward — picture that low shot in a caper movie, the thief gently moving on tiptoe. Now closer, I could hear them more clearly. One of them said, "I don't know what's happening to me. I'm just kinda scared and shaky. What if I freeze — mess it all up?" Then there was a pause. A moment later, the other said, "Honestly, I bet that happens to everyone one time or another. I think we're all just pretending to not be freaking out and you're just having a harder time pretending right now."

A second later the curtains rustled — they were hugging — then one of them said, "You know what I love about you?"

"Do tell," said the other, solicitously.

"It's like . . . ummm . . . how do I explain this? It's like you hold me steady, but without holding me still."

After a long pause, the other said, "It's an honor to hold you steady."

I still think about that moment. Not even that thick blue theater curtain could keep their love from radiating outward.

CHAPTER 13

ANNIE

2000
Plattsburgh, NY

There I was, white-knuckling the wheel and driving out of town, in full disbelief that I was doing it. But movement was the only thing I felt capable of. Movement away from Amanda's fallen body, which kept dropping from the sky in my mind, as if on a loop. My vision was filled with her foot catching the side of the pool, that awful angle, and I was stunned at how much adrenaline the human body could produce. Did it ever deplete? The tips of my hands had gone numb, as if my body was pulling all the heat toward my core. Was this survival mode, outside of my control? Or was I a monster?

Even as I was driving, in that first hour, I could sense that this decision would haunt me. And still I felt incapable of anything else. Life had just reared up, taken its first bite out of me. Running felt like a reflex. But then I wondered: If running was my reflex, what did that say about me?

An hour and a half passed in a blur. When I saw a sign for Plattsburgh, the name sparked. Amanda had an uncle there, visited him every other Thanksgiving. I had hated those years, loved the ones when she stayed home and we baked pies. We discovered I was a pretty good baker — precise with measurements.

I didn't want to go any farther from Amanda. And maybe if my body became still, my brain would follow suit. Would pipe down and let me think. (Also, I had to pee.)

I exited the highway, followed the signs for downtown. The temperature had dropped, and the street was dusty with crushed salt. I drove slowly along the main road until I spotted a café. I paused in front, peered inside: empty but for the guy working in it.

I parked the car and tried to calm down and think. I had the cash from my last paycheck bagging groceries in my wallet. I had some clothes — fuck, I had some of Amanda's too — in the trunk. And I had my car. I could sleep in my car.

It wasn't much, but I'd never had much.

I got out and walked to the café. Halfway there I noticed the HELP WANTED sign on the door. I froze. Was that a sign from the universe that I should stay? But that was a crazy thought. I could hear Amanda telling me how unhinged I sounded.

I went inside. The cheapest thing on the menu was drip black coffee. I filled it with cream and sugar and found a seat in the back. The place was more hippie than anything in Bolton. A surfing sticker was on the wall to my left and I ran my fingers over it, thought of the ocean in Malibu and the beachfront homes of Hollywood's biggest producers.

Amanda, I'm so, so sorry.

I couldn't be near that sticker. I stood and walked to the front, asked where the restroom was. The guy was reading a book, his elbow on the counter. He didn't look up, just pointed toward the door at the back of the shop. His apathy was comforting; nobody would notice me here.

The bathroom was down a hallway, and when I saw there was a shower stall in it, and what my brain did with that information, I realized how dedicated it was to building a new life. I pulled back the flimsy blue curtain, leaned forward, turned the handle. The water came out fast and hot.

The sink was adjacent to the shower. I washed my hands and stared in the small, square mirror, which looked like a weapon, its edges rough. Before I could block its arrival: an image of Amanda, broken, followed by a swarm of thoughts — *how is she?, where is she?, is she okay?, of course she's okay, but what if it's not and what if she's de—, no, no, no, her eyes were open, she's okay, but how could I, really, how could I?* I stared at myself long enough that, just like when a repeated word loses meaning, my face became just skin and bone. Then I stared through myself until I didn't know who I was anymore. Then back into focus I came. I was wearing a D.A.R.E hoodie under a tattered jean jacket — Amanda had always called it my "*RENT* look."

I gripped the sides of the sink and imagined going back to Bolton Landing. Imagined what life would be like: I'd pick up shifts again at Tops, help Amanda with whatever terrible thing had happened, live with my mom again.

Or I could —

See what this was like?

See if I could become someone new.

And if it wasn't working, I'd get in the car and go home. Which is probably what I would do anyway. Probably tomorrow.

But, just for now, I needed a new name. Needed some distance from being Annie.

I thought about every play I'd done. All the books I'd read. The names began filling my head. Some were too old (Blanche) or too old-fashioned (Ophelia), but then one popped in — Cassandra — and it was everything I wanted to be: sophisticated, distinct, worldly. And the fancier the first name, the simpler the last. One of my favorite movie-star names had always been Harrison Ford. Amanda and I had once staged a scene (in her bedroom) from *The Fugitive.*

Cassandra Ford.

Cass, for short.

I walked back into the café and asked for an application and the guy put down his book and looked at me. He wasn't getting up unless I was serious. I held his gaze, then he shrugged and went to get me the form.

That night I awoke in my car with my knees jammed into the gear shift and a crick in my neck. I sat upright and battered my fists against the steering wheel.

Why, why, why, why, why?

Such emotional outbursts were unlike me, but I was in a unique kind of agony. Like I'd had a heart transplant and was waiting to see if it would take. I wanted a new chance at life so badly. And also, I was terrified that I would get it.

A month went by like this: me sleeping in my car, working the first shift at the café, always just about to drive home.

But day after day, I didn't.

CHAPTER 14

CASS FORD

2000
Plattsburgh

The guy who managed the coffee shop was named Brett. Early one morning I was standing behind him as he struggled to unlock the door because of the cold. His hands had lost their dexterity.

"If you wanted, I could get started on everything before you got here," I said.

He didn't turn around, kept working the lock as he said, "Um, yeah, no, I don't know anything about you."

"I show up on time and work hard, what more do you need to know?" We were inside the back door now and I was hurriedly pulling it closed behind me.

"Literally anything," he said, flipping on the lights.

"I'm from Albany" — kind of a lie, although all of upstate New York could be considered Albany. "I'm just up here trying to do something different," I added.

Cass had become a fascinating character to play. She was me, but more of a loner; she liked to hang back and observe, looking for the next door opened by the universe. I wondered what Amanda would think of her — if she would like the tweaks I'd made. I kept telling myself that soon I would drive back and tell her everything. How I'd created this alternate version of myself and tested her out in the world. A play, of sorts, but with a limited run.

Amanda. I wished she was next to me right at that moment, talking to Brett. She knew how to say all the right things — she knew how to speak *boy*.

"There's never anybody here before, like, six thirty," I said, trailing behind Brett, uprighting chairs. "If you give me the key, I could be here by five forty-five, get everything done. You wouldn't have to get here until six fifteen, six thirty, whatever."

He stopped what he was doing and looked at me. Now only half-skeptical. I'd finally offered him something he wanted: more sleep. More sleep also happened to be my motive. I shrugged my shoulders as if to say *so simple man, c'mon,* then stole a glance at the tattered leather couch along the far wall that I imagined sleeping on for the next however long if I could pry those keys from Brett.

"Why though? Why would you want to do that?" He was behind the bar now, filling the green plastic watering can at the sink. He handed it to me, and I carried it to the tallest plant, near the front window, giving myself an extra minute to think.

"I'm a terrible sleeper," I said, which had become true since I'd abandoned my best friend, run away, and started sleeping in a car. "And I'm always standing out back in the freezing cold waiting for you to get here."

Back home in my cozy twin bed, I could sleep and sleep and sleep. I needed that. If I slept well, then I could think better, and good sleep and strong thinking would no doubt lead to better decisions than the ones I had lately been making.

When the first customers arrived, I glanced at the clock — 6:44 — and looked over at Brett to reinforce my earlier point. His response: a not-unfriendly eye roll. It gave me a glimmer of hope. He turned his attention to the customers, two men, offered them his grumpy *hey*.

They ordered and found a seat in the back corner near the cream and sugar station. The night before, Brett had asked me to prune the flyers along the wall. I walked over and began removing past-date events.

"The thing about writing —" I heard one guy say, and my ears perked. I paused, my fingers on a thumbtack, and tuned fully into their conversation. "— is that it's unlike other creative endeavors. It's not about you, it's only about the story and the words. To be an actor or musician, you must perform — you're trading on yourself — but not the writer. Most readers don't even consider the author.* I love that about writing."

Hello, universe. This felt like a door flinging open. The flyer at my fingertips slipped from beneath the thumbtack, falling down the wall and lodging into the baseboard with a surprisingly noisy thud. The man paused midsentence, glanced over.

"My bad," I said, bending to collect the flyer. Prying it from the wall took a few seconds and I hoped the older man would continue talking, but right then Brett called my name from behind the bar.

For the next few minutes I stood behind the counter, staring into space, unspooling my new future. It made so much sense. All

---

*****Note from Cate:** You know what, ironically, makes readers care about who has written the book? A pseudonym.

the books and plays I'd read. I knew what made a good story. Plus, I'd spent years imagining Amanda's inner thoughts based on her words and actions. Maybe writing, not acting, was my destiny. Maybe that's what would have happened in Hollywood: First we would have starred in movies, but then I would have started to write, too. Maybe I would have become the first —

"Earth to Cass!"

Two fingers were snapping in front of me, and I landed back behind the bar, Brett holding up a jug of milk and shaking it to show me how empty it was.

"Oh, got it," I said, and started moving toward the back, noticing that the two men were standing, putting on their coats. I scooted around the bar and half jogged to get the milk, thinking about what to ask the writer before he left.

I squatted in front of the back fridge and moved the tubs of cream cheese until I found a gallon of whole milk. I hustled back out and caught sight of the front door closing behind the men. Brett was impatient for my delivery, and I handed him the jug as I passed, jogging out into the freezing-cold morning in my T-shirt and coffee apron.

"Excuse me," I half yelled. My skin pricked as a gust of wind hit me. The guy who had said the thing about writing was parked in front of the café, keys in hand. He looked up, a flash of concern moving across his face. Desperate is how I must have seemed. But my superpower was, and had always been, an irrational belief in my own manifest destiny.

"Do you teach writing?" I asked, which must have piqued his interest because he pocketed the keys. "I do," he said. "Over at Plattsburgh," and he said this slowly, letting the question of *why do you ask?* smuggle itself inside.

"I want to be a writer," I said, wondering if maybe this had always been true. The cold was becoming unbearable in my short sleeves, but I could tell it was an asset in motivating him to make a snap decision. I cupped my hands together, blew into them.

A minute later I was walking back into the café holding the professor's business card, my teeth chattering. Brett looked at me curiously.

"What was that?" he asked as I joined him behind the counter.

"Just making dreams come true," I said.

At the end of the day Brett called my name as I was leaving. I was slow to respond, assuming he had another chore for me. He was wiping down the espresso machine as he said, "They're on the counter there," then shifted his eyes a few feet away, to where we put drinks for customers. Sitting there was a set of keys. Glorious, those keys — that heavy bundle of metal that I eagerly grabbed and held in my hands, tossing them once into the air. I snuck a glance at the leather couch, where I would sleep that night.

"Thank you, Brett," I said, my words slow and sincere. And as I said his name, I realized that maybe I'd never said it before — that he might even think I didn't know it.

"You're welcome, Cass."

CHAPTER 15

BRETT STEPHENS

2000
Plattsburgh

I knew something was up with Cass from the beginning. One of the first days after she started working at the café, I saw her in her car. It was after dark, and I'd forgotten something at the shop. I was walking through the back alley, which opens into a small parking lot with a chain-link fence and those hazy yellow streetlights that always make things feel ominous. I glanced over my shoulder and did a double take: Cass was sitting with her eyes closed in the front seat of this red Honda.

I stopped, looked closer. Her eyes were closed but not like she was asleep. Like she was meditating, though nobody did that back then. A force field of energy was radiating out, and I couldn't help but step closer. Then I could see that she was rocking back and forth, ever so slightly. I quickly looked away. I don't know, it just felt . . . private? Like she was trying to harness the world's energy to produce a miracle or something. I didn't want to get in the way.

What I learned that night: This girl, whoever she was, was processing something big. I wasn't wary or afraid of her after that. When she finally asked for the keys, it seemed like such an easy fix to a big problem, which was getting her a safe place to sleep. I should have thought of it myself. Of course, I was more of a jerk back then, so I made her sweat a little bit. But it seemed clear that whatever was happening with her, the only person she was endangering was herself.

CHAPTER 16

SIDNEY COLLINS

2000
Plattsburgh

Lawyers, we get a bad rap. We're just storytellers. The only difference is, unlike a book or movie, we don't say whether the story is true or false. That's for other people to decide. Besides, they say each time a memory is recalled, the mind slightly alters it. This memory I'm about to share may no longer resemble the truth, so frequently have I retrieved it. What I can promise is no conscious embellishments. Just clear-eyed recollections.

I remember the classroom in which I first saw Cass was bright from the artificial ceiling lights. The desks were the ones most high schools had, shaped like a kidney bean; slipping in and out of them was an art form. Older me looks at those desks now and sees a tweaked lower back, but at the time, I moved easily while grabbing my backpack off the floor, twisting out.

I was pursuing a prelaw degree, and taking an arts elective felt inconsequential, but in a good way — like you can try without worrying about failure. I loved Creative Writing 107. Everyone is always turning their hobbies into jobs, but not me. I still love a good turn of phrase, but the law pays my bills, and the law is enough pressure.

The semester was nearly halfway over when a new student joined. It was a small class, just a dozen people. We pulled those awful kidney bean desks into a circle so we could see each other's faces. The class had good vibes. We'd each already workshopped a piece, and everyone had been kind and thorough with each other, which I can personally confirm never happens in law school. "I love your use of em dashes," a classmate once told me at the end of his critique of my work. He nodded, impressed. I've loved 'em (haha, joke) ever since — my signature punctuation.

That afternoon, I was earlier than usual. I had just pulled the desks into a perfect circle when a woman walked in. She had light brown hair down to her elbows, parted in the middle. As she sat, she tucked the right side behind her ear. For a moment, she didn't look at me, like she hadn't noticed I was in the room, then she quietly raised her head and made eye contact, and I took in the richness of the brown, the perfect eyebrows — the way her eyes sagged at the corners. She nodded once, then ducked her head, fixed her hair again. My first emotion was confusion: Who was this person and were they in the wrong class? But right on its heels: I want to look at her again, more, for a longer time. I stared.

She lifted herself slightly from the chair and dug something out of the back pocket of her jeans — a piece of loose-leaf paper. Folded into a square. Like a note to be passed in class. She opened it once, twice, three times, then smoothed it down against the desk. It was blank.

"Do you have a —"

"Pen?" I interrupted, already rummaging through my bag, because providing was what I did best. I twisted out of the desk, took one big step, lunged with the pen outstretched. She barely had to move — just a slight lean forward. I put myself in rewind, sat back down, then said — and I debated whether to say it or not, but ultimately thought, *Chances, they must be taken* — "A writer can never be too prepared."

"Are you?" She uncapped the pen, scribbled

on the top corner of her paper to make sure it worked. (It did.) "A writer?"

"When I'm in this class I am, but no, pre-law," I said. I'd had a flitting thought as I said it that I hoped it would impress her, this very adult thing I would be. She leaned back as if hit by a stiff breeze and said, "Wow, that's very grown-up," and a tingle of excitement danced up my spine — our brains worked on the same wavelength. But with her tone, I couldn't decipher if she liked grown-up things.

"What about you? Are you a writer?"

"You know . . . I don't know yet." She put the pen in her mouth, seeming to forget it was mine, although I appreciated the gesture because it made me notice her mouth — a plush lower lip, thinner upper. "I think I might be."

"How'd you get in this class? It's so late to add," I said just as Professor Moore walked in. He looked harried, which I'd come to realize was probably his natural state. He used his hand to sweep the hair out of his eyes. "Oh, good, you're here," he said to the new girl. "And hello, Sidney," he said to me. "You two have met?" He gestured between us.

"I'm Sidney," I said. "Lender of pens."

"I'm Cass." She paused, and I could see

her brain churning, then a small smile. "Auditor of classes."

Professor Moore was unpacking his bag, but at this he jumped back in, said, "That's right. Cass here is going to be sitting in for the rest of the semester." He winked at Cass and thankfully the gesture came across as fatherly instead of creepy. "She's a writer, but she's never been taught-taught."

Then Cass looked at me, lifted the pen and single sheet of paper, and steeled her face as if going into battle. I grinned. I was grateful for Professor Moore because between me and him, Cass was clearly aligning with me.

When class ended, and we were all packing up our things, Cass was out the door first. Scrambling, I shoved everything into my bag and pulled out a spiral notebook I hadn't yet used. A plain red cover — nothing fancy. While hustling after her, I almost stopped myself, my older sister's words ringing in my ears. *Why don't you just chill, maybe let things come to you for once.* She also said I had no sense of humor, which is blatantly ridiculous. She'd called this "advice" but what it sounded like was criticism, a proxy for *you're so annoying.*

But my sister had dropped out of college the year before, was back home reassessing her life, whereas I loved what I was doing and was kicking ass. Quietly excelling in undergrad, applying early decision to NYU for law school, so why was I letting her old words haunt me? I hadn't been cool in high school — too lanky and odd with my short hair and slacks. And yet, as far as I could tell, being cool in high school was a death sentence. No pain to fuel you later.

"Cass!" I called out at a half jog. The girl was slippery, already around the corner and somehow, despite her striking beauty, blending into the crowd. The writing class was in the student union — she'd already merged into the food hall. But I had my eyes on her: She was wearing slip-on checkered Vans (or knockoffs), a detail so specific to this memory that I have never, in all the years since, seen someone wearing checkered Vans and not thought of this moment.

She looked over her shoulder, slowed, waited for me.

"Hi," she said, sounding cautious, curious. "Sidney?"

"Yes, or Sid . . . both work."

Everything about her body language was asking, *Why are you following me?* As an answer, I immediately held up the spiral notebook, presenting it like those name cards chauffeurs hold up at the airport. "I had this extra notebook in my bag, and I thought, if you still think you might be a writer, maybe you'd want it?" I realized then that a cheap spiral notebook was probably a dollar at the student union.

She squinted, but the corners of her mouth lifted. Reading people was something my law professors talked frequently about. Why do people do what they do, say what they say — how a lawyer must stay one step ahead. I wondered if Cass would be one of those people who rejected gifts because they believed it indebted them, made them feel inferior, or if she'd be someone who welcomed the generosity of others. This beautiful, mysterious girl was about to give me one piece of evidence about herself.

"Thank you," Cass said, gently taking the book in her hands. She hugged it to her chest. "That's really nice of you."

"No problem at all," I said, because seriously it wasn't. A moment passed, then another, and I quickly started to feel anxious. *What now, what now, what now.* I hadn't planned any further than giving her the book. The anxiety didn't seem to reach Cass. After a few more excruciating seconds, during which I practiced the ancient lawyerly art of *letting the other person say too much,* she filled the terrible silence. "Well, I have to get going." Then she lifted the book as if to say *thanks again* and off she went. I liked the way she walked. At that age, so many kids kept their heads down, or rounded their shoulders to take up less space. Cass walked with purpose. It was in that red notebook that she began the first draft of *The Very Last*.*

Just when she reached the main doors, I yelled after her, "Wait up!" Then I jogged to open the door for her, asking, "Where can I find you?"

An otherworldly level of patience is what it took to not go downtown to the coffee shop where she worked the very next day. And when I did allow myself to go, the day after,

***Note from Cate:** I debated whether to add a footnote here or let it go, but there's something about fully surrendering this piece of *The Very Last* origin story that I couldn't stomach. Memory is a strange thing, but here is mine: I don't remember Sidney giving me a notebook. My recollection is that Amanda gave me a notebook — *"To put all those big, juicy thoughts in,"* I remember her saying — at the end of senior year that I never used, so it was in my backpack when I left Bolton Landing. The fact that I wrote the first draft of my book in a notebook given to me by Amanda always soothed me in some small way.

I tried to be low-key — slip in without Cass noticing. I ducked inside with my head down. I wanted to find a discreet seat, probably in the corner, that allowed me to see what I was working with. This is the lawyer in me. I found a spot along the back wall between two oversized plants. The shop's decor was busier than I expected: pillows, plants, advertisements for concerts and farmers markets — stickers on the wall. The bohemian vibe wasn't really my style.

When I sat down, I scanned the room for Cass. No sign of her. Just a dude with greasy black hair behind the counter. But then I heard a door behind me fling open and a moment later I saw her from behind — a crate of milk in her arms. She craned her neck toward me. Why, I don't know, but eventually I learned that, like me, she always had her head on a swivel, always wanted to know what was in her blind spots.

That sly smile, the crinkle of her eyes — a trademark from those earliest days. She lifted her eyebrows — a greeting — then walked away and stocked the fridge with milk. I watched, waited. She'd come back, I knew it. But she didn't. She busied herself behind the counter with various tasks for the next hour, then the shop was closing. I stayed anyway. I stayed even as the dude with the greasy black hair started wiping down tables and stacking chairs, ominously making his way toward where I was sitting.

"Still here?" Cass appeared again from the back room, arms finally empty.

"Well, I came to see you," I said.

I'm a very point A to point B kind of person. A few times I thought about packing up and leaving without talking to Cass — who didn't seem interested in talking to me anyway. What kept me there? The belief that someone like Cass should be mine, that I was good enough for her, that she should realize it, too.

Cass laughed softly. She seemed to respect the directness of my approach, and I could sense that she was debating with herself about what to do next. "You know what, why don't you come out back, sit with me for a while?"

Winter had come quickly that fall. "Out back?" I said. "For a . . . *while*?"

"Aren't you from around here?"

"Burlington," I said.

"You'll be fine, come on," she said. "Unless you'd rather not." And the way she said this last part, like she really didn't care either way, felt callous — hurt my heart a little.

"So, where are you from?" I asked once we were out back. The coffee shop's back door led to four rotting wooden steps that looked out on a row of black trash cans and a narrow alley lined with a chain-link fence. We sat on the last step, just wide enough to fit the two of us shoulder to shoulder, which I was thankful for because then we could share warmth. Growing up in Vermont didn't make the cold more bearable — it simply made me more respectful of it.

"Got a smoke?" Cass asked. I chuckled; I'd just been thinking, sitting there, staring at the alley, that it seemed like the quintessential setting for a smoke. But no, I didn't have one. And come to find out, Cass wasn't even a smoker. She just thought it felt like the right thing to say.

"Do I look like a smoker?" I asked.

"No, you don't, you actually look more like —"

"Careful," I jumped in. I wasn't sure I'd like the end of that sentence.

"I was going to say . . ." Cass paused, dipped her head so she could see my eyes, which seemed kind of flirty to me. "I was going to say that you look like the CEO of the cigarette company who's too smart to smoke."

I liked that. Gone now was the sting of her earlier indifference, replaced by a buzz from this compliment.

"Why thank you." I smiled and bumped my shoulder into hers. "I feel seen."

"You're welcome." She fake-lit a cigarette, fake-took a drag, fake-passed it to me. Since I'd never held a cigarette, I pinched my fingers, brought them to my lips, sucked deeply, passed it back. Cass continued, "The list of things I know about you: you're from Burlington, you're prelaw, you appreciate very specific compliments, and you drink hot chocolate."

That's what I'd ordered while waiting for her attention. I guess I'd been secretly getting it — I felt that buzz again.

"Pretty much sums me up, actually," I said. She was right — the cold was nothing to me then. All night, I'd happily sit out there with her. I would tell this girl anything. She had this casual yet insightful, whimsical yet serious, chill yet chic vibe that felt completely natural coming from her but would have felt obnoxious and cultivated on anyone else. She did not seem native to the area. My previous girlfriend — not that I was thinking of Cass as my girlfriend at that point — but my previous girlfriend wore puffy coats and hiking boots and always seemed in reaction to her environment. Cass, though, blended seamlessly. At least, that's how it felt in the early days. That first night she was wearing a knee-length winter coat, cream sweater underneath, knit hat,* just effortlessly smoking her imaginary cigarette.

"What else do I need to know?" she asked.

I took the question seriously. What could I share that might impress her? I ticked through a list: I had one sister, a stay-at-home mom, and my dad worked for the Environmental Protection Agency. Maybe that I played basketball in high school? Then I remembered my law school application — *bingo*.

"Well, I'm starting at NYU Law next fall," I said, which wasn't yet true, but would be soon, I was sure. I pinched my fingers and reached for the fake cigarette, excited to be able to show her that even though I had serious career pursuits, I could be playful, too. Telling her about my future filled me with a tingly feeling. Who even was this girl?

At this news, Cass nodded in appreciation. She looked off to the left a little as she took a drag — exhaled out of the side of her mouth. Fake smoking was a talent and she had it.

"New York." She put an inflection on the

***Note from Cate:** I was always channeling Amanda when I dressed. Looking effortless, Amanda would say, comes only from an absurd amount of effort. Another *Cosmo*-ism, I'm sure.

end, like it was a question she was considering. She seemed to lean into me a little more, or maybe that was my imagination,* some wishful thinking, but my body reacted like it was a purposeful touch.

"Interesting," she said, putting out the fake cigarette on the railing.

***Note from Cate:** This was, in fact, her imagination.

CHAPTER 17

SIDNEY

2000
Plattsburgh

Just three weeks later, I asked Cass to move with me to New York. Reckless and crazy, I would tell myself whenever the idea popped into my head. My rational self would counsel my impatient self that it was too soon, and the idea would disappear for a little while. But then she'd do something, say something, that made my heart a beating thing and there it would be again — *Do it, ask her, fucking go for it!*

We'd been seeing each other every day because I was doing all my work at her café. I helped shut the place down. My textbooks spread across two tables, papers tucked neatly inside, Cass coming by every so often to check on me, bringing me coffees on the house. Then, once all the chairs were put up and the floor was mopped, Cass and I would go for a walk — if it wasn't too cold — or I'd take her somewhere for dinner and we'd talk. Well, *I'd* talk, mostly. I was still waiting for her to trust me with whatever had happened to her. The fact that something had happened was obvious. *In due time,* I told myself, a phrase that would essentially become my mantra.

"How about sushi?" I asked Cass one of these nights after she finished wiping down the counter. Brett had left a few minutes before, so it was just the two of us — it felt secretive, which turned me on.

"Sushi," Cass said, rolling the word around in her mouth. "Raw fish, you say?"

"My treat," I added, even though everything we'd ever done had been my treat.

"I've actually never had sushi." She was walking toward me, and as she said this, she tucked a strand of hair behind her ear — a patented Cass gesture, I had realized, which she seemed to do whenever she felt vulnerable in some way. Watching her walk to me, I wanted to grab her hand and pull her closer, but of course I didn't. We hadn't yet touched in any meaningful way.

"Is it good?" she asked while untying her apron.

"It is if you like raw fish," I said with a laugh, and she flashed me a look — she didn't like to be on the outside of things. "Nah," I said. "You don't even need to have raw fish. We could get shrimp, or avocado and cucumber. You'll like it, I think, although how well do I *really* know you?"

"Right at this moment, you know me better than anyone else in the world," she said, which was an interesting thing to say. I wanted to ask a follow-up, but also, I was playing the long game, so instead I said, "Sushi it is?"

Sushi in Plattsburgh was not the best introduction to the cuisine, I lamented as we sat at a two-top in an otherwise deserted restaurant. The server was a young woman with pale skin and jet-black hair — she walked sullenly toward our table with two large plastic menus, clearly disappointed we'd decided to eat there.

"Welcome to Sushi Land," she said as flatly as possible, extending a menu first to me, then to Cass, who looked up at the young woman and, I swear, it was like Cass was pouring energy and light into her, like Cass's attention had reanimated the girl.

"Thank you," Cass said with a focus I rarely saw from her — she often seemed to be drifting away on her thoughts.

"What do you like here?" Cass broke eye contact with the server to scan the menu, which had lots of pictures. "I need help, please."

I'm a confident person, so I don't feel shame in saying that I was jealous. Taking Cass to try sushi for the first time, well, I wanted to be the one to teach and advise her, to make recommendations. That was the whole point: to share something new, together. For the rest of her life, anytime she ate sushi, she'd think about the first time she ever had it — with *me*.

"My favorite is the shrimp tempura roll," the girl was now saying, stepping a little closer to Cass and turning so they could look at the menu from the same angle. She even bent down a little. Shrimp tempura, not exactly a connoisseur's choice, but she was probably right — it was probably the best thing for Cass to order.

"You're charming," I said when the girl was out of earshot. Cass was studying the menu, which she'd asked to keep. She shrugged. "I know what it's like working in a small town."

Beneath the table I was twirling my thumbs. As I mentioned earlier, a key part of being a lawyer was playing with the silences. Or rather, enduring them. If you were always pouncing on a witness, my professors would explain, you would never know their second thought — and the second thought was where the useful information lived.

"I used to think," Cass began a moment later, and by watching her I could tell how hard she was working to formulate this thought, to share this in a way that would make sense. She looked away and started again: "I used to think I was going to act, like really act." She looked directly at me for a moment, then away again. "My plan since I was a kid was to move to Hollywood and be an actor; it may sound silly, but it's something I've always wanted to do. Acting is just about making someone fall in love with you so they'll follow you anywhere — on the stage, I mean, or on the screen. Maybe also off it, I guess, if you do it well enough."

She stopped talking, but her attention seemed to be on some memory only she could see. I kept twirling my thumbs until the silence had stretched so many beats that it became its own sound. Finally, Cass looked back at me and said, "Does that make any sense to you?"

I said, piecing it together as I was speaking, "So . . . you . . . want to be a movie star and you —"

"Want*ed*," she interrupted, really enunciating the *t*. I looked at her blankly, not because I didn't understand but because I was interested in why she'd pounced so quickly on that part. (Follow people where they lead you.) When I didn't respond, she explained, "The movie star part, you said *want,* present tense, but it's past tense, want*ed*."

"You don't want to anymore — be a movie star?"

"It's not that I don't want to be, it's that —" She stopped abruptly. And I gathered that she knew precisely how to finish the sentence but decided not to.

"I don't know," she said, shaking her head. "It's complicated."

As we said good night, standing a few feet apart on the sidewalk, I was purposefully standoffish. Just to see how Cass would react, if my distance would bring her closer. I stuffed my hands in my pockets, rocked back on my heels, and told her I would see her tomorrow. Cass was looking at me with curiosity — obviously I wasn't as good an actor as she was — but said nothing.

"Good night, Sidney," she said. Just then my coat pocket started chirping, which was still an unusual phenomenon at the time, and I pulled out the little silver flip phone — MOM, it said — and lifted it toward Cass.

I thought I noticed an emotion flash across

Cass's face.* She took a long inhale, which I couldn't decipher, then turned and walked back the way we'd come.

Stepping back inside Sushi Land, I answered the phone. Twenty minutes later, Mom and I were finally saying goodbye, which was good timing because Annalise (Sushi Land server extraordinaire) was walking toward me. I gave her a quick wave and pushed out into the cold night.

My car was still parked in front of the café. I hustled that way, burrowing my chin into my coat and blowing hot air to warm my face. I did that repeatedly, my breath no

***Note from Cate:** When I read this part from Sidney, I was shocked at how astute her observation of that moment was. I remember it well. A few things were tied up in it, for me. Reading the word "Mom" teleported me to Bolton, which as you can imagine was not a place I wanted to be reminded of just then. The mind works quickly. What Sidney read as a "flash of emotion" was for me a series of intricately connected thoughts: Mom-childhood-Bolton-Amanda-accident-fleeing-coward. This call from Sidney's mom was *absolutely* the reason everything happened later that night. (Not unrelated: I was jealous. Imagine having a mom who called for no other reason than to just hear your voice. Just *imagine*.)

match for the freezing wind, until I was on the same block, then I glanced up, my eye drawn immediately to the soft glow in the window of the coffee shop. I peered through the inch of glass not covered by blinds. Cass was sitting on the corner of the couch, a notebook on her lap. I stepped backward as my mind flew through explanations, trying to make one stick, then I looked again and yes — absolutely Cass. Whatever games I was playing earlier felt stupid. I knocked on the glass. How would she react to me seeing her?

She looked up, but sat unmoving and her deep embarrassment hit me like a sonic wave through the glass, and then it disappeared. Had I made it up? She was uncurling herself from the couch and padding toward me in socks, no shoes. Her head was down the whole way, so I couldn't read her face. Then she was at the door, unlocking the deadbolt, opening it just wide enough for her face.

"Hi," she said, and it was the softest I'd ever heard her. She met my gaze for only a moment, then looked down, and even though there were so many other things to think about, I couldn't help it — my mind began fixating on how much freezing air was seeping inside. Cass was wearing black socks pulled up to mid-shin, white cotton shorts, and a hooded gray sweatshirt with the small Champion logo on the breastbone. She looked cozy like an underwear ad, and I wanted to touch her — but first we had to stop the flow of cold air.

"Can I come in?" I asked, and in response she stepped aside, and I turned sideways and slipped in, helping her close the door behind us — a relief. Without a word, she shuffled back to the couch, and I followed her. In those few seconds, the coffee shop stopped being a place of business and became an intimate living room. We sat and the lamp's small halo of light trapped us in its glow.

Cass held the closed notebook on her lap and was looking down at it. I was sitting arm's length away and slid closer, cutting the distance in half, then I leaned forward and took off my coat, laying it behind me on the couch.

"Am I imagining this?" I asked, swirling my finger in the space between us like I was calling for another round at the bar. Cass seemed caught off guard, and I wondered if maybe she'd been preparing some lie. Now I was making her consider this other thing, and she wasn't ready. As we sat there, the question of why she was shoeless in the coffee shop after hours seemed secondary to some other, bigger feeling.

"Imagining what?" she said finally, and I thought, *Okay, she needs me to spell it out, to buy herself time.*

"It feels like there's something really big on your mind," I said. "There's like a weight, a thickness, that's vibrating off you." Then I added, just to give her a release valve if needed, "Although I could be imagining it — that's a possibility."

She shook her head. "No, you're not imagining it." She could have gaslit me, and I half expected her to, saying something like, *What? No. I don't know what you mean.*

She looked down, quietly moved the notebook to the side, slowly bent forward over her legs, and for a moment I thought she was going to be sick. A second later she interlaced her fingers against the back of her neck. She looked like someone who thought the plane was going down. Then she started squeezing her elbows in tight, pulling on her neck, and I could see her eyes were pressed shut and her face was contorted like she was bracing herself for pain or maybe already enduring it. A moment later she began rocking back and forth, her toes pressing into the hardwood.

I slid myself even closer and put my hand on her back to steady her — just to let her know I was there. I watched as my hand began rising and falling, her breaths deep and fast. Whatever she was feeling, it seemed big and scary, and she was just holding on for dear life.

I kept repeating, my voice a whisper in her ear, *I'm here for you, I got you.* Twice, I tried folding myself onto her back and wrapping my arm around her, to steady her, but she was shaking so violently — the position was awkward. How long did we sit like this? Long enough that I went through every possible explanation — death, murder, rape, insanity, a blend of all or none, something else my mind couldn't even imagine. She sobbed; I categorized. I tried to convince myself that I didn't need an explanation — that the honesty of her pain and vulnerability was enough. But that wasn't true — I wanted to know.

Eventually, her breathing slowed, became more regular. A minute after that, she released her neck, began slowly pushing herself upright. Her eyes were swollen, and her nose was running. She covered her face with her hand, held it there for another few minutes, her shoulders still lifting and falling with quieter sobs. Finally, she cupped both hands over her nose and mouth like someone facing a terrible, monumental decision. My right hand was resting gently on her bare knee. A second later her hands dropped and she turned to me — a decision had been made.

"I left home," she said. "It's been a month or so, and I've been living out of my, my car." She paused, and her hand covered her eyes, but only for a moment, to steady herself. "My best friend she's . . . she's . . . I don't know what she is, she's hurt really badly, maybe even worse, I don't know."

Tears were dripping, but I wouldn't say she was crying. Crying is an action. This felt passive — she was leaking.

"And I left. I just left. I took the car and drove away," she said, like she couldn't believe it, like she was hearing it for the first time — baffled by herself. "The two of us, we were going to go to LA together. It was a whole thing we'd had planned for years, to get out of that town, and when it happened, I just felt out of control, like I had to leave." Her eyes flew to mine, then she said it again, "I *had* to leave."

"Okay," I said. "It's okay." (Was it okay? I didn't know yet.)

"My whole life, I've just been waiting for it to start, and I had all these big dreams of who I was going to be, and now I think —" She hiccupped then and flashed me a look like, *And now I'm fucking hiccupping — my entire life has imploded, and I can't even explain how because I'm hiccupping.* She waited, hiccupped once more, then started again: "And now I'm trapped — I'm trapped either way. If I go back, my life will be nothing, just cleaning rooms like my mom or working at the grocery store, figuring things out with Amanda, but now, I think it's even worse because I'm — I'm not even doing any of that. I'm like a ghost or something."

Her eyes were rimmed red, and her face was so puffy she looked like she'd been stung by a bee.

"How are you a ghost?" I asked.

"I play it out in my mind every night: I imagine that I make it big and what would happen if I did, you know? Amanda would see me, or someone from home would, and then they would come for me, I know they would."

"Who would come for you?" I was still trying to understand if she'd done something illegal. That's how I was trained to think.

She hopped over my question and continued. "Everyone would find out what a terrible person I am — I'd be the one who did that awful thing." She shifted her voice to a whisper, like someone gossiping about her: "*Can you even believe it? Who could do that to their* best *friend?* And now I'm trapped in my own life. Unless I go back, and then I'm trapped in that other life."

"Is it that bad?"

Her eyes flew to mine, and she said, slowly, "Yes, it's that bad."

"Tell me, then. I can handle it, whatever it is."

After I said this, she dropped her head against the back of the couch and took a few long breaths, steadying herself. Then she told me, in vivid detail, reliving each beat of that afternoon: the boat ride, the old house, the zip line, the pool, everything. And somehow it was both better than what I'd imagined, and immeasurably worse. When she was done talking, she twisted her shoulders and put her arms around me, pressing our bodies together, and she asked me if I could help her, please could I help her. I told her I would — of course I would.

That night in the café, I inhaled the scent of her hair, and it smelled like apples,* and

---

*__Note from Cate:__ I was obsessed with the Bath & Body Works line of products scented Country Apple. To this day, whenever I pass a store, I go inside and find the Country Apple Body Splash because it transports me back to Amanda, who also loved it, but hated that she loved it. (Apples, New York, cliché, etc.)

I ran my hands through the long brown strands again and again. Eventually, when she seemed calmer, I separated her from me, and now our lips were only inches apart. It felt trite, but I took my thumbs and brushed the remaining tears from her eyes. Being close to Cass lit my body up. I couldn't help it; I wanted to taste her. I tilted my head and slowly, so slowly, slow enough that she had time to pull away, I put my lips on hers. An electric current shot through me, and then I was slipping my tongue into her mouth and willing her body to respond.

"Come with me," I said, breaking from the moment, wanting Cass to know how serious I was about her — how committed I was to being the person who got her through this awful time. She was touching her mouth as if stunned at what just happened. *Funerals,* that's the word that was going through my mind. That age-old thing about how grief and sadness turn people on. What was happening between us here wasn't strange — it was part of the human condition.

"Come with you where?"

I could feel her leaning away, but I firmed my hands against her back and held her steady.

"I'm leaving for New York after the semester," I said. "Come with me. It'll be a fresh start, for both of us. You can become whoever you want to become."

She reached down to the coffee table, and my eyes followed, and there was the spiral notebook I had given her after her first class. She touched the cover, lifted it open briefly, then said, "I want to be a writer."

"Okay," I said, then added, "I think there are a few writers in New York." I meant this last part as a joke and Cass smiled. I could feel her body softening into me and I kissed her again and she finally kissed me back.

"Is that a yes then?" I asked.

She whispered into my ear, the feel of her breath sweeping down my spine, *"It's a yes."*

CHAPTER 18

Cass

2000
Plattsburgh

My first few nights inside the café, even though the blinds were drawn, and the place was filled with plants, I dared only to use the small lamp next to the couch. No easy sight lines. You'd have to press your face to the glass to see me.

I believed I had a measure of privacy. And each night I stared at my open notebook and waited for something to happen. For writing to happen. But so far, nothing. It had been thirty-nine days since I left Amanda, and I was filled with shame. It seemed to have gotten infected, my shame. I felt feverish. I needed it out of me.

That's how I was feeling the night Sidney knocked at the window. I was fidgety and stuck in my own head, reliving the moment. I had drawn a picture of myself going back to the island. A stick figure in a terrible little boat. Zooming across scribbled waves. Another stick figure, legs at unnatural angles, inside a lopsided pool. I stared at this picture, kept tracing the lines.

Then, a knock on the window. Before I looked up from the couch, I had this passing thought — *please don't be Sidney* — but of course it was. Her long face pressed up against the window and this deep annoyance radiating off me. What I wanted was to see Amanda standing there, one hip turned out, or even my mom, with one of her luxurious hugs that was supposed to make up for all the other stuff, *okay baby?* I padded over and unlocked the door, just a little, but she slipped inside. She was either not good at reading body language or believed herself capable of overcoming it.

When we sat on the couch, I realized how bad of a state she had caught me in. She was tugging off her coat and setting it aside. It hit me hard then, the need to say things. I'd swallowed this story whole, an entire life. And here was someone who wanted to listen.

I remember rocking on my heels, trying to hold it all in, press it all down. But not possible. Then I was speaking, a torrent of words; and I was sobbing, my eyes puffy. Finally, I was coming down, coming back. And

Sidney was close to me, and she felt safe, like dry land. I was surprised to find myself feeling glad she was there. Her body felt good against mine. Her lips were soft and gentle just like I always imagined a woman's would feel. I liked it.

"Come with me to New York," she was whispering in my ear. "I'll make this new life real."

What I said: *Yes.*

What I thought: *Another door opening.*

What happened: a second seismic shift in my story.

CHAPTER 19

SIDNEY

2000
Plattsburgh to Bolton Landing

My piano teacher once asked me if I could feel the music. I was at her house — on her piano. She was sitting facing me. I loved playing. Every note corresponded to a movement. Instant feedback about whether I'd done it right. I usually had. But I didn't know what her question meant — did I *feel* the music? When I said nothing, she said, "What I'm wondering is, do you have an emotional experience when you play?"

She had played with the Boston Pops. A local big-deal lady in our Vermont town. She wore only these flowy dresses and chunky necklaces that made no sense to me, so it wasn't odd that her question didn't, either. Sure, I could feel the emotion of the music, I just didn't find that part interesting. For me, playing piano was the satisfaction of repetition and practice. I liked hitting a button and seeing the correct letter appear — like a typewriter. Which is what I said to her. That had clearly been the wrong answer; she slowly stopped answering my mom's calls to schedule lessons.

Maybe this helps explain why I went to Bolton Landing, because if I didn't have "it" — whatever "it" was — then I needed to compensate. I needed to overprepare. And also, a lawyer must have as full an understanding as possible. That night in the café, Cass seemed to purge herself of the full story — that she'd left her best friend, Amanda, broken in a pool, that her real name was Anne Marie Callahan. But the best lawyers don't just have the same information as their clients; they have more.

I told Cass I was spending the three-day weekend with my family in Burlington. Instead, I drove to her hometown. I'd already started planning her future. And what she needed to truly escape her past was a stalwart representative (read: me) who could see every angle and block all incoming traffic before reaching her.

Which is why I needed to know.

The car ride to Bolton was ninety minutes, almost all highway, and I soon found myself pulling into a Stewart's just outside town so that I could get my bearings. My first stop was going to be the Bolton Central School office, where I would introduce myself as a new state university hire — a recruiter made the most sense, but I'd play it by ear. A few questions was all I needed to ask. Just tiptoe into an understanding of the town, its people, how it operated, and go from there.

The office was just inside the main entrance, and I poked my head in with a casual hello. I was wearing pleated, high-waisted khaki pants and a blue button-down, because that seemed like what someone holding my position (college recruiter?) would wear. The woman behind the front desk had brown frizzy hair and I could picture the salon she went to, an unattached white building on the side of the road with those glossy photos of permed women in the window. She saw me enter and gave me the thinnest of smiles.

And then I was surprising myself by saying, "Hi, I'm Sophia . . ." — the lie just appeared on my tongue without forethought — "I'm with SUNY Plattsburgh, the theater department. I was recently hired as a recruiter."

Mmhmm, was all the woman responded with, which was a-okay with me because her full attention, her committing my details to memory, was actually the opposite of what I needed. Temporary access — that's all I was going for.

"I was hoping for a few minutes with the drama teacher, to tell her about our program," I heard myself saying. *Smart,* I was thinking, *just go right to the source.* Cass had mentioned that she and Amanda were the leads in all the school plays; she hadn't said much else about the experience, except their future plans to go to Hollywood.

"Him," the woman said, looking up.

"What's that?" I was standing now with my hands on the welcome desk, about waist height.

"It's a him, the drama teacher — Mr. Riley." She really was barely looking at me, multitasking, with much more focus on whatever was happening on her computer. Without looking away from the screen, she was pointing over and behind her, saying, "He's probably in his office behind the theater, down the hall, through the double doors, and it's on the right."

"Thank you," I said, backing out of the office. I'd been expecting more hoops to jump through, but this was going to make my life easier.

Mr. Riley was, in fact, in his office. The black door was halfway open — a *Twelfth Night* poster taped to the front. Before knocking I paused and looked at the date of the performance — it was the previous autumn, which made me smile because no doubt Cass had appeared in the play. Then the poster was starting to fall, and I lunged forward to pin it to the door, and the noise caught Mr. Riley's attention and then he was standing, helping me and saying, "This thing just won't stay up, maybe I should get stronger tape." He was using tan masking tape, which was really just like using hope, but I kept quiet about it.

"Must have been a great performance," I said, tapping my finger against the poster.

"Oh goodness." He brought his hand over his heart in a dramatic flourish. "The story behind that play — you wouldn't believe it even if I told you. I'm Richard Riley, by the way. How can I help you?"

What a great name, I thought. He was an unexpected figure for a small-town drama teacher. I'd imagined a middle-aged woman who'd watched a lot of movies, but Richard Riley was really playing the part in a black turtleneck and gray ascot and well-tended salt-and-pepper beard. He seemed like someone who'd actually worked on Broadway.

"I'm Sally Carver," I was now saying — the lie spontaneous. In the split second before I was speaking, I realized I could get better information, and faster, if I pivoted away from being a college recruiter. "I work for a research firm down in the city and we've been hired to . . . put together a database, kind of like a census, of high school drama programs — for state budget purposes."

I was obviously constructing this reality as I went, each stepping-stone appearing as I was speaking, but the idea of being from a "research firm" felt vague enough and "budget purposes" serious enough that Mr. Riley would comply, and on the off chance he tried, it would make it difficult to track me down after the fact.

"And you're doing all that in person?"

"Oh, no, no, of course not — my sister, she, she lives in the town over," I said. Gosh, I was good at this. "So coming here, it's an excuse to expense a little trip home." I brought my finger to my lips and raised my eyebrows. He chuckled and brought his thumb and pointer to his mouth and pulled across, indicating my secret was safe with him. Now I had his trust.

He pulled out a folding chair he kept tucked away, then I asked him every bureaucratic question I could think of — participation numbers, attendance, budgets, promotion, process, all of it. Mr. Riley took the questions seriously, pulling out a binder at one point to confirm some numbers. I had a notebook in my bag, and I jotted down everything he told me. At one point, I forgot that the whole thing was an act because I really wanted to know the answers to what I was asking. If someone hadn't put this database together, they absolutely should. Then I closed my notebook, signaling the work part was over, and glanced back at the *Twelfth Night* poster taped to the door. His eyes followed mine.

"Okay, so, *now* can I hear the story behind that play?"

Transparently: I was fucking impressed with myself. Sitting there, just a few feet from him, my question felt perfectly natural. Not nosy. Or too prying. Who could resist following up on some local drama, especially when the idea of that drama had been introduced by someone else — in this case, Richard Riley himself! Maybe Cass didn't want the truth, but I wanted every drop of it.

He leaned back and interlaced his hands behind his head, shaking it in disbelief. "It's heartbreaking," he began, then paused. Before continuing, he pointed to the poster. "That was the final play starring, probably, the two best kids I ever worked with here. They'd been the leads every year, and they were best friends, basically inseparable.

We'd even talk about it in the teachers' lounge, always just the two of them and no one else. Sally, I even *chose plays* based on what would best fit them; never did *that* before in my teaching career. I was absolutely convinced they were going to make it big."

"Wow," I said — a quick verbal cue that I hoped would keep him talking.

"I know," he said, then he suddenly got up and walked to the door, peeking his head one way then the other before pulling the door closed. "Town is still torn up about the whole thing," he said, sitting back in his chair. "Anyway, so the two of them, they both had that 'it' factor, as they say, but one was a verifiable star and the other was riding the coattails just a tiny little bit." Here he pressed his fingers together and squinted to illustrate the slight, but not insignificant, difference in talent between the two girls. (Which was Cass, which was Amanda? — a question I wanted to ask but couldn't.)

"But that's beside the point," he said. "And I don't want to keep you. No doubt you want to get back to your sister."

My sister, my sister, my sis— I'd almost forgotten about her! But I recovered and said, "Oh, no, I have a few minutes. What happened?" Injecting those two words with just the right amount of curiosity was the game, and I nailed it.

"It's just the craziest thing," he said. "Just a month or so ago, one of the girls rushes into the Big 8 — this beaten-up motel down the road — and calls 911, right? Tells them to get to Hideaway Island immediately, tells them her friend is hurt, tells them where, the whole bit. Of course, they rush help out there, find the girl exactly where they were told she would be, get her to the hospital."

Like a true performer, he stopped there — end of Act I, quick intermission, everyone catches their breath.

"Okay," I said, and I drew out the word like it was an invitation to continue.

"Okay, so," he reset. "One girl is in the hospital, but the other — the one who made the call? — *POOF!*" He brought his hands together and mushroomed them out. "Gone. Nowhere to be found, just disappeared."

Cass.

"Just . . . gone?" I said, feigning shock, because it felt like what someone hearing this for the first time would say and do.

"Nobody, not even her mom — though, to be fair, she was never winning any Mom of the Year awards — has heard from her since. Vanished."

"What happened to her?" I asked.

Mr. Riley tossed his hands in bewilderment, said, "Your guess is as good as mine. I've heard every possible theory whispered around town; they're saying she tried to kill her friend, then fled when it didn't work, which I don't believe for a second. They loved each other. And also, then why would she call 911? I've even heard some people say that the island is haunted, and she probably drowned trying to get back. Honestly, it's a mystery."

Loved each other? I thought.

"What do the police think?"

"No clue. They'd very much like to talk to her, of course, but because her friend didn't die, it's just an unfortunate accident in their mind."

"That makes sense," I said. "So, the other girl, she's alive?"

"Yes, Amanda. But paralyzed from the waist down. Absolutely tragic." He looked again at the *Twelfth Night* poster and said, "Shakespearean, the whole thing."

CHAPTER 20

SIDNEY

2000
Plattsburgh

The way I saw it back then, Cass was a once-in-a-lifetime woman. I'd never been to New York before, didn't know how big the sea of fish could get, and I was convinced it couldn't get better than Cass. What I needed — and what she needed — was to stop looking back. Releasing her from the albatross of Amanda — that would be my gift to her. She would have true freedom. With me.

I drove directly from Mr. Riley's office to the coffee shop in Plattsburgh. Two minutes before closing, I was pushing through the front door, expecting to see Cass in her apron, stacking chairs. But no, just Brett. He didn't seem a fan of mine — or of anyone, really. He pointed toward the back door, and I walked wordlessly past. I assumed Cass would be sitting on the steps where we'd shared that fake cigarette, but no luck there either. I kept walking, to the parking lot, and there she was, inside her dinged-up red Civic. She was twisted around, looking for something in the back seat, so she didn't see me. I opened the passenger door, folded myself inside.

"No, you can't," she said, now facing front. "I'm leaving. And what are you even doing here? I have to leave."

She'd been crying — her eyes were puffy — and she turned her head like she didn't want me to see. As if I hadn't already witnessed her rock bottom. I reached over and touched her arm. She looked down at my hand, held her eyes there for a beat, then looked at me, quickly shaking her head.

"I'm going back," she said, motioning that I needed to get out of the car. It didn't feel good — being shooed away like that.

"This is all wrong," she was saying next. "I've made so many mistakes."

I put my hand on the door handle and thought about just getting out. Why was I letting her treat me this way? Who was she to me, anyway? That is, besides the most beautiful girl I'd ever seen. I cut her a look, let her know I was hurt. Her shoulders sagged.

"I'm sorry," she said, slowing herself down. "I don't mean to disappoint you. I really,

really don't. But I have to go back home now."

Her face was open, and I knew for certain she was leaving. That she would hit the gas as soon as I got out of the car — a flash of red, speeding back to a life that would trap her forever.

"Oh, Cass," I said, and I let my face crumble. "That's what I'm here about."

She looked confused. "That's what you're here about?"

"Amanda," I said. I covered my eyes with my hand. I was a terrible actor. The whole thing felt absurd, and I expected my next sentence to move us in some other direction. But then I was stumbling ahead, saying, "I went to Bolton Landing today."

"You wha—"

"I'm sorry," I cut her off. "But I needed to know. So I could help you. And, Cass, what I found out — I am so, so sorry."

I dropped my head and started shaking it, slowly, infusing my movement with pure devastation so she'd understand that sorry was actual sorrow — and about something much more consequential than a covert day trip.

Still, I wasn't sure I could do it — say the words aloud. Weaving an entirely new existence for Cass with a single sentence. Did

I have the stomach for it? But then Cass's hands were reaching for mine, and that went straight to my veins. She looked stricken, her eyes imploring, and I just committed — committed myself to the moment and what was needed of me.

"Amanda is dead," I said. "Pneumonia in the hospital — a week after the accident."

All in. I went all in on Cass.

Then I steeled myself, shutting down all thought — no soul; I was just a body across from her — and holding steady as her eyes searched mine, desperately looking for an escape hatch. One second, two seconds, three. Then she dropped my hands and turned away, silently letting herself out of the car. I watched through the window as she opened the trunk, rummaged around. Then she slammed it shut, disappearing through a gap in the fence and into the row of trees behind the parking lot.

CHAPTER 21

CASS

2000
Plattsburgh

I hadn't touched Amanda's things yet. I think on some level I thought I was going back — of course I was going back! — so maybe I figured why disturb them. Or maybe that's not right. Maybe I thought not using Amanda's things was a tiny patch of moral high ground I could claim. See, now there's a line even I wouldn't cross. And somehow, all the while, I never thought of myself as a bad person. I was just struggling, figuring out how to do life. Or maybe that's what all rotten people tell themselves.

Then that terrible afternoon. Sidney saying those words. Saying, "Amanda is dead." That's what she said.

A minute prior, I was just a stretch of highway from seeing Amanda again; now, I'd never —

I couldn't even think it. And no matter how hard I looked at Sidney — truly begging her, with all of me — she wouldn't take it back. Then suddenly, I needed to get out of the car; maybe I could trap the idea of Amanda being dead inside. I got out and opened the trunk, quickly grabbing Amanda's bag, the Strand tote, from the back right corner. Only once the trunk was closed did I exhale. I couldn't let any more of the car's air, tainted as it was, into my body.

Inside the bag were three meticulously rolled sweaters, tidiness being Amanda's lone streak of OCD.

I squeezed the bag to my chest and disappeared into the row of trees behind the parking lot. Despite my best efforts, the reality of Sidney's words had escaped the car and were, I was disturbed to acknowledge, surviving contact with the outside world. And so now this idea of Amanda being dead, I ignored it. Just let it be this thing in the world. Like words across a banner, pulled behind a plane: AMANDA IS DEAD. Written in the clouds. Either way, a thing apart from and outside of me. I could look up and engage or I could not.

I found a thick tree and slid down the trunk. I held the bag to my chest and that stupid thing Amanda always said about fashion kept running through my mind, how it's about matching your outside to your insides. Currently my insides were melting. I brought the bag to my face and screamed into the canvas:

I'm sorry, I'm sorry, I'm sorry, I'm sorry.

Maybe an hour later, I'm not sure, I finally pressed myself to standing. I felt wobbly. I was hollowed out everywhere except my head, which throbbed. I was walking carefully back toward the car and there, still, was Sidney. Exactly where I had left her.

I expected to feel annoyed, angry even, but I wasn't. Maybe it was okay for something to be easy for once. For me to just let things happen because it was there, and it would feel good — being touched and held. Imagine being wrapped in someone's warmth, the rush of their blood against your ear. Then Sidney saw me, and she was getting out of the car, walking toward me.

"Cass," she said, pulling me into a hug, squeezing. "I'm here for you. I got you, okay? I got you."

My chin was on her shoulder, and I nodded into her collarbone. We stood hugging for a few seconds. Then I brought my hand to the back of her neck and guided her lips to mine. Amanda being dead — I just couldn't look in that direction for a little while.

That night, when Sidney brought me back to her apartment, we went straight to her bed. She knew what she was doing. When I finally touched her, slipping my hand inside her jeans, she was dripping wet, and my eyes flicked to hers, a reflex.

"You do that to me," she said, and I realized it turned me on — being wanted that much.

That night, Sidney fell asleep with her arm across my chest. I was staring at the ceiling, terrified to have no more distractions. Again, those three words appeared above me: AMANDA IS DEAD. Black letters, font like on a marquee. I closed my eyes, but the words had already seared my vision. I cried until the pillow was wet against my cheek.

Later that night, I started writing *The Very Last*.

CATE KAY

The Very Last

Jeremiah and Samantha had just finished their overnight shift at ANC. The morning sun was turning the skyscrapers golden, and Samantha hated to miss the show, but

Jeremiah had forgotten his sunglasses in their car, which they kept in monthly parking in the basement of the building and mostly only used on the weekend. They took the elevator deep into the bowels of the garage. Four floors down. The car wasn't much — an old green Mazda they'd nicknamed Pacino because it was scrappy. Pacino had taken some licks: dinged bumper, cracked rearview mirror, floorboards worn through. But it gave them freedom to get out of the city, listen to music, feel the wind in their hair. They were California kids at heart; they needed a pair of wheels.

Jeremiah was in Pacino's front seat, leaning across and rummaging through the glove compartment. Samantha was waiting, her back against a thick cement pillar. She was thinking about the mixtape he'd made her years before, just before they'd driven east to chase their dreams. He'd titled it *Freedom at Last.* They'd taken a spin, listened to the songs, arguing about where to place the best song on a mixtape. She said third track; he said fifth.

She looked at her watch: 6:44. The sun was up. Samantha couldn't know, but these were the last seconds before the city exploded.

From up above, Flight 1602 was

descending into La Guardia. A nine-year-old girl with shiny brown hair, wearing rainbow jellies, had her face pressed against the oval window. She thought she noticed something weird happening on the ground and she reached for her mom. But just as she did, the plane shook, and the girl's mom pulled her away from the window. A second later, a cloud like a big mushroom bloomed above the tall buildings, growing upward and outward and the pilot told them they weren't going to land, that they were going to keep flying, and all the people around them started crying.

Standing in the garage, Samantha felt a pulse of energy within the concrete pillar. The structure seemed to vibrate against her back, a distant rumble. A subway car running near them, she thought. The vibration felt similar, but this energy was on fast-forward somehow. Her whole body became alert.

"Get out!" Samantha yelled, her voice unrecognizable. She lurched forward, grabbed for Jeremiah, pulled him out of the car. They huddled together against the pillar, covered their ears. The lights blew out first. Then, sections of the ceiling fell — thick slabs of concrete — and crushed the cars around them. Pacino's door was still open, and Samantha watched as their green car was flattened by a chunk of the building. Who cared about a cracked rearview mirror now? She pressed her eyes closed and held on to Jeremiah.

CHAPTER 22

AMANDA KENT

2000
Bolton Landing

The summer before sixth grade, Annie and I spent the first week of July playing *Super Mario Bros.* on the original Nintendo system. Playing video games made us feel restless and irritable, but we couldn't seem to help ourselves. We'd mix up a batch of Crystal Light and lie on my den carpet with our heads on pillows, alternating turns and shrieking each time a turtle shell or mistimed jump sent 8-bit Mario plummeting upside-down into the underworld.

At some point, Annie sprung off the floor and said, "I can't take it anymore," then she ripped the cartridge out of the console and faced me. In her best Terminator voice she asked, "Permission to destroy?"

I leapt to my feet, glad for this sudden change in the day's trajectory. I pinned my heels together like the officers I'd seen on TV, rolled my shoulders back, said, "Permission granted, sir," and watched as Annie flung the cartridge across the room like a Frisbee. Not exactly a well-conceived plan of destruction. The gray square hit the far wall and dropped, still in one piece. Annie raced over to collect it, and we inspected it together. Nothing seemed amiss.

"Maybe we see if it still works?" Annie said, already putting it back in the console. She shut the lid and hit Play, and we stood back and watched as the game tried to bring itself back after our murder attempt. The screen blinked; the game was straining to build the full expression of its world but was unable to — something internal had broken.

Annie and I glanced at each other. I was waiting for her to tell me how to feel about purposefully breaking something of value. "We had to," she said, shrugging. "It was like we were disappearing into the game."

The reason I'm telling you this story is because the morning I woke up in the hospital, it felt very much like I was a video game that wouldn't load properly.

As I was first waking up, I was curious, like I was a detective solving the mystery of what was happening to me — the who, where, when, why of it.

Who: me, I think; yes, me.

Where: unclear to start, but I heard a rhythmic beeping and saw the fuzzy outline of a machine that told me . . . hospital.

When: rewind, rewind, rewind — the zip line, the fall, those were the nearest memories.

Why: I'm hurt, but how badly was not a question I was ready to consider.

(Sometimes, even now, I'll wake up feeling the same as that morning. Just my brain's way of messing with me. When I feel that happening, I force myself to sit upright and turn on the bedside lamp. Then I breathe deeply many times, and the panic usually subsides.)

Back to that very first morning. I had one eye open. Someone had curled themselves into a chair in the corner of the room, huddled beneath a too-small blanket. Was it Annie? I couldn't tell. On the windowsill next to the person who was probably Annie was a coffee cup from the local shop, Spot, and seeing the logo of the brown dog with its red tongue calmed me. The familiarity made me feel safe.

My throat was dry and painful, and I wondered if I had strep or maybe laryngitis and that's why I was in the hospital, not because of the zip line. I was trying so hard to stay awake, keeping my one eye fixed on the coffee cup, but then I was being pulled under again, swimming back toward a memory.

Toward Annie. She was wearing the blue peacoat she found at Goodwill that had these buttons that looked like sideways wine corks. It was free period, and we always went to Spot during free period. The key to coffee, Annie said, was adding enough cream and sugar so that it was more like a milkshake.

We had a love-hate relationship with Spot. We loved how close it was to school and that they served coffee out of this old trolley car painted blue with yellow accents. We hated the name and logo. (The coffee also wasn't very good, but we didn't know that back then.)

"Just, like, who names their dog Spot?" Annie said the first time we went together — sophomore year, I think. "Did they sit down to think of dog names and just run out of energy?"

"Maybe the process overwhelmed them," I said, and she gave me that look of hers, one eyebrow slightly lifted, when she saw we were about to have a bout of cleverness.

"It can't be more overwhelming than, you know, actually having a dog, can it?"

"I don't know, let's give it a try. What would you name your dog?"

She dropped her head back and looked to the clouds for an answer. A few seconds later, she said, "Um . . . Lucky? . . . Patch?" — apparently she'd seen *101 Dalmatians* — then she paused, added, "This is harder than I thought." It was unusual, Annie not having the perfect comeback, and I watched with amusement as she put both hands on the sides of her head and looked at me in horror.

"Oh my god, I'm so bad at this," she said.

(She was never bad at anything.)

"You try. What would you name your dog?"

That was easy. My dad had dogs around his shop, so since I was little, I'd been dreaming about the day I could have my own and what I'd name them. Then at one theater camp in middle school we did *A Midsummer Night's Dream* and I knew.

"Puck," I said. "I'm gonna name my dog Puck."

Annie leapt to her feet and looked at me, impressed. "Oh my god that's perfect! Did you just come up with that on the . . . *Spot?*" She winked at me after this last word, trying to win back some cool points with a lame joke.

After that day, every so often, we'd be sitting

on one of the benches that looked like it was salvaged from a train station and Annie, out of nowhere, would just say a name: Cicero, or Poe, or Henry V, or Hamlet. The first few times it happened, I was lost and in need of more context. I'd respond, "Wait, what?"

"Persephone," she said one afternoon during March of senior year. I know for certain it was March because when a cold gust of wind blew a few minutes later, Annie said, "March," while subtly shaking her head and I knew to finish it with "in like a lion, out like a lamb," and we high-fived without looking at each other — our tradition throughout every March since fourth grade when our favorite teacher Mrs. Rogers had us cut flowers and lions out of construction paper and taped them up in the hallway outside her classroom beneath the proverb, a project that delighted us to no end.

In response, I furrowed my brow, which she properly interpreted. She interlaced her hands behind her head, said, "I know, I know — it's not a dog name."

"It is, however, a great name for a human character."

She nodded. A minute later she tried again: "Dante."

"Hmm," I said, really considering this one; I took my position seriously. "A strong candidate for sure, but really only if you get, like, a Doberman."

Annie sighed. "Yeah, I think you're right." Then she looked at me and said, "Do you think I owe the owners of Spot a formal apology?"

I was waking up again and now Kerri was right there, holding my hand. She seemed both relieved and terrified that I was awake.

"Hi," I croaked.

Kerri instantly started crying and lifted my hand to kiss it. My hand felt weird, like when I woke up in the middle of the night and my arm was asleep and it felt like someone else's arm.

"Where did Annie go?" I whispered, sure she'd been there earlier, curled up in the chair.

Kerri just looked at me, didn't say anything.

And I swear, this is when fear started seeping into my bones, when the pieces started to slide together — the hospital, my throat, the zip line, the heaviness of my body, Annie there with me in the pool, but then gone.

How big and scary this must be to have chased her away.

"I don't know where Annie is," Kerri said finally.

CHAPTER 23

SIDNEY

2005
New York City

I knew *The Very Last* would be huge. Cass finally let me read it after four and a half years of writing and editing and rewriting. That entire time, everything about the book — the premise and characters and setting — was unknown to me. She could have been writing a romantic comedy for all I knew, though I doubted she was, as romance didn't seem a priority to her, no matter how tender I tried to be. That she would fictionalize some version of her past was also a concern. So, when she finally gave me the book, I was nervous, and I stayed up all night reading it, terrified until the end that something in it would give her away. I put the final page on the stack and looked at her — she was asleep on her side, her back to me.

We lived in a one-bedroom in Harlem.

Cass worked at a coffee shop around the corner. I'd put myself on an accelerated track at NYU, summer courses, too, and graduated in two years instead of three, was already working my way up at a prestigious law firm.

Early that morning, I touched her shoulder and gently shook her awake. She looked sleepily back at me until she saw the stack of papers on my lap, and then she pushed herself upright, suddenly alert.

"You read it," she said. I could hear the hope in her voice. She cared what I thought, and that made me feel better about us; our relationship always felt like such a tenuous thing. Aside from storytelling, Cass's greatest gift seemed to be absence — that she could easily vacate her physical body. She was almost always somewhere else, and I had started to take it as a personal affront. Had I not given her enough?

Seeing her that morning in bed, fully present, desperate to know my reaction to her work, I fell back in love. "It's a bestseller," I said, and as the words came out, I vowed to use every lever at my disposal to make it so.

"You think?" she asked, which was unlike her, seeking repeated positive reinforcement from me.

"We need to make a plan," I said instead.

"I actually submitted it," she said, turning on the lamp by her side of the bed. She was impatient — always had been. Whoever first used the phrase *putting the cart before the horse* was talking about someone very much like Cass. How could she send a copy of this manuscript without first checking with me? No doubt she sensed my disapproval because she added, "Just to this one literary agency — it's my top choice: Eloquence."

"And whose name did you use as the author?"

"A pseudonym."

"What pseudonym?"

"The one I want to use —"

"Which is?" I was annoyed and didn't try to hide it.

She clenched her jaw, then eased it. "I was getting to that. I decided on Cate Kay."

"Cate Kay," I said, testing it out, trying to mentally poke holes in it. "What does it mean?"

"It doesn't mean anything. I just like the way it sounds."

CHAPTER 24

CASS

2005
New York City

Nearly five years without Amanda. That's 1,825 days. A microscopic number compared to how many times I'd thought of her. She was in every nook and cranny. Each time I sat down to write — always in a cheap spiral notebook, always by hand — I could hear her laughing at my persistent pen-clicking. She'd reach over, steady my hand. She had noticed all my little compulsions.* Writing amplified these tics. I'd click my pens to death. Literally, the spring would fly out the top. Whenever this happened, I thought of Amanda, which was followed by a cold wave of guilt. A potent one-two punch.

*****Note from Cate:** She even knew that if allowed to keep my straw wrapper, I'd fold it into the tiniest square possible.

She was with me, always.

I infused her into my book, of course. Where else was Amanda going to go, all the little details I loved about her, if not into my book? I had no other outlet for her, and she was taking up too much room inside me; I had to offer some to the universe.

So I wrote a story about two friends, partners, who had a dream together, but are eventually separated by disaster. One loves the other, but the love isn't returned — not in the same way, anyway. And I made the disaster that would separate my two soulmates big, so big that the world would understand that no one was to blame; it was the universe that had ripped them apart.

I wrote and wrote and wrote. The book was an homage, but also a Hail Mary. Did I think it would ever get published or become a bestseller? Absolutely not. The odds were infinitesimal; and also, yes, it was a certainty. I was of two minds. Other times, I swear it didn't matter either way — the writing of it was the point. But mostly, I thought of the book as my escape hatch into another life, and perhaps I believed that was possible because I'd already done it once: escaped into another life.

CATE KAY

The Very Last

Roger Riley was ANC's most famous anchor. He was known for his well-kept salt-and-pepper beard and steady demeanor. He was on-air the morning of the blast, broadcasting from the network's Atlanta headquarters. Midway through a routine weather update, his producer got in his ear and frantically explained the news coming out of New York. Roger relayed everything to the viewers in real time, trying to keep the tremble out of his voice. He knew this was a history-altering event. The death toll would be stunning.

Detonated in Midtown New York. Shockwaves felt in Philadelphia. Cell phone signals down. Broadcast signals down. New York is cut off from help and information.

This last piece is what Roger worried most about. Survivors needed to shelter in place; the air was deadly.

He had been on-air for an hour, no commercials, when his producer came back into his ear with unbelievable news: Two young ANC reporters had survived the blast and so had ANC's mobile signal. They had a working camera and mic pack

— they could broadcast from the ground.

"Will the signal reach New Yorkers?" he asked. Protocol be damned. His producer wasn't sure, but she thought it was possible. He nodded and looked into the camera:

"We have just received word that two young members of the ANC team have survived the blast and are broadcasting live. Their names are Samantha Park and Jeremiah Douglas. They are risking their lives to share what is happening on the ground. Let's go to them now . . ."

* * *

"This is Samantha Park with Jeremiah Douglas behind the camera," Samantha said, eyes level, keeping her voice as steady as possible. "We are broadcasting live from downtown Manhattan. We believe a nuclear bomb was detonated in Midtown at approximately 6:45 a.m."

They'd been outside for two hours, and Jeremiah was feeling dizzy and cold. Atlanta had just told them they had three minutes off-camera — Roger Riley was interviewing a nuclear expert in the studio. Jeremiah tried to hold steady, but the camera pitched forward and crashed to the ground. He dropped to one knee.

"This is real, huh?" he said. Samantha had been having the same realization. She knew he was talking about all of it — the day, the explosion, the air, which they could feel poisoning their bodies in real time.

Samantha ran over, put a hand on his shoulder. "What do you feel?"

"Kind of like altitude sickness, except way worse: dizziness, headache, nausea," he said. "But then also this other thing. It's like my insides are — I don't know how to describe it exactly."

Right then, a swirl of wind — the air seemed possessed in those first hours — blew a paper cup into Samantha's foot and she grabbed it, looked up, was absolutely stunned to see that they were in front of their favorite coffee shop. She spun once around, trying to get her bearings. How?

She looked at the cup in her hand, swiveled it until she was looking at the logo: *Spot*. She imagined the cup with coffee — enough milk and sugar so it tasted like a warm milkshake.

She was thinking of all the nights she and Jeremiah had stopped here, at first thrilled at their new job, then game-planning world dominance, then complaining about internal bureaucracy. She thought of Jeremiah walking in on a recent Sunday morning, casually wondering if they should go back home — maybe this city living, this big-dream stuff, wasn't all it was cracked up to be? Samantha had laughed, then abruptly stopped. "Wait, you're serious?" She had promised him they would talk about it, but they hadn't.

While Samantha was lost in thought, staring at the empty cup, Jeremiah managed to bring the camera back to his shoulder. Their three minutes were over. A cold sweat was covering his body, but they were coming back on air in *three, two, one*. He trained the camera on Samantha's face: She was having a moment. He had noticed, seconds before, the way her face had twisted, the way it always did when she was trying not to cry. Now her chest was rising and falling, and she was cradling the cup as if to warm her hands.

"Sam," Jeremiah whispered, wanting her to know they were live again. When she lifted her head and saw that he had the camera, her eyes got big before regaining focus.

"I'm sorry," she said, looking at the sky. "In this moment, more than anything, I want to be professional, for all the survivors who need information, for you at home, for everyone who deserves to know what's happening here. But we've been so disoriented in the aftermath, and we've just found Spot, our coffee shop — the best one in New York. And we've — I've — just gotten knocked sideways for a second."

Samantha bent down and collected the rest of the scattered white cups, stacking them in her hands. Then she walked through the blown-out front of Spot. Jeremiah followed her, capturing her as she tenderly placed the stacked cups on what was left of the counter.

She wiped her eyes and addressed the camera: "We're still in search of emergency services and will continue heading toward city hall, where we hope to find more information and answers for everyone about survivors and what to do next. For now, everyone, please stay sheltered. It's dangerous out here — for many reasons."

CHAPTER 25

Melody Huber

2005
New York City

My role in this story is obvious: I'm the agent who saved *The Very Last* from the slush pile. I've recounted the events of that day a hundred times, at every dinner party I've ever attended. The price for my invitation. But usually I hold back, remove some of my favorite details — not everyone deserves to know everything. But here, now, I won't hold back.

The day I discovered the manuscript, and subsequently Cate Kay, began as one of the worst of my professional career. I was thirty years old and had been in publishing, at the same literary agency, for all eight years since graduating from Brown. The first two I spent as an intern at Eloquence, then two more as an assistant, then the last four as the least productive agent in the agency's history.

Perhaps I'm exaggerating. But I don't think so. In four years, I'd sold just five books. For context, one of my colleagues once closed two deals in one day, and the top agent sold twenty-one books one year. How was I so terrible at the job I'd wanted since I was a little girl? No idea.

It was the Thursday heading into Memorial Day weekend, which was the start of summer and when the agency world slows to a crawl.

"Why hello, Melody," was how the founder of the firm, a sleek, gray-haired man named Dempsey Carroll, greeted me each morning, and he did so again on this one. He was chatting with the woman who runs the front desk, and I was just trying to get past them to my cubicle without having to look anyone in the eye. Being unable to sell in a selling business steadily erodes your confidence, and at this point my ego was in font size two. I assumed everyone around the office was equally embarrassed by my performance.

"Good morning, Dempsey," I said without looking up. I was wearing a modest blue-and-white flower sundress that hit around mid-shin with a pair of basic flats. Everything about me back then screamed average. Because of the way Dempsey had greeted me — like every other day — I did not expect anything out of the ordinary. Looking back on it, I'm certain that all the other agents expected me to quit that spring instead of continuing to pull a paycheck during the summer doldrums. *Some self-respect* is what they believed I should have. As for me, I did have self-respect. I respected my*self* enough to continue getting paid for as long as possible. Especially since I worked hard, even if it wasn't producing results.

On my way to my desk, as I did at the end of every week, I gathered the slush pile into my arms, which always made me look like a disorganized mailroom attendant, tan envelopes spilling every which way. I sat down and stacked all the mail into a neat pile. When I did this, I felt like a dealer at the end of a shuffle, tucking in every wayward card.

"Hey, Melody-girl." Dempsey appeared suddenly by my side — and, before you ask, *yes*, I did hate that he called me *Melody-girl*, but when you can't sell shit, you find it hard to accuse your boss of belittling you with his language. When I looked at him, he'd twisted his mouth into a strange shape, then said, "Hey, when you get a minute, come pop into my office."

That's not the kind of invitation you delay on, so I gave the slush pile one final tap, then said, "I can come now." Reading unsolicited manuscripts was one of my favorite parts of the job, and I looked forward to gathering the pile each week and lugging them home. Going to garage sales was also my thing, that sense of possibility with each stop, and a slush pile tapped into the same energy for me. Luckily, none of my colleagues felt the same, so the wasteland of buried gems was all mine. That morning as I walked away from my desk, I glanced back at the crisply stacked manilla envelopes with longing. How much I'd rather be opening and reading them than following Dempsey Carroll into his bigwig office.

"Grab a seat," he said, gesturing to one of the chairs as he did that annoying thing of half sitting, half standing against the corner of his desk. He smoothed his tie and folded his hands in his lap. (My first thought: *Did he see that in a movie?* My next: *Oh, this isn't gonna be good.*)

Why couldn't I sell anything? I was as confused as anyone. Reading was my favorite activity, and always had been. I was meticulous and had good taste. And yet, all the data would suggest I was in the wrong profession. I'd started to believe maybe I was, too.

Maybe, I'd started thinking in that last year at Eloquence, being a literary agent was less about the words and more about schmoozing and glad-handing, at which I would proudly admit I was terrible. Most days I spent entirely at my desk, reading, writing letters to authors I admired, following the trades, making lists. I loved it. My fellow agents spent their time out of the office, at endless coffee and lunch meetings with authors and editors.

I had never been popular. My eyesight was bad — a genetic thing — and I was fitted for those thick glasses that some babies have to wear, and as I got older the easiest way to explain who I became is to point back to that and say, "Now imagine her as a full-grown person." During school lunches, I read my favorite book tucked into a bathroom stall, and even back then my mom would say, "Melody, shouldn't you try to make some friends?," which I now see as foreshadowing my early failures as an agent.

I remember looking at Dempsey with desperation. He could see the panic bleeding into my eyes, and he didn't like it; it made him uneasy. I felt a surge of fondness for him in that moment, even though I was increasingly certain what was about to happen.

"Melody, kiddo," he said. (Again, I was thirty years old.) "This just isn't working out the way we wanted." He stopped there, hoping this was enough, hoping that I'd fill in the rest for him. A pen was nestled in a groove on his desk, and he lifted it. This seemed to provide him comfort. I felt like I'd swallowed an ice cube that was slowly melting its way down my throat and into my stomach, freezing me from the inside.

Back then, my entire, meager existence was dependent on being a literary agent. I'd moved to New York after one summer home in Chicago, and in those many years I'd made only one friend — a girl I'd gone to college with who happened to live in the same terrible building as me and whom I met up with about once a week so we could both tell others we "had plans" and thus convince ourselves that we were thriving in this lonely metropolis. If Eloquence fired me, not only was I out of a job, and money, and a reason to stay, but I was also out of the only professional field for which I'd ever thought myself qualified.

Staring at Dempsey's sad, sad eyes, I realized: He probably wouldn't write me a letter of recommendation, either. My stomach was cold. I looked at the ceiling. I was going to have to move home and become a librarian. This was the backup plan that my subconscious had concocted years ago, but that I never allowed myself to form into a full thought . . . until right then. A librarian in my hometown. I didn't want to imagine it. Bookworm life was for me, but I'd hoped New York would transform me, Anne Hathaway–style, into the most urbane version of myself.

"We're going to give you a week of severance for every year you've been here." He sounded proud of himself for this. Eight weeks of my embarrassingly low salary.

And that's how the principal agent at Eloquence fired me without actually saying the words. Of course, most things in life are conveyed without using precision, which is why I loved books so much. The people in them were scared and rarely said what they meant, but the best authors used words like swords to slice through it all.

Dempsey stood and so did I, mirroring his movements so I could get out of this sticky moment.

"You don't need to stay the day, obviously." Dempsey was in the doorway now, gesturing toward my desk. I was now also in the doorway, and that's when I saw the stacked brown envelopes and the rest of the items on my desk, mostly just junk. Those manuscripts would be my going-away present.

"Do you need any help with your things?" Dempsey was biting his inner lip, and though social awkwardness was my calling card, even I could tell the correct answer to this question was no. "I'll be fine," I said. A few minutes later everyone saw me leave with that final slush pile, and nobody tried to stop me; if anything, they were probably relieved that I was clearing the mailroom floor one last time. I took this as tacit agreement that the manuscripts were now mine.

Picture me in my shoebox apartment in a Hell's Kitchen walk-up (fifth floor), the apartment so small the bathroom door only partially opened before it hit the sink. Now picture me at the round table in the kitchen, enough surface area for a single plate and a glass. Or for a stack of manuscript envelopes, which were in front of me that night. How much hope did I have for this last set of diamonds in the rough? More than was justified. Of the five books I had sold, none were from the slush pile, though I had found three clients from it and was hopeful for their futures.

More than once that night, I wondered what I was even doing opening this mail: If I found something amazing, I no longer worked for Eloquence. But I kept opening, kept reading, kept hoping, kept telling myself I would cross that bridge if I came to it, which I probably wouldn't.

When people have asked me, over the

years, to explain how I discovered *The Very Last,* I don't think of it as a moment; I think of it as the final scene in a long movie, one that began with me in the back seat of every car ride I took as a kid, buried in some book. A world exists where I leave those envelopes on my desk at Eloquence. This version of my life is not difficult for me to imagine; I have pictured it every day of my life since. Am I the most successful literary agent in the world, or am I one everyday decision from becoming a librarian in Cook County? I am both, always.

Seventeen, the number of manuscripts in the pile. I counted them before opening any and pulled one aside, as if it were a tarot card. My chosen one.

The first ten manuscripts I opened were all bad in the same way, and I dropped them on the floor at the base of my stool. I had six manuscripts left in the stacked pile, and the one "special" manuscript that I'd separated and propped up like a picture frame against a (garage sale) lamp.

My guess is you've assumed this envelope held Cate Kay's manuscript. It didn't.

I finished my dinner (microwaved), sat back down on the stool, and took a deep breath. I had only a few envelopes left, and savoring each was paramount. I lifted the next one and looked at the return address: Cate Kay. Crazy, but I remember thinking that was a great name, and my interest was immediately piqued. The address was local to New York, a law firm somewhere near Columbia University. I carefully slid my finger under the flap, then tenderly removed the pages, like they themselves were the work of art. First, the title page.

And then, that first propulsive sentence: *With time, Samantha Park would become a legend.* Okay, I thought to myself, strong start; I'm interested in how this woman becomes a legend.

I kept reading. In the background of my mind, hope began swirling, even as I told myself to calm down, that the story would likely crash and burn. The premise was ambitious. It was unlikely that an unknown author could pull it off *and* stick the landing. But by the final paragraph of the first chapter, I was hooked.

CHAPTER 26

AMANDA

2000
Bolton Landing

The first months after the accident I spent hours daydreaming alternate scenarios for my life: I never take Annie to the island in the first place, or she comes back with the first responders — or, or, or. Living in these alternate worlds was a momentary relief, but then my reality — the endless rehab and my uncooperative legs — would come back into focus.

For a long time, the last image I saw before drifting to sleep was Annie, her face hovering above mine in the seconds after the fall. One of the things I remember feeling when she first appeared in that pool was relief. She was blocking the sun, and I couldn't blink my eyes for some reason — probably shock — so I was thankful for her, for that small mercy.* Then she moved and the sun hit me again. At first, I thought she would be back in a few seconds, then I thought maybe a few minutes. Finally, I figured it would be longer.

I was always thinking about the distance between me and Annie. Wondering how far apart we might be at any given moment — thousands of miles, hundreds, tens? She couldn't be just a town or two over, could she? No, not possible. I would hear her voice. Sense her. Smell her.

Waiting in line at the store, I'd find myself daydreaming, my mind creating a map of the country, and I'd place a stick figure of Annie in some possible location (at times Los Angeles, at times somewhere random like the middle of Texas) and I'd draw a

***Note from Cate:** When I read this detail, I had to stop for a few minutes to collect myself. This crystallized how little Amanda *actually* needed from me after the accident. I was running away from the story my brain had created, but all Amanda needed was for me to . . . stand still and block the sun from her eyes. And I wonder how many other things in life I've misjudged this badly. More than I could stomach, I'm sure.

mental line from me to her. Another kind of zip line, I guess.

At other times, to comfort or torture myself, I don't know, I'd think of all the moments there was no space between us: a night in our sleeping bags, a kiss on her cheek, my arms thrown around her. I had become so dependent on her love. But then I could feel her affection dimming — at first imperceptible, then undeniable — and I had become desperate. Stupid, reckless, trying to be the coolest version of myself, the one I thought she loved most. Whenever my mind goes down this path, I end up on that zip line. All roads lead to it, I guess.

The accident altered everything about my world, even giving me a new unit of measurement: One zip line, which was approximately sixteen feet. The distance of my fall into the pool. I find that I'm always measuring the space between things: usually an object and the ground, vertically, but sometimes even between two things, like parked cars, laterally.

There's a pizza shop in town, Iggy's, and they hung a shingle about a year after the accident, red cursive lettering on wood, and now I can't go by Iggy's or see someone eating Iggy's or hear someone talking about Iggy's without falling again from that zip line because their sign hangs, according to my subconscious calculations, at the precise height above the sidewalk as the zip line was above the pool. What I've come to understand is that the feeling of those few seconds — my entire self at the mercy of the universe — will never go away. I've tried. I've closed my eyes and relived it, purposefully calling it to mind a hundred times in a row, my stomach turning like I was on the open seas, and what I can tell you is that the hundredth time was just as potent as the first. Eventually I had to realize no dilution of that memory would ever occur.

And still, I'm always thinking about those last few days together. Annie thought she was good at hiding her emotion. She thought she was hard to read; seriously, she thought she was. It was one of her weaknesses. (Hindsight being twenty-twenty.) But she could never keep emotion from those crisp brown eyes. I could see she was scanning me for flaws, in the name of self-preservation, because she wanted to stop loving me. That's a tough vibe to hide. It felt like she was peering at me through binoculars, from behind a wall.

Which was the worst, seeing as I loved her so much. When she laughed, she squinted, and it was so adorable. Plus, that brain of hers, the higher plane she occupied, I was always trying to keep up.

In other words: She made life exciting.

A few days before it ("it") happened, we were standing at the trunk of Brando, loading a bag for the trip, and she asked me, "Did you have any different dreams before you met me?"

I wasn't sure how to react. I hated that I'd hurt her at junior prom, and I wished I hadn't, but also I was mad that she was letting it affect our friendship so much. I thought we were better, deeper, stronger.

"You do realize you're not the first person in the world to want to move to Hollywood, right?" I glared at her because, I mean, *Fuck her,* then I added, "Would you rather go alone? Is that what you're trying to say?"

I wanted to clasp my hands over my mouth after I said this, put the question back inside. I didn't want the answer. But Annie wasn't confrontational; she preferred coded messages. It's one reason she liked acting: Characters never say exactly what they mean. That would be so boring.

"Feisty," she said. "I like it."

I was relieved that the weirdness had passed. Hashing out our feelings in advance of Los Angeles seemed like an amateur move. We would get to Hollywood and get settled, and then we would talk.

She was about to shut the trunk when I asked her to wait. We'd forgotten our sleeping bags: mine was red and hers green, in honor of Christmas. We loved Christmas. As I tucked them snugly in the back, I thought — as I often did — of the night we slept in my red sleeping bag on the balcony of a motel during a theater field trip. Some clerical error resulted in us staying at a motel instead of a cabin. The room was filthy in a way that jumpstarts the imagination: dark spots on pillows, stains on the comforter and mattress (we looked), yellow patches on the carpet. We were horrified at the range of bodily fluids on display.

At bedtime, we tried to get comfortable without touching much, just lying stiff on our backs staring at the ceiling. But above us were dark stains that seemed to be alive, so after a while Annie asked if I was still awake, and I said there was zero chance of sleep.

"Wanna sleep outside in your sleeping bag?" she asked, and it seemed like a genius idea. The room had a balcony with two plastic chairs, a table, and an ashtray and so we moved everything to the side and unrolled my sleeping bag on the cement. We were somewhere in the middle of New York

State, surrounded by lakes and trees, and we angled ourselves so we could see the stars, bright above us.

We talked and talked. About a lot of things I don't remember, and the night drifted on. We didn't have a clock so who knows what time it was, and just as I was falling asleep, I heard Annie's voice again. "Oh yeah," she was saying. "I've been meaning to tell you." I gave her a *mmmm* to let her know I was there, but also, I was in that in-between place, my eyes closed. She was talking about the week before, when she'd gone to the nearest town to run some errand.

"I go by that movie theater. You know the one that's next to that one shop with all the weird baby dolls in the window, and we're always wondering how it's staying in business? And they have that old marquee up above, right, and I'm going by, and I read it and it says, '*Elizabeth* with Cate Blanchett,' except, oh my god Amanda, they spelled it with a K — Kate Blanchett."

"Those fucking morons," I whispered without opening my eyes. But her story was alive inside my mind. I was picturing it: the black letters against the white background, the understandable and yet utterly horrifying mistake of spelling out "Kate Blanchett."

"We just cannot, absolutely cannot, live

in a town that spells Cate Blanchett's name with a K."

"No, Annie, we absolutely cannot," I said.

That anecdote — Kate, not Cate — became synonymous with *We gotta get the fuck out of here*. A hundred times over the next few years, something would happen — a boy crushing a beer can on his forehead, for example — and we'd look at each other and one of us would say, "Cate with a K," and the other would reply, "Cate with a motherfucking K."

Standing at the back of the Civic just days before we were supposed to leave town, I looked down at my tightly rolled sleeping bag that I'd had since I was twelve years old that would now make the long drive west. And because I badly wanted to feel like the version of Annie that was enamored with me, and us, and our big dreams, I said, "Cate with a K."

I knew I was in trouble when she didn't respond immediately, when she slammed down the trunk lid and said, "Yup."

CHAPTER 27

JAKE FISCHER

2006
New York City

The first time I saw Cate Kay's name was in a review of her now-famous debut in the *New York Times*. It was just after lunch, and I was walking back to my desk at *Vanity Fair,* where I was a senior writer. As I passed another writer's empty cubicle, I saw the book review section face up on the edge of the desk and paused on seeing the massive question mark that anchored the page. THE VERY LAST: A RUNAWAY SUCCESS was the headline, then beneath it, more intriguing to me, the subhead: IDENTITY OF AUTHOR OF BREAKOUT HIT REMAINS A MYSTERY. I skimmed the page: "Even the book's editor is in the dark as to who the elusive 'Cate Kay' is."

My first thought was *No way*. I brought the section back to my desk and dropped into my rolling desk chair, momentum pushing me to my phone. I scanned the article. My takeaway: the book was no literary masterpiece, but compelling and selling like hotcakes. I laughed at the ridiculousness of the book's tagline: "*The Road,* but a beach read!" (Absurd though it was, I later had to admit that it conveyed exactly what *The Very Last* was.)

Back then, I was always on the hunt for a story to pitch my editor, otherwise I might get saddled with some trivial assignment. A colleague had been a senior writer, same level as me, then got bumped to writer-at-large. When I went to the editor-in-chief, not to complain, but to simply ask for clarification, he pointed out that she had two cover stories under her belt while I was still looking for my first.

Sometimes landing a cover story was luck and timing. One of her covers was a short Q&A — a fucking Q&A, for God's sake! — with the movie star Ry Channing. Her best friend from high school was Channing's manager, and the thing was meant to be no more than one page near the back of the issue, but then the planned cover story had fallen through, and Channing's latest movie, *Beneath the Same Moon,* was taking off and . . . voila. Now, was that a daring feat of journalism or a heavy dose of luck and an exercise in networking? Granted, in journalism the daylight between those two could be slim.

I lifted the receiver on my desk phone and punched in my brother's number and realized, as it rang, that this was quite possibly the first time I had ever called Brian at his office. A woman answered, and even though I'd never seen my brother at work, I pictured him at a desk, no doubt wearing his wire-rim glasses and one of those silly vests he thought made him look erudite.

"This is Brian's brother, Jake, is he available?"

"One moment please," she said, then some terrible music started playing, because silence terrifies people. I'm always noticing the little ways society protects us from the menace of silence, like with Muzak in elevators. Humans: we built the Pyramids and made all the world's information instantly accessible, but apparently if we stand together quietly, we'll short-circuit and melt.

"Jake?" came Brian's voice.

"Yup," I said. "Hey, bro."

"How are you?"

I once read that in their lifetime most people spend about the equivalent of two days saying goodbye at parties. Two whole days. No thanks. Not me. But one of my friends

— a bigwig at Goldman — once told me to think of niceties like the few warm-up minutes before a run. Which is probably why he had a $3 million loft on Gold Street, and I was renting a walk-up in Chelsea.

"I'm good, I'm good," I said. "At work, got a little something brewing. How are you?" I did my best to make this last part sound sincere, but it might have come across a little forced. Thankfully, my brother knew me, so he said, "I'm fine — so what's up? Why are you calling?"

"Have you heard of Cate Kay?" I was looking down at that newspaper, at the big question mark. In response, he laughed, then said, "Have I heard of her? It's all anyone's talking about in my neck of the woods."

"Obviously it's a pseudonym, this Cate Kay, but I figured all of you inside publishing must know who it is — some guy that just wanted a fresh start? Stephen King playing games or something?"

Then my brother goes, "So you assume a guy wrote *The Very Last*?," which is absolutely the exact thing my brother would say, latch on to the most unimportant detail of the conversation and make it the centerpiece.

"Fuck off, man," I said. I see now that I was leaning a little too hard into the straight-guy stereotype: former jock, fraternity at

Cornell, steak medium rare, etc. But I didn't want anyone guessing my secret. I added, "I'm just using the generic 'guy' here."

"Right. Well, as far as Cate Kay goes, it's apparently a total mystery. Nobody in publishing has seen anything like it. Crazy thing is that nobody at Atria — not even the book's *editor* — has any idea who the author is. That's pretty rare."

"Yeah, that's what the review in the *Times* said," and here I hoped he would read between the lines, which was: Do you have information that hasn't already been published in the newspaper of record? And when the line filled with silence, I resisted the urge to fill it. Finally, he chimed in with, "I *did* hear that the mystery runs deeper — apparently even her agent, this woman fired by Eloquence who discovered the manuscript, is also in the dark."

I jotted down "Eloquence."

"Okay," I said, "but somebody's gotta be getting paid — there's gotta be a bank account cashing these checks."

"That sounds like a question for your ilk, Jakey," my brother said, and that was my cue to exit the conversation.

Two quick phone calls and I could tell you who wasn't hiding: a woman named Sidney

Collins. First, I spoke with Dempsey Carroll at Eloquence, who seemed much more caught up in the proprietary rights his agency did or did not have over *The Very Last,* which he claimed was submitted unsolicited to him and physically carried out of the office by an agent named Melody Huber on the morning he fired her.

When I reached Melody, she was in the process of launching her own agency, Slush, which as many of us now know, became one of the most successful literary agencies in the industry. On the phone she sounded quiet, and younger than her thirty-one years, but there was something persistent and precise in her communication, and I could see why she would make a good agent. I pictured a birdlike woman, with thin bones and pointy features, an image that seemed to fit her surgical language. And when I finally saw a photo of Melody a few months later, I wasn't too far off.

The ethos at Slush, as she explained it, was to prioritize discovering talent, instead of relying on publishing trends and milking existing stars for everything they were worth. She and her agents would focus on reading, not schmoozing. I was too jaded to believe this nonsense, even though I could tell from Melody's voice that she genuinely did.

In the end, I was both right and wrong about Slush. Melody did discover many hidden literary gems . . . and then she went on to milk them for all they were worth. Like *The Very Last,* which became a movie trilogy, then a limited TV series, then a line of action figures, then a theme park, and a thousand other products, no doubt; I once saw a line of canoes painted to look like the ones from The Core, which made me wonder if the book had licensed itself out to nuclear bombs as well.*

"Do you have an inkling as to who Cate Kay is?" I finally asked toward the end of our conversation, which I'd front-loaded with questions about Slush, so that maybe Melody would think that the entire piece would be built around her nascent agency.

She laughed at the question, then said, "The one thing I know for certain is that the author is a woman."

*****Note from Cate:** We did not license nuclear bombs. But — point taken. I will admit that I green-lit — or Sidney did, without asking me — an absurd amount of consumer goods. Much of this I regret. Exploiting the books commercially was a by-product of never receiving public credit for them. Money was a proxy — an inferior one, I'll add. Give me credit all day, every day.

"How?"

"The writing," she said simply. "A man would have centered the experience of Jeremiah instead of Samantha," which was at that point a meaningless observation to me because I hadn't yet read the book.

"I look forward to reading it," I said, making a mental note to pick up a copy that same day. Maybe, as Melody was alluding to, there were clues in the text. "One more question if I may," I jumped back in.

"Yes?"

"Who do you work with, if not Cate Kay? There must be somebody on the other end of your calls?"

"Of course," she said, and nothing in her voice suggested this was a big secret as she said, "That would be Sidney Collins."

I scribbled down the name in my notebook, spelling it like the city, *Sydney*.

"And you're sure this Sidney Collins — you're sure this person's not the author?"

"When it comes to Cate Kay, there are only two things I'm sure of: she's a woman, and she is not Sidney Collins."

"You're certain?"

"I take it you haven't spoken yet to Ms. Collins?"

"I have not."

"Well then, you will see for yourself."

This chat with Melody Huber was one of the only of its kind. The next time I got her on the line she was much less forthcoming. Most of her answers were along the lines of, "I can't tell you that, Mr. Fischer," or, "I'm not at liberty to say," and I quickly gathered that Sidney Collins had called around to everyone with hands on *The Very Last* and asked them not to cooperate with any media attempting to uncover the identity of Cate Kay.

After three weeks of calling every day, I finally convinced Sidney Collins* to meet me at Blue Star Café in Harlem. I arrived right on time, scanned the space once, twice. Then came a voice from behind me, smooth and assured. "Mr. Fischer, I believe?" I spun, and there was Sidney Collins, looking like she planned to go running after our meeting. Beneath the ball cap, I couldn't see her eyes, but she was long and lithe. Not unpleasant to look at, but not remarkable, either.

*Note from Cate: That was the only major interview Sidney ever did. She liked it too much, for one — the attention. And also, she saw how this one article was cited and aggregated and spun forward. She had planted her flag as the public guardian of the Cate Kay empire. No more media needed.

"So," I said, settling into the seat across from her. "The famous Sidney Collins."

"I prefer 'infamous.'" She smirked and lifted her cap slightly to scratch her hairline. And now I could see her eyes and they were exceptional, a velvet blue. Then she tugged her cap back down, and the gesture seemed to suggest business, like a baseball manager with one foot on the dugout steps. She leaned forward and said, "Listen, Jake, let's just get right to it. First, as I said in our brief conversation on the phone, everything is off the record — including that comment I just made about preferring 'infamous' . . ." — and here she winked at me as if to say *I know all your little tricks,* and I felt exposed because I had, in fact, filed away that detail as material. She continued: "If I want something on the record, I'll specify. If you want something on the record, you can ask. We clear?"

"This ain't your first rodeo," I said, because acknowledging the dynamic seemed like the next best move.

"Actually, it is," she said. "If by rodeo you mean media circus."

A clever turn of phrase. I decided to buy myself some time, so I asked Sidney if she needed anything — a scone or muffin? — then excused myself to the counter for a coffee and a regroup. The young woman helping me was striking, with shimmering brown eyes beneath a red cap that had the shop's logo. She* greeted me warmly, which was unusual for New York, but I just didn't have the brain space to engage.

What I needed was to establish some simple facts I could print, basic stuff that Sidney would be paranoid to reject, and build from there. Get a couple points on the board, I told myself while pouring cream until it turned my coffee off-white. Black coffee was for the insane.

"Can I write that we had coffee?" I said while slipping back into my seat.

This question seemed to surprise her, which made me feel better. She wasn't invincible. "Yes," she said slowly, like she was still searching for my angle, to cut me off at the pass.

"Okay." I pretended to jot something down in my notebook. "And can I write how you take your coffee?"

She squinted at me now, turned her head slightly while keeping her eyes fixed on mine. "Why would that matter to anyone?"

"It's a detail," I said. "If I can't tell them

*Note from Cate: Yup, that was me. Guess Sidney was playing a sick little game with Jake. I had no idea.

anything new about Cate Kay, I can at least tell them how her . . . his . . . lawyer takes her coffee. Everyone likes to know how people drink their coffee." As I said it, I realized how true this last part was, and I made a mental note to pitch a front-of-book piece that would just be a list of a dozen celebrities and how they took their coffee.

"Yes." She tilted her cup and peered inside. "You can write that I take my coffee black."

I learned almost nothing from that coffee with Sidney. Cate Kay was maybe a single person, but also could be a pair, or even a group of people. Sidney seemed to enjoy the battle of wits we were engaged in; me dissecting each of her words for information, she stripping them of their specificity. I did, however, come to understand why Melody was convinced Sidney wasn't Cate Kay. Many reasons, really, and probably Melody's had something to do with Sidney's lawyer-like mentality, whereas mine was something more subtle. Sidney gave off an air of virtue that could only exist if she was doing all this for someone else.

The article I eventually published for *Vanity Fair* was meh. No new ground broken on Cate Kay, just a few empty roads traveled down. Because of that article, the world knew a couple places from which Cate Kay almost certainly hadn't come (for example, I found no trace of her at Sidney's alma maters, SUNY Plattsburgh and NYU), but was still properly baffled about where she had. More than anything, the piece read like a profile on Sidney Collins, which is probably why she kept my contact info.

And no, it did not make the cover.

CHAPTER 28

AMANDA

2006
Bolton Landing

I might have taken physical therapy more seriously if the location wasn't so depressing. Picture every single-story senior living center you've ever driven past thinking "God, I hope I don't end up there" and, bingo, you know the building. Physical therapy is already a bad time: some part of your body isn't working properly. (In my case, many parts.) The least they could do is have some big windows looking onto the Adirondacks — an inspiring view for the daunting climb ahead. But no, the building was at the far side of an icy parking lot behind a strip mall in the town over. I guess if someone slipped and fell on the way inside, they were already in the right place.

Janet, though, I loved her. Physical therapist extraordinaire. Short blond hair, stocky build; I came to learn she did triathlons on the weekends, and that made perfect sense to me. I could picture her sucking on one of those goo packets while stripping out of a wetsuit. In the first months we worked together, I was skeptical of her. She was so energetic, so positive, so hopeful — traits I would come to love and depend on her for, but not what I was feeling after three brutal months in the rehab hospital. We clashed.

After about a year together, she was in her plush leather rolling chair, and she scooted herself to me, chart on lap.

I hated those charts. They were filled with shorthand, these seemingly innocuous combinations of letters that packed a devastating punch such as SCI (Spinal Cord Injury) or ADL (Activities of Daily Living). I'm wary of all acronyms now. My diagnosis was Incomplete Quadriplegia, meaning all my limbs were affected, though my legs much more than my arms.

"Let's talk about goals," she was saying, eyes down. Clearly this was to be our come-to-Jesus moment.

My entire life to that point had been wordplay with Annie, usually infused with cheekiness and sarcasm, so I said, "My goal is to invent time travel. Yes, I would go back to the accident, but that's not why I'd want to invent time travel. I think America had a real before-and-after moment with JFK's assassination, so back to 1963 I would go."

That got her eyes up, and I could see there was a little glimmer in them. I thought of Annie — of course I did.

"JFK?" Janet said. "A little cliché, don't you think?"

That's when I knew we would be okay. And a few minutes later, when she got back on task and asked me, "But, seriously, Amanda — what do you want from this journey?"

I responded, not as unkindly as I might have, that I'd like her to never again use the word *journey* except if referring to the band. It called to mind voluntary trips, far-flung travel. Juxtaposed with my actual circumstances, it only served to remind me of how terribly earthbound I'd become.

She nodded, considering. Was I just being my snarky self, or did I have a point? Her mind was churning.

I added: "And it's not that I don't understand that I am on a kind of . . . journey — to use your shitty little word. It's just if I think of it as this yearslong thing, of all the work ahead, I think my head might explode. The only way for me not to melt into a puddle of sadness is to just think of this session and what we're going to work on *today*."

She looked me right in the eyes and said, "I get it," and I never heard her use the word *journey* again.

"What do you want to work on *today*?" she asked next, and something immediately popped into my mind. I lifted my right arm off the chair and held my palm open to her, tried to touch each finger to my thumb, but it was clumsy. Then I mimicked turning a page on a book — the kind of intricate dexterity needed, I wanted it back.

"Can we work on turning a page?" I asked. Reading had never been my thing as much as Annie's, but that could change. Plus, if I could turn a page, then I could also button a shirt — it was a two-for-one.

She sat up straighter, her face brightened. A simple, reachable goal with a powerful metaphor smuggled inside: I was speaking her language. Plus, almost every time I came into PT she had her legs up on her desk, nose in a book.

Slowly, so slowly, Janet made me better. But I think I made her better, too. (At the very least, she's not going around crushing people's souls asking them about their "journeys.") Physical therapy became the only place I allowed myself a modicum of normalcy, perhaps even optimism. Ironic that I found my first slice of blue sky in that sad little building. I'd leave sessions with a glimmer of something different, but then later that day Kerri would come home from school, her energy harried and stressed that she'd abandoned me for so long. Like I was a puppy who might go on the rug. She'd drop her backpack in a rush, and no matter what I said to her, I'd be forced to remember that I was siphoning her life force. Back into darkness I'd spiral.

What many people don't understand about serious injury or illness is that what you're really coming to grips with isn't the physical limitations (although there is that); it's how the physical limitations alter your interactions with the world. At first, you can only take. You take people's time, their physical energy, their emotional reserves. You're in a state of need and you *take, take, take* without giving. And taking without giving, that messes with your head. You start asking yourself what the point of your existence is. A drain on the world's resources, on the resources of those you love, nothing else.

But eventually — and it may take years, as it did for me — you discover ways to start giving again. Honestly, you'd be shocked at how many ways exist to *give* in this world if that's all you're looking for.

But enough of that. Back to my girl Janet.

It was more than five years after the accident, and we were quite obviously coming to the end of our *journey* together. We'd hit a dead end: I wasn't adding additional movement or dexterity, and Janet wanted me to acknowledge this. But I wasn't ready. One of our last sessions together, I arrived in a sour mood. She hadn't seen me yet because she was reading the final pages of some book. I parked my chair right in front of her and still she didn't look up. After a moment, she lifted one finger, acknowledging my presence. She must have been on the last page, because a minute later she let out a satisfied sigh and tenderly closed the book.

"Was it *that* good?" I asked. I meant it snidely, but she rose above, took my words at face value.

"Loved it, loved it, loved it," she said in a singsong voice. I ducked my head to try to see the title, and Janet lifted the book, showed me the front: *The Very Last*. By someone named Cate Kay. The title struck a chord, and I remembered Kerri mentioning it the week prior — she was on the waiting list for it at the local library.

"Do you own that copy?" I asked, thinking of Kerri, how it might make her smile if I brought a present home. A gift — a way to give, to hold the demons at bay.

"You want to borrow?" Janet was thrusting the book at me, desperate to encourage a healthy impulse. I took it from her, looked at the black and tan cover, the crumbling CITY HALL subway station sign. *Cate Kay.*

"I'll bring it back soon," I said.

She waved me off. "Books are meant to be shared," she said, then slapped her knees, ready to get to work, and asked the question she'd asked at the start of every appointment the last many years: "What are we working on today?"

"Walking," I said without hesitation.

She leaned forward and said, "I just — I don't think that's the best use of our time."

"*Our* time?" I said cruelly, even though one of my favorite things about working with Janet was how we were a team. She flinched. A wall went up.

"If that's what you want," she said, standing.

That afternoon before Kerri came home, I opened the book and the first thing I noticed was that the dedication said "For a . . . ," which perplexed me because it seemed unfinished. *For a . . . what? For a . . . who?* The TV was muted, and I was in the den. Dad was back at the garage, so no one else was home, and I started reading: *Chapter 1:*

The Big Apple. Samantha and Jeremiah are in New York City and they're talking intimately like only best friends do, and then — *bam!* There it was. On the very first page. Their exchange — about the sunsets of New York — sent me cartwheeling back in time; me and Annie in a boat in the middle of Lake George. But then just as quickly, I'm returned, and slightly bewildered. I read the scene again, same experience. Reading is not quite what this feels like; it's more like remembering.

The whole book was like this, a remembering of various moments with Annie, and then that climactic scene with Jeremiah wearing those black Converse!* When I finished, a satisfied sigh is not what I released. I let the book tumble from my hands; it bounced off a wheel and landed awkwardly on the carpet — spine propped in the air; pages bent blasphemously.

We kept envelopes in the kitchen drawer, and I rolled over and pulled one out. This

---

*Note from Cate: I once asked Amanda why she almost always wore those black Converse, and she said it was because they gave off an air of classic, low-key confidence. "They got it right with these," she would say, lifting her foot and admiring their simplicity.

was new for me, this desperate need to get something inside of me out, and I carefully tore away a piece of lined paper from a scratch pad and wrote a quick "note" to Annie — I'm sorry, to *Cate Kay* — then folded it precisely and tucked it inside an envelope.

When Kerri came home that day, she was confused to find *The Very Last* crushed like roadkill in our den. (It's possible I ran over it on my way to the kitchen, then again on the way back.) She picked the book up, tried smoothing the pages.

I never returned it to Janet. Kerri read it, apparently none the wiser about the book's author, then *The Very Last* stayed on my bedside table to keep my anger fresh.

Every night I would look at that book and silently scream. That's not a metaphor or an exaggeration. I'd pause before transferring myself into bed (okay, who am I kidding? — it was more of a flop) and stare at the book that Annie had written instead of staying with me, thought of every shred of us she'd shared with the world instead of sharing herself with me. I'd let the pain and anger swell, then rage at the gods — all without making a sound.

I would picture her sitting inside her fancy house, brimming with creative fulfillment, or maybe out for drinks with her new, sophisticated friends — all of them sipping on brown liquor poured over a single big ice cube. Like the city folk.

CATE KAY

The Very Last

Jeremiah collapsed outside city hall; the camera crashed to the ground, leaving viewers with a shot of the curb. Samantha knelt next to him, shaking his shoulders, trying to wake him up. But then she heard the crackling of audio and looked up: two firemen, in full hazmat suits and gas masks, running toward them. They looked like astronauts. Samantha squeezed Jeremiah's hand, held it for a moment, hoping his eyes would open. But a second later the men were pushing into her space, covering his mouth with an oxygen mask. She stood, backed away without a word.

She glanced at the camera, still by his feet, then toward city hall. She hated herself for the thought, but she knew she needed to keep going — to finish the story they had started. After all, they'd come this far, hadn't they? The world needed to see what happened next, and only Samantha could show them. She bent over and grabbed the top handle of the camera, lifting it up, careful to keep the lens pointed away from Jeremiah. She took one step backward, then another, unwilling to fully commit to this terrible course of action, but as she framed a shot of city hall, she told herself that this decision was essential, maybe even brave.

Love didn't always mean staying. She walked toward city hall, talking to the viewer about what she hoped to find inside — a working subway station, survivors, information. What those hundreds of millions of viewers didn't see was Samantha glancing over her shoulder, catching a glimpse of the soles of Jeremiah's black Converse, her tears mixing with the dirt and dust and God knows what else.

CHAPTER 29

Cass

January 2007
New York

When *The Very Last* took off, I didn't know how to feel exactly. I tried to tell myself it meant that Amanda wasn't mad at me. How could she be if she was helping me from another dimension? But I couldn't always make that logic stick.

My first royalty check was Powerball money. One day my account said $2,100 — from my small book advance and my job working as a barista in our Harlem neighborhood — the next it looked like the number on a calculator you forgot to reset to zero. Many, many numbers. And all of it was mine. Accounts were in my new legal name (Cass Ford), and so were my credit cards. I had full access. But it was Sidney's law firm that handled everything, could keep tabs on the back end. She made that clear.

I hated how brilliant she was at her job; how good the sex was. Because the relationship had bad vibes. We lived in a one-bedroom apartment three blocks from the Blue Star Café, where I was still working even as *The Very Last* was rocketing to the top of the bestseller lists. She oversaw my life so thoroughly, but I'd not yet tugged at the restraints. So, it's no surprise that Sidney wasn't planning to tell me about Ry Channing's invitation.

And if not for a blizzard walloping New York, I'd probably have never known.

The day was cold and slate gray. I was working at Blue Star, but by midafternoon the place was empty. Eight inches of snow had already fallen, and they were calling for two feet. Nobody was on the streets. Closing early was a no-brainer.

I cleaned up, stacked the chairs, and locked the door behind me, stepping out into a snow globe. I walked in the middle of the avenue — no cars in any direction. Nothing could match the eerie thrill of a snowstorm, and I thought of Amanda pulling me along on an orange plastic sled into town, the two of us pretending we were on an expedition in Alaska. Survival not guaranteed. I imagined Amanda next to me now, wearing a red knit beanie, snowflakes on her eyelashes, loving every minute of a big storm. We never wasted a snow day; we squeezed adventure out of each one.

My tears were hot on my cheeks. I paused and tilted my head back, blinked and blinked. AMANDA IS DEAD, still written in the clouds.

A few minutes later, when I got into the apartment, I caught Sidney at our breakfast table, cell phone open in front of her, call on speaker. She was obviously surprised to see me and scrambled to bring it to her ear, but not before I heard the guy on the line say, "You've seen Ryan's letter to Cate, she thinks an in-person will make the movie unstopp—"

When the call ended, I said, "Let me see the letter."

Sidney reached for her work bag, tugged out a piece of paper. I leaned against the counter and began reading: *Dear Cate, I find myself thinking of you frequently. Which is odd, of course, I'm aware. But there are a few reasons for this, which I'd like to explain if you come out to Los Angeles.*

I paused, glanced at Sidney. She rolled her eyes, said, "It's ridiculous, I know," which was not at all my sentiment. I kept reading: *The main reason I think you should come is because everyone thinks it's a terrible idea.*

But I have this feeling that you don't listen to what other people say —

"I'm going," I said. I handed the letter back to Sidney.

"Don't be crazy," she said. "Secrecy isn't exactly Hollywood's strong suit."

"I'll be careful," I said. (Also — what did Sidney know about Hollywood?)

"It's not about being careful," she said. "They chew people up, spit them out — I don't want that to happen to you."

"It's not *Hollywood,* it's one person. I'm going," I said. Sidney didn't understand me at all. "And . . . question for you: When, exactly, were you planning to tell me that the *star of the movie adaptation* wanted to meet with me?"

She ignored the question; selective engagement was her specialty.

"What about everything we've carefully built to get to this point?" she said. "Everything is in place the way you wanted it to be. You're going to risk it all just because some prima donna can't stand not having exactly what she wants?"

"That's not what I read," I said, although the idea of Ry Channing wanting time with me was not an insignificant factor in my decision-making. She carried herself with a kind of swagger, and her hand gestures made me hopeful she wasn't totally straight. (If you know, you know.) I had watched *Moon,* then everything else she'd been in.

"She wrote that meeting with me would help the movie," I said. "And weren't you saying just yesterday that the quality of the movie is 'crucial' to the success of the next books?"

She stared at me. I held her gaze. Finally, she stood up.

"You just want to get away from me, don't you?" she said, lifting her coat off the back of the chair, slipping it on. "That's what this is about, isn't it? That's what *all* of this is about." She hammered these last few words, drew a circle with her finger. "Fine, go fuck up your life again," she added. "See if I care."

Then she walked out, slamming the door behind her.

My face was pressed against the plastic oval as the plane landed. Los Angeles, finally. More twists and turns than expected, but I was finally here. My heart ached for Amanda. I turned on my cell phone as we taxied to the gate. I had seven missed calls from Sidney. Earlier that morning, I'd slipped out of bed, then the apartment, without saying goodbye, and she sounded sad and disappointed in her first message, then angry in the next few. I powered down my phone and stuffed it deep into my bag.

The sun, the light — I had my hand out the window the entire cab ride, letting it catch the breeze, thinking about Amanda. Would all the weirdness between us have melted away as we drove into Los Angeles? Would we be starring in romantic comedies right now, happily complaining about the absurdity of the movie biz, or would we have burned through all our cash, gotten jobs as waitresses, and become bitter about our failed dreams?

I thought about how Amanda would have loved sushi, but not as much as what loving it said about her, as well as parties in the Hollywood Hills, which I'd only read about, and bottomless Champagne, which she would have been thrilled by, but mostly she would have loved knowing that Champagne was a place, not a grape. I could imagine her telling people that fact like it was a trivia gem until realizing most people already knew, and then she would have laughed at her naïveté and made that part of the story, too.

Los Angeles Amanda became real to me. She was still a good time, just like she always was — I mean, *had been* — but in LA, she would get sharpened. And I wanted so badly to know this version of her, to marvel together at the idiocy of our previous selves. I'd accepted Amanda's death as a fact, but only intellectually — a trick that had kept me from the kind of grief that forces you beneath the covers.

In the back of that taxi, I opened a cheap spiral notebook — by then I'd gone through dozens of them — and wrote my best friend back to life.

CHAPTER 30

RYAN*

January 2007
Los Angeles

There I stood, just a few feet from Cate Kay. She'd materialized so unexpectedly that all I could do was stare blankly at her. Even though she would already have known what I looked like, I still found myself wondering what she saw and whether the real me was satisfactory. Brushing my teeth, washing my face, neither of these things had happened yet. I was wearing what I had slept in. These were facts I was suddenly aware of as I absorbed the woman in my backyard.

"Hi." She waved like she was tracing a rainbow. I smiled because the gesture was

*****Note from Cate:** Ryan will not be pleased that she's been off-screen (off-page?) for such a long stretch of this story, but now she's back. Let us give her our full attention.

purposefully awkward, ironic even, and I liked her already for calling attention to the strangeness of the moment. Discreetly (I think), I looked her down to up. My view from toe to head: suede Puma sneakers, blue jeans, white T-shirt, faded leather jacket, light brown hair in a messy bun, bittersweet eyes.

What I'm saying is, she was effortlessly cool, and I was having trouble believing she was Cate Kay. Not possible, I kept telling myself. That the author of the hottest book in the world also had sun-kissed cheeks and a jawline like a mannequin and was standing in my backyard with a look that could only be described as a smirk. Like she was waiting for me to process it all. Or maybe it was a defense mechanism. Either way, I needed to say something.

"Hi back," is what I managed. Then, a beat later, "You're really, really early. Like, so early I haven't even brushed my teeth."

"I was excited, I couldn't sleep, so I took an earlier flight . . . well, actually, *the* earliest flight — first of the day, five twenty." She put down the bag and I realized there were things hosts were supposed to do for guests, and I was failing at all of them. Into action I sprung, collecting her bag from the ground, gently touching her arm as I passed. "Let's get you settled," I said. But my brain was replaying the touch, wondering why I had done it. As best I could understand, it was to introduce the idea of . . . *I'm happy you showed up early at my back gate.*

The guest room was across the hall from my bedroom. A dark purple Turkish rug was the star of the show, laid at an angle in front of a low-slung wooden bed frame. On top was a white duvet and six colorful pillows. No such thing as too many pillows, my mom had argued two years ago, and I can't say, back then, I had an opinion on the matter. "This is you," I said, carefully placing her bag on the bed. "I'm just across the way," I added. Now that my bellhop duties were done, and far too quickly, I was scrambling for what to offer next. Space, yes, maybe she needed space.

"I'll let you do your thing," I said. "The bathroom is just there, in the hallway, if you're one of those must-shower-after-they-fly types. I'll be out back with my terrible coffee."

"Are you?" She was now on the opposite side of the bed from me. She was unzipping her bag, and she seemed to know I was confused by the question. She gave me an extra second to rewind to what I had said before the coffee thing. Ah!

Me: "I'm not, but I really want to be."*

"There's still time." She was rummaging through her bag, but she lifted her eyes to mine and they were a bright brown — shimmering like if diamonds were brown. Being the first to look away felt like a fail. I willed myself to hold her gaze. We held eye contact for many seconds, and I swear it felt like we were both refusing to be the one to end it. Or maybe it wasn't like that for her. But when she looked back down into her bag, I felt like I'd proven something to her.†

"I'll be outside," I said again as I was leaving the room. My hand curled around the side of the door, pulling it shut behind me.

"Ryan," she said, and I turned back. The door was still in my hand. I raised my eyebrows, *hmmm?* She was holding her toiletry

---

*__Note from Cate:__ If you are not a person who showers after a flight, and have never considered wanting to be that person, then you are more like Amanda.

†__Note from Cate:__ When I first read this part from Ryan, I was shocked that she remembered this moment. I had also felt like looking away was a failure, and I remember thinking that I was the one who had failed. But she's wrong in why it started. I wasn't testing her; she was just so beautiful that I must have been staring.

bag, and I resisted the urge to tell her that I liked how my name sounded in her mouth. That was something a character said in a poorly written drama. Not in real life.

"I'm Cass, by the way," she said.

Cass. There it was. Cate Kay's real name was Cass.

"Hi, Cass," I said with a smile.

CHAPTER 31

Cass

January 2007
Los Angeles

The hottest movie star in the world was standing barefoot in her backyard wearing basketball shorts, her red hair pulled back. Wide-set eyes, a dusting of freckles, she was just slightly off from symmetrical, which made her that much more striking. Seeing her standing there like that — seemingly without vanity — I wondered what I would have been like if I'd become a movie star, how precious I'd have become about how people saw me. I hoped in this alternate universe I was as chill as Ryan seemed.

The air was different in Los Angeles. You could feel the ocean, which reminded me of the lake, which made me think of Amanda. I took the bag off my shoulder and let it rest on the patio by my feet. I felt unburdened for the first time in six years — glimpsed for a moment the feeling I was chasing, I was pining for, when I'd run away from Amanda. Wide-open space. A smile tugged at the corner of my mouth. I tried to suppress it. Didn't want to be the crazy person grinning in the backyard of a movie star. A movie star who seemed like somebody I'd be friends with in another life. (Or maybe this one?)

When Ryan grabbed my bag, I felt her fingers graze my elbow and my body turned on, but my brain built an explanation: a mistake, possibly, or just a kind gesture.

I watched Ryan's movements, studied her legs as she walked, her fingers as they gripped the sliding door, the way her hands found her pockets after showing me to the guest room. Her body was delivering clues about who she was, what she wanted — I just hoped I was reading them correctly. The subtlety of it, both electrifying and exhausting.

"I'll be outside," she said, dipping her head just so, turning to leave.

"Hey Ryan?" I said, before the door closed behind her. She paused, leaned back to me, tipping on one foot.

Whoa. I had jumped in the deep end. I was feeling so much like my old self, I almost introduced myself as Annie.

CHAPTER 32

RYAN

January 2007
Los Angeles

How long would Cass stay? She had said a week, but then a week did not feel long enough. I told her she could stay as long as she wanted. That my schedule was wide open until the following month, when shooting for *The Very Last* started in Charleston.

I wanted her to stay as long as she could. We spent those first days ordering food in, lying outside by the pool reading, staying up late talking. So much talking, and so deep, that I sensed she'd been desperate to speak, to share herself. I realized I'd been desperate, too.

Talking to a profile writer about "the real me" was about as far from intimacy as one could get. My favorite, and scariest, stories from childhood were too sacred to have them published in a magazine. They'd be poached and "written up" for some nascent online site, then woven into my Wiki page. Eventually, that transformative afternoon when I was caught trying to shoplift the new Mariah Carey cassette in the pocket of my Umbro shorts (true story) would become some stranger's casual piece of trivia. Not mine at all anymore.

The Umbro story, these were the kinds of stories Cass and I shared as we sat in my living room one night drinking red wine. Unspooling our lives. How we came to find ourselves on the same green velvet couch, our legs either tucked under us (Cass) or extended on the coffee table (me).

I knew she had secrets — I knew she *was* a secret — but I also knew everything she was telling me was true. Too much detail, and too much pain. I've read enough scripts to smell a made-up life when I hear one. Hers was just boring enough to be real, just dramatic enough to be compelling. A hardscrabble childhood in a small lakeside town in New York. An absent father, a preoccupied (the nice way of putting it) mother, an obsession with getting out of there. And then some awful, unfortunate stuff I hadn't yet gotten the full scoop on.

Neither of us knew much about wine, except that it seemed like the sophisticated thing to drink. We landed on a cabernet sauvignon instead of a pinot noir because the description of pinot suggested that sometimes it could be "dainty" and at this we looked at each other and said, "Nah," and started laughing. Big and bold were the descriptions for the cabernet. We liked that better.

The bottle was on the coffee table. I leaned forward, poured myself a little more, offered some to Cass. She extended her glass, and I channeled every wine-pouring scene I'd ever watched. I even spun the bottle at the end to keep it from dripping on the sofa. Well executed, I thought.

Cass had underpacked, unaware of how chilly Los Angeles nights could be. This was fine with me because now she was sitting a few feet away in my heather gray Kansas Jayhawks hooded sweatshirt. She was holding her glass in one hand, the other twirling one of the hoodie's drawstrings.

The more casual she dressed, the more beautiful she became. Her laugh was rich, and she was quick to it. My favorite part was how she squinted while doing it.

I wondered what she was noticing about me. Whether she found me as nuanced and dynamic as I found her.

We hadn't yet talked about the book. I wanted to, but I wasn't sure she did. The book seemed tied up with the mysterious part of her life. For a few seconds, we said nothing, each took a sip of our wine, pretended to understand and savor it. Then Cass said, "So . . . ," injecting the tiny word with steroids, so it was robust. I waited. She dropped her head against the back of the sofa and looked at the ceiling. "You know, I wanted to be you," she said. "Still want to be you, actually."

"Me?" I wasn't sure what she was getting at. Wanted to be me as in *Single White Female*? Even though I ruled it out instantaneously, a pang of fear echoed in my body. (Thanks a lot, fame.)

"I mean an actor," she said quickly, sensing my weirdness. "It's why I said yes immediately to coming out here. Even though Sidney said it was, and I quote, the stupidest fucking idea ever, I wanted to come meet you and see what my life could have been like if it hadn't gone completely off the rails the way it did. Of course, Sidney is terrified that now, after how careful we've been, I'm going to fuck it all up." At this last part, she glanced over at me with her head still back, hair spilling over the back of the couch.

"I'm talking too much," she said, lifting her glass. She smiled softly.

Was she flirting? I wanted to touch her hair, run it through my fingers.

How to respond, how to respond, how to respond — I wanted something that kept us on this track but didn't scare her away. "Do you want to . . . 'fuck it all up'?"

She was holding eye contact as she said, "I want," then stopped. Was that the beginning of a sentence or its entirety? Both, probably. We were still looking at each other, one second, two. Then her eyes darted up and to the left. She started shaking her head, subtly. "I want so many things I don't think I can have anymore, and I'm trying to — move through all that wanting."

Wanting things, I could relate to that. I often wished a life in Lawrence could satisfy me. But I needed more. It wasn't just about money or fame; it was something else.

"Cosmic bigness," Cass whispered. I stared at her, unnerved. Had I heard correctly?

"Wait," I said. "Say that again."

"I don't know, it's just —" she started, but I interrupted.

"No, I mean, what did you just say?"

"Cosmic bigness?"

"Oh my god," I whispered back, meeting her eyes. The phrase defined some unnamed thing within me. "That's exactly what it is."

"I know," she said. *"I know."*

"Is there a cure?" I asked.

She shook her head. "No known cure."

"So, we're doomed?"

"'Fraid so." She took a big gulp of wine.

We watched each other over the rims of our glasses, then I asked, "So why does Sidney think us meeting would ruin everything . . . and what's 'everything'?" (I wanted more information on this Sidney Collins.)

Nobody except Janie and my sister knew that I was gay. Matt, if I'd told him, he would have laughed, told me I had a morbid sense of humor. My mom and dad and brother, no way. They were too immersed in midwestern, middle-class culture to understand. They'd think it was some Hollywood affect rather than the way I'd felt since seeing Julia Roberts in *Notting Hill* when I was a kid. Watching her stand there, just a girl, asking a boy to love her, I realized I wished she'd been asking a girl to love her. And I wished that girl was me.

But this was the 2000s, and short hair and tuxedos were not going to make me America's sweetheart. I did what was needed, wore couture gowns and painted smokey eyes. But whenever I walked the red carpet I imagined — and this is embarrassingly true — that the cameras were Julia Roberts and my goal was to make her want me.

Now I wanted Cass to want me. Gone

were my thoughts of platonic allyship. Did she know I wanted her? And how could I make sure she did? These were the thoughts going through my head as we worked our way through the bottle of wine.

"Sid, well, things with her are impossible to describe." Cass sat upright again. She switched which leg she was sitting on and draped her arm over the back of the sofa. I couldn't help but notice her hand was now so much closer to me. Just a few inches from my left shoulder. That obviously had been the purpose of the readjustment, no?

I fidgeted so that I could bring my body a little nearer to the tips of her fingers. Her nails were unpainted, her hands tan* and slender. She continued, "What's everything? Um, I guess 'everything' is this wall we've built between me, who I am, my identity, and the book and all of that. There's a bunch of layers so that it would be impossible to identify me as the author — Sid's the only one who knows, I guess until now. She said the only way people could find out who I am is by human error."

*Note from Cate: My mom once explained our complexion as "Black Irish," courtesy of some long-ago Spanish traders who had settled in the country. I brown easily.

"And I imagine she's worried you" — I pointed at her — "are the human who might commit this error?" The gesture was multipurpose. It reached its full potential when my lifted hand dusted her forearm. Lingering on her arm felt too bold. I let my hand slide off and onto the back of the sofa. Now our forearms were running parallel, separated by just a few inches. She was speaking again, but my focus, and my eyes, was on the space between us. I pictured a ruler measuring how far apart we were, imagined a tiny pencil behind my ear to record the number. Was it two inches exactly? Maybe even less.

I tuned back in midsentence. "— she says it's about the business, but I think actually it might be about you."

Shit. That's a sentence I wish I had heard in full. "Wait." I shook my head — maybe best to be honest? — "I was, well, my mind wandered for a moment. Can you say that again?"

She raised her eyebrows. Flirtatious, yes, almost definitely flirtatious. I bit my bottom lip in a way I hoped was subtle and sexy, not cheesy. People bit their bottom lip for all different kinds of reasons.

"I was just saying that it seemed to me that her concern about blowing my anonymity was just the pretense, and that really

Sid was against this trip because she was jealous."

"Of . . . me?"

We both know the answer to that, was the look on Cass's face. Fair enough; I had been fishing for a compliment. The pieces of the puzzle were starting to look like a picture. Maybe Cass and this Sid had been something to each other. Maybe they still were. And maybe coming to meet me, to see what life was like in Hollywood, was about more than just the book and the movie. Maybe Sidney was beautiful and brilliant and everything Cass wanted, but I was sensing not.

Enter: Ry Channing.

A public relationship was not possible. The allure of Cass, beyond her sexiness, was her commitment to anonymity. Right on the heels of Sarah, she was the anti-Sarah. And my train of thought was chugging along, moving quickly enough that I couldn't vet each step, and the next thing I said was, "I mean, how bad could it have been, this thing you're hiding from?"

A cold frost descended on my cozy living room. It was a dumb thing to say. But in those brief seconds, I was playing out the entirety of our relationship. Eventually, Cass's mysterious background and need for anonymity would become an issue. Maybe

I wanted reassurance that it was all being blown out of proportion. We were both young. It was a sample-size issue. Maybe this thing felt like a big deal now, but she'd come to realize it wasn't? If not, then dating me was off the table.

As the last word left my mouth, I could sense Cass retreating. Then I could see it, her arm lifting from the back of the sofa and crossing with her other arm against her chest. For someone paid to charm millions with a look, I'd managed to alienate Cass with just a few wrong words.

"I think I'm gonna head to bed," is what she said instead of *Why the fuck did you ruin the night?*

"Wait, Cass, don't." I was in full retreat. "I'm sorry, that was a stupid thing to ask, and you don't owe me an explanation."

"It's not that," she lied. "I'm just . . . exhausted — it's late my time." She stood, extended her arms overhead. Let out a big yawn. It sounded authentic, and caused me to yawn, too. "See?" She seemed pleased my body had inadvertently confirmed her fake rationale.

By the time we made it to the hallway — me in my doorway, she in hers — she had softened again. I tried to shake off the weird energy but couldn't. I dragged her into my inner turmoil and said, "I'm sorry I asked you that." I gestured my thumb back toward the living room, where the two half-drunk glasses of wine would stay overnight. "I know how annoying it is when people pry."

This last part was true. She was already shaking her head and brushing away my words. Her head dipped a little, and she looked directly at me. Then she tucked a strand of hair behind her ear. Maybe she was waiting for me to move toward her, but I couldn't be the one. Not after stumbling so hard just a minute earlier.

A beat, another beat, her eyes searching mine. When nothing came, she said, "Good night then, Ryan," and turned into the room. The door closed noiselessly behind her. Picture me standing there for probably a full minute, wondering if she was just on the other side of the door.* Wondering if she was also waiting, hoping I would softly knock.

*****Note from Cate:** I was.

CHAPTER 33

Cass

January 2007
Los Angeles

We never talked about the book, or the movie, or really anything about our work* except when I asked questions about what it was like being a movie star. "Like being a person, except delusional," she said, to which I responded, "Deluded, how?" And she said, tenting her fingers and drumming them together, "You're always in a state of believing something that isn't really true?" Then she jumped into the pool, and I took that to mean she wouldn't be elaborating.

I wanted her. But I was scared. And my fears were constantly shape-shifting: Was she feeling how I was feeling? Was she acting like she liked me? Did I deserve this, this state of wonder, or was I horrible for

---

***Note from Cate:** I was not thinking about work.

feeling lightness again? The truth was that I thought about Amanda less those weeks in LA, and about Sidney not unless forced to.

Ryan said she wanted me to stay. *As long as you want,* she'd said. I texted Sidney that the studio had asked me to extend my trip because it was so helpful to Ryan. They said my contribution was invaluable. I texted her about how much we were getting done, how well it was all going. She knew it was bullshit, and I knew she knew it was bullshit. I just didn't care — I wanted another few weeks with Ryan more than I wanted a life with Sidney.

Her responses were perfunctory. I was grateful for the emotionally distant medium of text messaging, a baked-in excuse for brevity. And I kept reminding myself that she didn't own me.

Not exactly.

CHAPTER 34

RYAN

January 2007
Los Angeles

The first night after Cass extended her trip, I was lying in bed, wide-awake. An hour passed, then another. The entire time I was poised, always just a moment from climbing out of bed and knocking on Cass's door. My senses were heightened. I was listening deeply. Every creak of the house, every branch hitting a window had me wondering if maybe it was her coming to me.

I was wearing just an old T-shirt and thong, and my skin was alive against the sheets. I imagined what would happen if she slipped into bed next to me. The energy of it felt like a tornado, with me at the center. I thought at once that it was my imagination and also that it was the realest thing I'd ever felt. Across the hall, she must be listening for me, for my footsteps. Nothing else made sense.

Then finally, like a dream, I got out of bed. The clock read 1:57. The wood was cold on my feet, and I shivered, nervous. With every step toward her, I was in disbelief that I was upright. The cover of night made me curious. Was I real? Was this real? I kept telling myself it was.

I knocked so softly on the door. Softly enough that if she was asleep — but she couldn't be asleep — she wouldn't hear me. I pressed my ear to the wood. A long second passed.

"Come in," came Cass's voice from inside, a faint whisper. I turned the knob gently, letting myself into the room, releasing it only after pressing the door closed behind me. My eyes had just started to adjust. I could see Cass on the left side of the bed, right leg flung over the covers. I tiptoed to the other side and as I got closer, she lifted the covers for me and I laid myself down, facing her. Her hair was falling in her eyes. I reached over and tucked it behind her ear, which I'd seen her do a dozen times and had fantasized about doing myself. I let my hand rest on her neck, her skin warm beneath my touch, and I made my eyes as soft as possible so maybe she could see how much I wanted this — her.

My body was a loose wire. I resisted the

urge to wrap myself around her. *Wait, wait, wait,* I told myself many times. Wanting everything to be perfect. We lay staring at each other for many seconds and my heartbeat was a sound that seemed to fill the room. Then she was moving her body toward mine. We were only centimeters apart and still the only place we were touching was my hand on her neck. She leaned into my ear and whispered, "What took you so long?" Then she brought her lips closer, so they were hovering next to mine, a molecule apart, if that. And I waited for her still, waited some more. But then I couldn't help myself, and I pressed into her, and she exhaled in a way that made me know for sure that she wanted me as much as I wanted her.

The thing I remember about that night is that no stop signs existed. Not even a yield. The moment our bodies came together — her hard nipples against my skin — we each escalated in turn. She brought her left hand to my breast. I reached for her hip. She slowly moved her right hand, which had been briefly gripping my neck, down the length of my body, pausing her open palm on my stomach and subtly pressing her hips into mine, then traveled farther until she was just outside of me. I arched my back — I wanted her to feel how wet I was — until she was inside. Then I exhaled slowly into her ear, whispered, *Fuuuuuck*. She turned my chin with her free hand and looked me right in the eyes, began rhythmically moving herself into me.

CHAPTER 35

CASS

January 2007
Los Angeles

Most nights that first week after we parted ways, I lay awake and whispered softly, again and again, *Come here, come here, come here,* believing with my full body that if I emitted enough desire, she would feel it across the hall. Finally, she did come. And that kind of ache, teetering on the edge of overwhelm, I'd never felt before. It was bold, but when I guided her hand down to feel me, my mouth was open by her ear and I thought for a moment I wouldn't be able to form words, that all of my life force had pooled to the center, leaving nothing else functioning, but then finally I mastered myself and whispered, "You're what I want," and I let the words blend together with my breath so that it was a feeling passed more than a sentence said.

It was the best night of my life.*

***Note from Cate:** Nothing compares to this first night with Ryan. We didn't fall asleep until dawn, and then just for an hour or two, the softness of her naked body wrapped around mine and me lying awake in awe at how good she felt, how I'd been as close to her as possible — inside her, even — and yet all I wanted was to be closer. *How,* I remember thinking that night, *could we get even closer?* (The second-best night of my life was when the local newspaper reviewed our play junior year and wrote that Amanda and I had "star power"; we sat on the dock for hours, feet dangling in the lake, reading the review aloud to each other.)

CHAPTER 36

SIDNEY

January 2007
New York

I built the entire Cate Kay world. The labyrinth of contracts and bank accounts and NDAs — all untraceable to Cass. One day, Cassandra Ford was just a made-up name; the next, a US citizen with discreet access to nearly unlimited resources. I thought securing Cass's privacy would unlock her love. Flawed lawyer-think, I see now. She never appreciated the genius of what I'd created — how I pulled at every loophole and knitted her an entirely new universe. But my skill set would never take Cass's breath away — a fact I was too blind to see for too long.

   She preferred me in bed, in the dark — not out in public. But just one week before she jetted across the country to Ry Channing (without even a backward glance, let me add), we'd had one of the more tender nights of our relationship. Anytime she offered me her full attention, I felt like one of those magic sponge animals — just add water — that instantly and rapidly expand. The fullest, most powerful version of myself.

That night, we were eating dinner at a downtown sushi restaurant that was in the basement of a brownstone and was so dark that the sushi rice gleamed on the table. We had to lean forward just to see each other's faces.

After sushi, we were in a bubble of warmth as we walked up the steps to the street. I was, however, preparing myself for it to burst — two feet of separation and Cass drifting away on some thought train she rarely invited me on. But that night as we walked toward the subway, she nuzzled into me, wrapping her arm through mine, leaning against my shoulder. I glanced down at our interlaced arms — took a mental snapshot. A surge of dopamine lit me up.

That night in bed, she leaned over and kissed me on the cheek, unprompted, and said, "Thank you for dinner and for everything you've done for me." All was right in my world.

So, imagine my . . . I don't even know what the right word is — sadness, anger, disappointment? — when a week later Cass dropped everything to accept Ry Channing's invitation. I was always the more mature one — I tried to rise above. I let her go. Let her have her space. She checked in, but her updates were painfully obligatory. I would glance at them on my BlackBerry and wonder how such a good actor — according to her drama teacher, anyway — was so terrible at pretending.

In my profession you learn that people are always building a web of lies around a kernel of truth and calling it honesty — it's transparent. So, when Cass tried convincing me that the trip to Hollywood was about the movie — well, I'm no idiot. If it was about *The Very Last,* she would have been gone for a few days inside conference rooms on some studio lot. She might have even considered inviting me along. I knew she went on that trip to Los Angeles searching — for infatuation, clearly, and for a version of her life she was hoping could still exist.

I was furious.

A partner at the firm noticed my discontent while Cass was away. He'd stopped by my office, twice, to find me staring out the window. Not necessarily an unusual position in which to find a lawyer, but I didn't even hear him knocking. He had to put himself in front of me to break my trance. The second day he found me like this, he dropped into the chair across from me and said, "Tomorrow at noon, be ready. I'm taking you somewhere to burn off whatever *this* is." *This* was said with disdain.

"Taking me where?" I wasn't in the habit of joining men on mystery adventures — certainly not in the middle of a workday. This guy, Jonathan, wasn't my boss, but he wasn't somebody you turned down, either.

"You played basketball in high school, yes?" he asked.

I was intrigued. "I did . . ."

"And I've seen you running, so you'll love this." He was already standing again. "Wear whatever you'd wear for one of your runs."

"Noon," he added, rapping my door on his way out. "Be ready."

"Soul . . . Cycle?" I said, trying to work out what those two words meant in combination. We were on an Upper West Side corner approaching a shiny white storefront with gold embellishments, and I'd never seen Jonathan this excited. He was backpedaling so he could watch me approaching. A first-timer, taking it all in.

"You're gonna fucking *love* it," he said, pulling open the door for me. He was talking a mile a minute — pointing out the lockers and changing rooms and explaining the transformation that would happen inside the darkened space down the hallway.

Jonathan had misjudged me. I wasn't a group fitness person. I liked to oversee my own physical punishment, and I'd never found a group class that wasn't mostly wasted time. Also, I hadn't been on a bike since I'd put baseball cards in the spokes as a kid, and I certainly had no desire to be physically attached to one. But here I was. I stuffed my feet into the weird shoes and clacked down the hallway.

The room was already filled — people were buzzing with anticipation like we were at a concert. Jonathan was in the back row, already pedaling, and he waved a towel to get my attention. I turned sideways and excused myself a dozen times until I was standing next to this gleaming torture device. He began gesturing toward the front of the room, but I was focused on figuring out how to get myself up and on. The pedals were spinning wildly — an apt metaphor for how I was feeling.

I felt a hand on my shoulder and heard a rich, velvety voice saying, "Here, let me help." I glanced to my right — there stood a goddess. Strong shoulders, dirty blond hair done in a Viking braid. She was missing only bow and arrow. She smirked, saying, "I promise it's not as scary as it seems." Then she was touching my hip — a measurement for the bike, I soon realized. She turned some knobs and gracefully manipulated the handlebars. "Try this," she said, steadying my forearm as I tried clipping in my shoes.

My reluctance melted, and I pressed my toes down until I heard one satisfying click, then another. Even as a kid my mom would stop people and say, "Oh, Sidney can figure it out on her own." She was always telling people I was so competent she'd never have to worry about me. But sometimes it's nice to be worried about. Even if it's just the gift of a sweat towel or a seat adjustment with a lingering touch.

"Feel good?" she was asking. I looked down. For no discernable reason, her hand was resting lightly on my thigh.

"Feel great," I said. And I did — nobody was ever helping me fix *my* problems.

"Brilliant," she said, then she was gone. I turned to Jonathan and before I could say anything, he jumped in with "I just *knew* you'd love this place."

I went every day for the next month.

CHAPTER 37

RYAN

February 2007
Los Angeles

So is Hollywood everything you dreamed of?" I asked Cass on one of the last days before I had to leave for Charleston. It was early afternoon. The sun was full strength. She was lowering herself into the pool. I was lying on the Moroccan tile, my right arm dangling in the water. She pressed her lips against the inside of my elbow, and I wished we were in bed again, but the sun had put me in a kind of coma, and I felt immobilized.

"Let's see." Cass crossed her arms on the tile and put her chin on her hands. "I'm next to, literally, the most beautiful woman in the world, the sun is out, we can have anything we want, and work hasn't crossed my mind in weeks — yes, I think it's everything I dreamed of."

Plenty of ways for me to respond to that.

But, of course, I couldn't get past the compliment. It made me wonder what other women, if any, Cass had loved, so I asked her how long she'd known that she liked women. She turned her head to the side, her left temple on her hands, and looked at me.

"How long have *you* known?" she countered. Her tone was light and flirtatious, so I didn't mind answering my own question.

"Hmmm," I said, my eyes closed against the sun, more relaxed than I'd been in years. "You mean in addition to *Notting Hill*?" I opened my eyes just long enough to wink at her before continuing. "I think fifth grade. Kansas. We were going on a school field trip, and the boys were asking girls to sit with them like it was the elementary school version of the prom or something."

The sun had me feeling almost stoned. As I told the story, I felt myself back there — that fifth-grade classroom with maps of the world on the walls, the dawn of my sexual consciousness.

"This boy named Mark asked if I'd sit with him, and I had this physical reaction like, *absolutely not,* because the only person I wanted to sit next to was this girl in my class named Ashley. We were kind of friends, but I wanted to be, you know, better friends, and so I told Mark that I already had a seatmate,

Ashley, then I turned to Ashley and said, 'Right?'"

"Oh God, I'm worried for you, Ryan." Cass leaned over and touched her lips to mine, armor against my impending devastation. "And what did your one true love say?"

"She said — and I kid you not, I'll remember it for the rest of my life — she said, 'I think I'll sit with Mark.'" I shook my head slowly, as if reliving the pain.

Cass pretended to stab herself through the heart, then let her body slowly slip beneath the water — a silent, lovesick death. *She absolutely could have been a movie star,* I remember thinking in that moment. One eye squinted open, watching her go under, resurfacing with her hair slicked back and beads of water clinging to the ends of her eyelashes.

"Fuck," I said. "You're aware of how sexy you are?"

"No and yes," she said, then smiled. "Although that was probably a rhetorical question."

"It was, but I like when you answer all of my questions — rhetorical or otherwise." I wasn't really thinking about *the one question* she'd left unanswered (for the whole world), but as soon as I said this, I could feel her body tense ever so slightly. I brought my hand out of the water and brushed her bottom lip with my thumb, left it there until she slowly opened her mouth and let me inside. She was watching me the entire time. Once the tension released, I said, "Your turn, please. How long have *you* known?"

She lowered her mouth to the water. Her bottom lip was just below the surface, her mouth half-filled with pool water. I waited. I was willing to be patient for this answer. After a few moments she lifted herself an inch. The water was at chin level. Whenever she decided to tell me something about herself, I felt relieved. I was one small step closer to knowing her fully. (But always it was hovering: *Why, why, why* did she need to be anonymous? What happened all those years ago?)

"It was summer theater camp, and I was probably a little younger than you were on the field trip. There was this small outdoor theater behind the local library, near the lake, and we'd break into groups and at the end of the week we'd put on a play. That was the whole camp. It was amazing."

Here she paused and lowered her bottom lip below the water again, filling her mouth, and again I waited, watching her closely and wishing I could be inside her head. She was so careful. With all her words. I was wondering if I should be more careful with mine. And yet Cass seemed to be handcuffed in some indescribable way.

"Amanda," she said after a little while, and hearing that name and the way she said it — *reverence* is the word that comes to mind — I felt certain she was telling me something important. I'd been letting the sun daze me, but now I propped myself on an elbow. I made it as casual as possible so that I didn't startle her back into silence with my sudden, undivided attention. She continued: "Her name was Amanda and that week she was the only thing I could think about. Every morning I would wake up early and pop out of bed, just because I knew I was seeing her. She had these clear jellied sandals, but she'd painted them herself, like an ombré rainbow or something, and they were the coolest thing I'd ever seen."

The way Cass spoke, with such precision, I was mesmerized watching her lips form the words. The way her pink tongue — were all tongues so pink? — peeked out between her teeth. When she mentioned the jellied sandals, she closed her eyes, and I knew she was conjuring them in her mind. "After that first summer camp, we were inseparable," she said. "She was the only friend I ever needed — and really the only one I wanted in that small town. We did everything together, but we were never . . . she never . . . we were friends. It wasn't like that for her, I guess."

"Are you sure it wasn't?" I couldn't imagine being near Cass and not wanting to touch her, to make her my own. This Amanda, maybe she just hadn't known it yet.

"Yes, I'm sure," Cass said, then she let herself slip under the water again. I leaned over the side to watch her, the ripples distorting her image, but I thought I could see the heels of her hands pressing into her eyes. *Amanda,* she was something big, I could tell. I wanted to know more, but I didn't want Cass to disappear into herself. I debated what to say next. Should I ask, or shouldn't I?

My curiosity outweighed my caution. Once she came up for air, I waited a moment, then asked, "What happened — with Amanda?"

She ran her hands through her hair. She dipped her head left and right, shaking water from her ears. I could feel the energy, thickened by the churning of her mind.

"There was an accident." She lifted her eyes and met mine, briefly, before dropping them again. She began cupping the water with her hands. "She was in an accident."

"Is she okay?"

She inhaled deeply. "No, she di—"

But just then a knock came from the back of the house. Janie appeared at the sliding door, pulling it open. In her hands was a thick binder. As she walked toward us, she held it aloft and shimmied it back and forth as if to say, *Here it is!*

It was the latest script for *The Very Last*. Janie didn't ask if now was a good time. Nor would she care. She sat at the outdoor table and started flipping through the pages. Cass lifted herself out of the pool, wrapped a towel around her waist, and joined her. "Wow, so it's really happening," she was saying, and I could hear in her voice how happy she was to switch topics.

Cass and Janie had interacted a few times by then. (Sorry, NDA.) During her most recent visit, Janie had cornered me in the kitchen and asked, "What's going on with you two?" And in response I took as big a bite of my toast as I could fit in my mouth.* I chewed slowly, then shrugged.

***Note from Cate:** I'm thankful that Ryan included these parts about her losing weight for *The Very Last*. We never talked about it, but watching her hardly eat for weeks on end made me question if I would have enjoyed being an actor as much as I'd assumed I would as a kid. I never considered the underbelly of it — only the shiny parts.

"Dude," Janie had said, which made me laugh. I liked being called "dude." It helped balance out the hyperfemininity I had to exhibit almost everywhere else. Plus, this *dude,* she said it like an exhale — it had so much loaded inside. If Janie had asked, I could have listed everything she'd infused it with. Instead, while still chewing, I said, "You worry too much. It's going to be fine."

She scoffed. "Do you know how famous you are now? I know you've been holed up in here, but it's bananas out there." She pointed to the outside world, and I pictured a frenzy of paparazzi and car chases. "You're telling me you've decided to date someone whose goal in life appears to be maintaining absolute secrecy concerning her identity? And you think I'm worrying *too much*?"

Okay, when you put it that way! I said something like "Point taken," but my brain was on the drug of love and no doubt that was distorting everything. A few hurdles, that's all they were. We'd figure them out.

Janie leaned into me and whispered, "To be clear, the only thing I'm worried about is you and your beautiful heart." Then she snatched the peanut butter toast out of my hand and said, "Wardrobe fitting next week, help me out here."

CHAPTER 38

CASS

February 2007
Los Angeles

That last week before Ryan had to leave for filming in Charleston, I kept waiting for her to ask me to join her. Crazy, crazy, I know. It had only been a few weeks. But I just wanted it — her, the life, the city. Every single part of it. Los Angeles felt exactly like how we — Amanda and I — imagined it during those long Adirondack winters, and I knew I'd love being on location just as much.

Early morning of our last day, careful not to wake Ryan, I slipped out of bed. I tiptoed across the hall, locked myself in the bathroom, and sat on the toilet staring down at my silver phone. I flipped it open, flipped it shut — open, shut, open, shut.

"Ah, fuck it," I said softly, then called the airline and rerouted my flight to New York to Charleston. Cart, horse, for sure, but I thought, why not twist the universe's arm?

I steeled myself. I knew what would happen next. Two hours after the charge hit the account, Sidney would notice. ("Um, because I'm not a reckless moron," she had responded when I once asked why she logged into my American Express account *twice a day*.) Then my phone would ring. And it wouldn't stop ringing until I answered. Better to just call her directly, get it over with.

It went straight to voicemail — a blessing. There was Sidney's commanding voice saying, "You've reached the mobile of Sidney Collins, Esquire, please leave a message after the beep." How humorless she could be, not even a wink in her tone. I took a deep breath, said, *"Sidney, it's me. I wanted to let you know that I'm not coming back to New York right now. I'm going to Charleston with Ryan for the filming, and we can talk about all this when I'm back. Okay? Okay. I hope you're . . . I hope everything is good there."*

I wondered if I was ever going back to New York. Did a world exist in which I would never see Sidney again? My left knee was bouncing rapidly. I bowed between my legs and pressed my eyes closed. A layer of fear, but beneath — excitement.

A minute later, I tiptoed across the hall, climbed back into bed, and pressed myself against Ryan's back, grateful for her warmth after the bathroom's cold tile.

We spent the day in bed, and I ignored my phone. Finally, early evening, I slipped away to get changed for dinner and fished the phone out of my bag. I was prepared for missed messages from Sidney — nobody ever called me except Sidney — yet there was nothing from her. But right there, right there on that little screen, was a number I didn't recognize. Three times it had called me, leaving one voicemail.

My stomach dropped so violently that my vision went fuzzy for a moment. An unknown number had never called this phone. My brain was off and running: Here it finally was — the police. I listened immediately. A man's voice:

"Hello, Ms. Ford — this is incredibly urgent. Please call me back at 212-555-3463."

I could not give myself time to spiral. The faster this was over — whatever *this* was — the better for my internal organs. I dialed the number, hit Talk, willing him to answer —

"Hello."

"This is Cass Ford," I said. I was marching on a direct path through this moment.

But then the line went silent, which almost made me angry, like come on man, let's get to the point as quickly as possible. The more open space my brain was given — even just a few seconds — the more horrible a scenario it would create. (This wasn't the local police, it was the FBI — no, no, it was probably the CIA . . .) Eventually he cleared his throat, said, "Thank you for returning my call. I know it's dinnertime in LA, so I'll get right to it."

Wait, how did he know I was in LA? The room's only window looked onto the backyard, but I stepped out of eyeline anyway. I made a mental list of who knew my whereabouts: Sidney, Janie, Ry—

I flashed back to the day before, in Ryan's pool, telling her too much about Amanda, the accident, tipsy on sunshine and infatuation.

But then he was talking: "We have a source here at the *New York Times* confirming you as the writer behind the pseudonym Cate Kay and that you were involved in a death in your hometown."

My skin became a hot plate. I looked down at the tile in Ryan's bathroom, hexagonal black and white. Yes, I'd told Ryan about Amanda, but — no, no way would she. I let my eyes run along the grout, following the pattern, looking for a way out. But there wasn't one.

I hung up the phone. Didn't say another word. Just snapped it shut on his questions and what it all meant. I looked at the flip phone and imagined the whole mess, the mess of my life, now trapped inside its shiny case.

Everything that had happened the previous few weeks with Ryan melted away. Just that morning, I'd been considering an exit strategy — out of this pseudonym and back into my life. I'd thought maybe I could release the next books under *my* name. I had felt excited; I was in control. But this, it felt like an invasion. I imagined the headlines, the follow-up stories, the whispers, and, worst of all, Amanda's name in print — but no Amanda to read it.

I called Sidney. I needed her. She'd always fixed my mistakes. She picked up on the second ring and said, "Hi, Cass," with the curtness I know I deserved. I leapfrogged niceties and explained the phone call, what the reporter had said, what was happening. I whispered, "Sidney, please, help, what do I do?"

She asked me to repeat everything, slowly, and hearing the calmness in her voice soothed me. I did as she asked, then waited.

"I knew this trip was a bad idea," she said. "Can't trust anyone in Hollywood."

"You think Janie had something to do with this?" I didn't want to say Ryan's name again and certainly not to Sidney.

"Not Janie. Ryan. Doesn't surprise me one bit. Actors *are* addicted to drama. Wasn't she just going out with that costar of hers? Truth is a mirage out there."

I flinched at the insinuation that I was just another in Ryan's long list of conquests, but deconstructing the psychology of the movie business was not what I needed right then. "What do I *do*?" I asked.

Thankfully, she moved on. "Okay, I'm going to personally go over to the New York Times offices and kill this story — whatever it takes. You should get on a red-eye home. Get out of that madness."

I scrunched my eyes shut and pressed the heel of my hand into my right eye until I was seeing stars. Leaving Ryan, I didn't want that — wasn't ready to commit to it.

"How, how — how did this happen?"

"You know how," she said. "But come home and we'll figure it out."

"Okay — yeah — okay," I said, then she told me she loved me, then I hung up and I don't remember if I said it back.

Ryan had a computer in the hallway, and I

threw myself toward it. A stack of cassettes crashed to the floor as I reached for the power button, and Ryan called out from the kitchen, "Everything cool?" It felt like I was at high altitude, like I couldn't get enough air. I had to deliberately pause and breathe once before I yelled back, "All good, just checking my email real quick," even though I was not someone who needed to check their email real quick — or at all.

What had this reporter guy found? Into the Google search box I typed *Amanda Kent and Anne Marie Callahan* then paused. My fingers hovered over the keyboard. A moment later I quickly added *dead, Bolton Landing* and clicked the search button, terrified of the results.

I turned off half my brain, which is how I always managed thoughts of Amanda's death, and scanned each result. Only one item was relevant: the local newspaper was building a digital archive and had recently uploaded their review of our play junior year, *Rosencrantz and Guildenstern Are Dead,* in which Amanda and I played (with "star power") the title characters, two traditionally male roles. Nothing else. Just this one result offering proof of our existence. I was about to click on it, read it again, when from the other end of the house,

Ryan stepped into the hallway, yelled, "Is seven o'clock good for dinner tonight?" In a panic, I fumbled for the mouse and exited the search results.

CHAPTER 39

AMANDA

February 2007
Bolton Landing

Although I didn't get out much, I did very occasionally meet some old high school friends for a drink — or many, many drinks. We'd meet at a bar in town that was carpeted, which tells you everything you need to know about the place. Yes, there was an old-school jukebox; no, the drinks were not good.

The last time I ever joined them was a Friday in late winter. Kerri was home for the weekend from Siena College, close to Albany, where she had a scholarship that she routinely threatened to give up in favor of coming home and taking care of me. She was serious; it was terrifying. I knew I needed to get my shit together so she could move forward with her own life, but I couldn't seem to. Perhaps my buzzing social life would soothe her worries.

"Amanda!" my friends called in near unison when I appeared that night in the doorway of the bar. Their overexcited greeting was, to my ear at least, an attempt to balance the terrible thought they'd all no doubt just had: *Thank God that isn't me.* One of them was already hustling over to hold the door open.

"Hey, everyone!" I called back, smiling like we were in the opening scene of some feel-good network sitcom.

The group was five of us, including Tommy, who could have been the inspiration behind Bruce Springsteen's "Glory Days." Did we know he'd been named a Section II all-star his senior year? It was a fact that came up more frequently than you'd imagine possible.

We were the only kids from our small graduating class who'd never left town. We wouldn't have admitted it, but we all had chips on our shoulders. Riddled with insecurities. When I got to the table, I ordered the first of seven cranberry vodkas.

Two hours later and we were all drunk. I closed one eye and took a big, long sip through the tiny black straw. So narrow! So cruel! Was it designed to keep drunk people from getting alcohol into their mouths as fast as they wanted? Probably.

I noticed that Tommy was leaning back

and squinting at me, his lips pursed. Then he said, "Okay, fuck it — I'm gonna ask," and this weird energy rippled outward. The others stared at him, then exchanged glances, and I sensed that they knew precisely what he was about to ask. They seemed aghast, and *thrilled,* by their friend's brazenness.

"You and Annie," he said, then paused, lifting his drink to just below his lips. "You two ever . . . you know . . ." — he raised one eyebrow — "fuck?"

He took a slow sip of his drink in a way that he no doubt intended to be alluring but was pure douche.

No one had said her name to me. We'd never, not once in six years, spoken of her. I think they meant this as a kindness, but it was a robbery — of the me from before, who was made up of approximately 92 percent Annie memories and stories. For six years, we pretended Annie never existed; six years of misjudged decorum down the drain because Tommy got drunk and his urge to inquire about potential girl-on-girl action simply could not be resisted.

Of course, that in no way justifies what I did next, which was grab one of the empty beer bottles and slam it against the side of the table. The glass shattered, spraying everywhere. My friends flung themselves backward as if in mortal danger, which struck me as a bit exaggerated, almost performative. They'd finally found their reason to disinvite me.

When I got home, I was knocking my chair into shit, and Kerri came out rubbing her eyes.

"Amanda?" she asked, and she sounded exactly like Annie had while standing over me in the drained pool — my name like a question, though it wasn't, both their tones icy with terror. I flashed back to that afternoon, and asked myself the question I always did: Is it possible that when I was lying on those wet leaves waiting for Annie that I both knew that she would come back at any second and also that she was gone for good?

"Amanda?" Kerri said again, this time more forcefully. I glanced over at my little sister; she looked world-weary, her shoulders rounded. I hated that I was to blame. As always, I noticed how this feeling, like all my feelings, was instantly cannibalized by the Blame Annie monster — an insatiable beast. Everything was her fault.

I needed to get to bed, shut myself down for the night. (How had Annie functioned with that nonstop brain of hers? I wondered. Mine was starting to get like that, churning and churning. It was unsustainable.) I clumsily jerked myself forward, crushing my hand between my chair and the coffee table. The pain was searing.

"Fuck this!" I screamed, tilting my head back, really holding the *i* in *this* like the lead singer in a heavy metal band. It was primal. But it felt good, too, and I suddenly realized that maybe rage-yelling could be the first step on my road to freedom. On my *journey*, if you will.

Kerri, though, she wasn't privy to this silver lining I had stumbled onto. She'd reached her wits' end, too. Perhaps screaming, like sneezing, is a social contagion, because a second later she let out a vicious roar. (Dad was out playing poker.)

At some point, I quieted and observed Kerri. Her hands were balled into fists at her sides; her eyes were pressed shut. She sounded like someone on the scariest part of a roller coaster — more depth emanating from her slight frame than I would have expected. A few seconds later she ran out of air, sucked in a big breath, and screamed — with what must be described as bitterness — "I FUCKING HATE ANNIE CALLAHAN!"

Then she doubled down: "I hate her, I hate her, I HATE HER!"

She quickly depleted herself, and we descended into an odd silence. With a firmness that surprised me, I said, "Kerri — don't ever say that again. Never, ever again." Then, after a moment, I added softly, "Promise me?"

Kerri looked shell-shocked. "What?" she eventually managed, her fists becoming open palms. "Why are you defending her?"

"I'm not," I said, because I wasn't, not technically. But something had been knocked loose inside me.

"Um, yeah," she said, crossing her arms, "you kind of are."

What was I feeling? The sudden presence of a ball lodged in my throat. And the clarity that if Annie walked in the door at that moment, I would have thrown myself at her, sobbing — *I'm sorry, I'm sorry, I'm sorry.* I'd been so foolish and reckless that day on the island, so insecure in who I was. I'd put her in an awful position. She'd been in love with me — for years. But instead of letting her go, sharing her with someone else, I'd done just enough to keep her: a hand on the cheek, a kiss on the forehead, a too-long hug.

What I could finally acknowledge, on that terrible drunken night, was simple:

Annie must be in pain, too.

The next morning I called the Bolton Free Library and asked when and where the next AA meeting was. They told me it was that evening at the community church.

CHAPTER 40

KERRI

February 2007
Bolton Landing

I never hated Annie. I have this memory of her from when I was little — young enough that I was still dragging a doll around. It was after school, I'm sure, because Annie was in our kitchen making her and Amanda's usual snack: a plate of tortilla chips with melted shredded cheese. The height of middle-school sophistication. Her face was pressed to the microwave, hands cupped around her eyes.

"Can I have some, too?" I asked. I remember I didn't really want any chips, I just wanted to be part of whatever they were doing. Amanda was in another room, no doubt preparing whatever fun thing was about to happen. They were always doing something fun. If it was nice out, they'd be in the side yard using Dad's old car parts to construct some action scene; if it wasn't, they'd be doing a fashion show in Amanda's room, or mapping out the rules of a game they'd devised.

So deeply focused on the melting cheese, Annie didn't answer. Not unusual for her. She could be like that: single-minded. Whenever I saw her reading alone, I knew not to bother. She was very different from Amanda in that way.

A few seconds later she popped open the microwave and removed the plate. I was standing in the doorway, worried I'd have to ask again. Too much like begging. I watched as she walked past me as if I were invisible, plate of nachos in her hand. I turned, deflated. Then, she grabbed the banister with her free hand and paused, looking back at me.

"You coming, little one?" she said, winking. Grinning wildly, I dropped my doll and followed her up the stairs. I'd eventually recognize this as classic Annie: playing each scene for maximum effect, escalating the tension, unaware of the extra seconds of discomfort it caused the other person. Or maybe she figured the payoff was worth it.

As we entered Amanda's bedroom, Annie announced, "I have hired us an assistant."

Amanda was sitting on the ground, fiddling with the VCR, which she must have unhooked from downstairs. She looked up, and I scoured her face for annoyance, found none. I loved that easygoing quality about her — about them.

"Let's put the kid to work," my sister said. I was ready for whatever menial labor was expected of me. Annie sat across from Amanda, put the plate between them on the carpet, the chips smothered in a spiderweb of orange.

"Grab the movie." Annie nudged me, pointing toward Amanda's dresser. On top was a video from the local rental store.

"What is it?" I brought it over, sitting down near, but not too close — I didn't want to assume equality.

"Get over here." Annie reached for my arm, and I scooted toward them.

"Here's the plan," Amanda was saying, now plugging the VCR into the small television she had saved up for that year. "We'll each have a role, but first we have to get our lines."

"They call this *transcription*," Annie said, handing me a notebook. I looked at what she'd given me: a cheap spiral notebook with a red cover.

Amanda glanced over, said, "No, not

that one — I'm saving that one,"* then she pointed to a different notebook and Annie swapped with me.

"We'll go scene by scene," Annie said. "First, we'll transcribe, then we'll act it out. Don't worry, we'll help you with it. It's actually helpful that you're here, Kerri, because we needed someone to play Helen."

"Who's Helen?" I asked.

"Helen Kimble," Amanda said, reaching to take the case from me.

I popped it open and saw the movie: *The Fugitive*.

"I'll be Harrison Ford, obviously," she said, pushing the tape into the VCR. My eyes darted to Annie. She rolled her eyes and I almost giggled but caught myself. This was serious actor business.

Twelve years later, when I was woken up to Amanda drunk and crashing around our living room, all I could think about was how tired I was, waiting for Amanda to find herself again. And that night when I screamed that I hated Annie, it had nothing to do with her leaving us. It's like I was mad that we'd

---

***Note from Cate:** That sound you hear is me exhaling — this, *this,* is the notebook in which I wrote the first draft of *The Very Last*.

ever had her — mad that she existed in the first place.

You know that saying, it's better to have loved and lost than never to have loved at all?

That night I was feeling very much the opposite.

CHAPTER 41

JANIE JOHNSON

February 2007
Los Angeles

After my first-ever meeting with Ryan, we were standing on the sidewalk in West Hollywood. She hugged me warmly and said, "Maybe you could be my West Coast family?"

At the time, she'd only booked a couple small TV roles, nothing massive, and nobody at my company thought she was big enough to work with, but I found myself drawn to her. She had warmth and this blend of confidence and vulnerability that's rare and which she projected effortlessly on-screen.

We did become family. I took that part of my job seriously. Los Angeles wasn't an easy place to build community, something Ryan and I talked about frequently, and so I decided early on that I would treat her like my younger sister. Coddling wasn't an older sister's job, but loyalty and protection were, and that's how I approached everything with Ryan — loyalty and protection, first and foremost.

When I asked at that first meeting what she wanted from her career, she replied, "Everything." I'd taken a big bite of my croissant, too big, and brought my hand to my mouth while I chewed.

"What does 'everything' mean to you?" I asked. She was younger then. I'm not sure she knew what *everything* would cost her. But I was glad to see she was taking the question seriously. Really thinking about it. After a few seconds, she said, "I know acting will get me inside the room —"

"*Some* rooms," I jumped in. No point in pulling punches.

"*Some* rooms," she agreed. "But that's exactly my point — by the end, I don't just want to be in the room, I want to decide who else is in it, too."

"Directing?" I needed to know what mountains we would be climbing.

"Directing, producing — all of it."

They'd served my mocha in a wide porcelain mug; each sip was precarious. I lifted it again, taking my time, and Ryan watched me intently. Ordering a mocha and croissant was a tactical move. I knew it conveyed warmth and confidence. My goal was to make Ryan want to work with me. The first step was to make her want the things around me. This all sounds Machiavellian, but it was basic strategy — like dressing chicly for a job interview.

I swallowed the rich chocolate, leaned forward, carefully placed the mug back on the saucer. "A question for you," I said.

"Anything." She had her elbows on her knees, really engaging.

"If we worked together, would you understand that I'd make moves behind the scenes, on your behalf?"

She looked surprised but adapted quickly. "You mean without telling me?"

"Maybe, perhaps," I said. "If it made the most sense, for our long-term plan."

I could see her brighten at the word *our*. She didn't hesitate in responding, "I'd understand, yes."

Family is what Ryan and I have been ever since. And it's the reason I called the paparazzi that last night, the night she and Cass went out to dinner. Ryan had just turned the corner in her career, was one of the most sought-after actors in Hollywood — another step on our climb up the mountain.

Falling in love with Cass, staying hidden

in her bungalow, was not going to get her where she said she wanted to go. I knew even just a few flashbulbs would send Cass back to New York if she was committed to staying hidden, and it seemed she was.

CHAPTER 42

RYAN

February 2007
Los Angeles

My plan for our last night together in Los Angeles was to ask Cass to join me in Charleston for filming. Janie had rented me an old, old house in the heart of downtown. The kind with a courtyard and sloped floors and exposed beams from the 1800s. Cass could write during the days. Take walks along the water. See the history. Asking her to come to Charleston with me wasn't a marriage proposal, but still, I wanted a setting for us that was more memorable than takeout on my patio.

We'd finally gotten out of bed for a snack — it was almost lunchtime — when I mentioned possibly going out for dinner. I could tell that Cass wanted to like the idea. So, I pressed.

"It's a local spot, not some scene-y place,"

I said, remembering the night at Jack's when Sarah had stood me up. I was excited to create a better memory there. "I'll wear a baseball hat and we'll be super low-key."

Cass was standing in front of the open refrigerator looking for something to eat. She decided on a handful of grapes. I motioned for her to share, and she held them protectively against her chest. "I don't think Janie would approve," she said. "Grapes have sugar in them."

"Speaking of things Janie wouldn't approve of," I said, pleased with myself at the segue, returning us to the topic of dinner. "Jack's, tonight, please? We'll get a table in the corner, there are plants everywhere. Just friends out for dinner. Nobody will see us, I promise."

"You're reckless," Cass said. It sounded playful. I knew I was bending her to my will. What I had on my side was an understanding of her deep desire to know fame. And because I still didn't know the full picture of what had happened with her, I couldn't calculate the cost of exposure.

I grabbed her free hand and spun her into me. I pressed my body against hers. "Please, for me, I *need* to get out of this house," I whispered against her slightly parted lips.

"You're going to wear a baseball cap? And

we'll be discreet? And you absolutely promise nobody will find out?"

I could do no such thing. But I said yes anyway.

We spent the rest of the afternoon in bed. An hour before our reservation, Cass went to get changed. I was in the living room, and I watched her walk down the hall. She must have felt my eyes on her because she glanced back, saw me looking, and raised her eyebrows twice, quickly. Oh my god, this woman. I wanted her again. I looked at my wrist, at an imaginary watch, and said, "No, definitely not enough time for what I'm thinking."

She gave me a look like, *My interest is piqued.*

When she came out of the bathroom a half hour later, I heard her power up my desktop computer.

"We good for dinner at seven?" I called down the hallway.

She came into the kitchen a minute later, and I sensed something had shifted. Her mind was a thousand miles away. She was standing by the counter looking at her phone. I came up behind her, put my hands in her pockets, my lips on her neck. "So here's what I'm thinking," I whispered, trying to reattach us to the earlier thread of me wanting her before dinner.

"It's okay." She spun to face me; my hands came out of her pockets. "We should get going."

I wore my Kansas Jayhawks hat with the brim bent around my eyes. Actors always go out with Dodgers or Yankees hats. It makes me laugh. As soon as anyone sees someone with one of those caps in LA the first thing they do is look closer like, *Wait, which famous person is that?* But a Jayhawks hat? Nobody is double-taking a team from the Midwest.

Jack's had the best Chianti and eggplant parmesan, which I told Cass even though I would order a seltzer and the house salad with dressing on the side. The menu was small and printed in cursive, which represented the vibe of the place. Farmhouse tables, family photos on the walls, plants in every corner, low lighting. We were tucked into a corner, and I was feeling good about the whole thing.

Cass still seemed distant, but I told myself that made sense. Being out together meant more eyeballs on us, which meant someone might recognize me, and next they'd wonder who the woman across from me was. They'd wonder if she was someone they should know. Let me remind you: Los Angeles is a big city, but Hollywood is a small town. We were taking a calculated risk, but if Sidney Collins had done her job like she said she had, then there was no way one dinner with me would bring the whole Cate Kay house of cards down.

"We made it," I said, smiling. She was wearing a green V-neck T-shirt. I loved her collarbone. I wanted to reach across the table and run my fingers along its edge.

"We did," she said, fumbling with her napkin.

Our waiter appeared, welcoming us. Young guy, slicked blond hair. I was trying to keep my eyes hidden under my hat. I was getting the feeling that he thought I was somebody. People aren't as discreet as they imagine. There's the whisper to someone else. Then a little while later, when that person thinks enough time has passed, they look your way for a few seconds too long. Then they offer an affirmative to their friend, and then there's this buzz that emanates from their corner of the world. You just pray they aren't going to come over and ask if you are so-and-so.

"I'm surprised," Cass said when he left.

"What are you surprised about?" I was trying to fully tune in to her, but my attention was split. My eyes followed the server back to the bar where, yup, he was whispering into the ear of the bartender. *Fuck,* I thought, *he's going to call it in — make a buck on us.* Coming here was stupid after all. But romance is risk.

"Ryan?" Cass was looking at me strangely. "What's going on?" I pried my attention away from the bar. I needed to let it go. I couldn't control what this guy did. "Nothing, we're all good," I said. "So, what are you surprised about?"

"You," she said, and then I actually did forget about the server and bartender. Now Cass was talking about *us* — my favorite topic.

"What about me?" I said as seductively as possible. Were we flirting now? I could do that.

"I'm actually serious," she said. "I thought you wanted to meet me for the movie. Because you wanted more insight into the book, the characters, and all that?"

I leaned back. I had a moment of panic that we were shooting the movie soon and Cass was right, I hadn't done my standard prep work. Too much sex and big, bold cabernets and late nights listening to music.

"That *is* why I asked to meet you," I said. "At least, that's what I told my agent and Janie so they'd try to make it happen. But it was something else, too, this thing I noticed in the book."

"What thing?"

"A lot of people here — in Hollywood I mean — are convinced that the author of *The Very Last* is a man. Mostly, probably, because men assume all successful things are done by men, but also because of the premise of the book: New York City, its destruction, the grittiness of life in The Core. It's a loud premise. And men tend to blow things up more than women."

"But both main characters are women and one of them is gay," Cass said.

"A 'smart' move to 'balance' the story" — I did air quotes around *smart* and *balance* and used my best big-time studio executive voice to let her know how logic inside this twisted business worked.

"However," I said, putting my right elbow on the table and lifting my pointer finger, "you have that one small exchange between Samantha and Jeremiah, from back when they are in high school — the misunderstanding over the word 'girlfriend'? When I read that, I knew."

I was certain she would be proud of my insight and thrilled that I'd read her work so closely. But instead, she said, "You knew what?" And there was an edge to her voice, and she was leaning back in her chair. I tilted my head, confused. Even sharper now, she said, "What did you think you knew?"

I replayed my previous few sentences, scanning them for errors, for a reason for this abrupt shift in energy. I couldn't locate my misstep, which set my heart bouncing. My response came out slowly, a stutter. It was mostly just *I, um, I, I.* Before I could get out a complete sentence, which I'm not even sure was going to happen, Cass jumped in with another question. She was leaning forward and lowered her voice as she said, "Why did you invite me here?"

Dinner had gone off the rails so quickly. I was tongue-tied. "What's . . . happening?" I hoped my bewilderment came across as sincere.

She looked nervously around the restaurant, then stared into her lap.

"Cass," I said sharply, hoping to regain her attention. Out of the corner of my eye I saw our waiter returning with drinks. I tilted my head from him just slightly, so he could neither confirm nor deny that I was the movie star he suspected me to be.

A tall glass, dewy with condensation, now sat on the table. And the bubbles of my seltzer were rapidly rising to the surface — a perfect metaphor for whatever the fuck had happened to this conversation. Images of the previous month flashed through my mind. I reassessed them, wondering if they'd felt differently to Cass than they did to me. Had I ignored her unease? I'd heard horror stories of what fame could do to your sense of entitlement — entitlement to things, yes, but also to people. Had I done that with Cass; was my self-awareness shifting out from under me?

She was rigid across from me. Her head was level, but her eyes were down. I reached my hand across the table, palm up, and said, "Babe?" I dipped my head slightly to try to pry her eyes upward.

I watched her hands, willing them toward mine, but they remained in her lap. She lifted her eyes. They were filled with tears. My chest swelled. A misunderstanding is all this was. She was coming back to me. Then she swallowed and said, "Don't, please." She pushed back in her chair, stood.

"Where are you go — ?"

"I have a red-eye back to New York. I'll send for my things." She dropped her napkin on the table, a blur of white that I stared at for a second, my brain foggy.

Then Cass was walking away, and I was still processing what she had said. She had a plane booked for that night? Was this some kind of last-minute plan, or backup plan, or the plan all along? I stood and followed her through the restaurant. I was calming my energy and keeping my head down. The only thing that draws attention quicker than a celebrity is public drama. Cass was walking quickly, dodging tables. I inadvertently made eye contact with our server and was about to give him a fake reassuring smile, but his eyes darted away. *Uh-oh.* I knew that look.

"Cass, wait," I whisper-shouted. "Wait, wait, wait."

But she was pushing through the front door. Now that I've had time — years, actually — to dwell on it, of course I shouldn't have followed her outside. But that day was a slippery slope of bad decisions. *"That's her! Hey, Ry, over here!"*

From the waiter's sheepish look, I had anticipated dozens of cameras. But it was just two guys. I made a mental note to call Janie as soon as I got home. But first I needed to get to Cass, talk to her, bring her back to me.

A black SUV pulled onto the street and slowed down, stopping up the block from the restaurant. Cass picked up speed, walking toward the back seat door. I was dumbfounded at the coordination — where had this car even come from? How did Cass know it was arriving, and when? She reached the door handle and pulled it open, stepping up into the car.

For a moment I thought she was going to get in without even turning to look at me. But at the last second, her arm gripping the door, she lifted herself up, her chin resting on top of the door's black frame, and glanced back. And I swear to God, she mouthed, *I'm sorry.* But I don't know, I just don't know.

CHAPTER 43

Cass

February 2007
Los Angeles

Those weeks, they couldn't have meant nothing to Ryan. Maybe she could get her eyes to fill with love, or her body to emit desire, or her words to be perfect on camera. But all three, always, every day? Only love — not its facsimile — could produce that.

I was telling myself this as we walked to Jack's, part of a larger campaign to convince myself that dinner was a good idea. I reverse engineered the logic: if I wanted to trust Ryan — and I did — then I needed to trust her completely.

And I told myself if anything appeared amiss, I'd leave immediately. Sidney had texted me the flight information. She said when I needed the car, to just send her the address, she'd have one on standby in the neighborhood.

Plan A: Ryan.
Plan B: Leave.

I fidgeted in my chair. In front of me was a linen place mat and coaster, and I spent a few seconds moving them until they appeared centered on the table. When I looked at Ryan, her eyes were down. She was tilting her head slightly, bringing her fingers to her right temple. If she thought the movement subtle, it wasn't.

I grabbed my napkin and placed it in my lap, tucked my phone into the napkin's folds. The ridiculousness of hiding my phone struck me — what was I even doing? Why was I being so reckless?

Then, sitting there, I had this crushing thought: Since Amanda, I've been nothing more than a visitor in other people's worlds. Sidney's in New York; Ryan's in Los Angeles; Samantha's and Persephone's in *The Very Last*. I'd abandoned my best friend, lost her forever, for what? To *not* discover who I am?

I kept my eyes down, continued readjusting the napkin around my phone. Thankfully the server was still explaining the specials.

"I'm surprised," I said to Ryan once he was gone. Maybe I should have just been straightforward, said, *Sidney thinks you've sold me out to the press.* That's probably what my mom, or even Amanda, would have said. A fastball down the middle. But not me. I could only tiptoe around, backpedal my way into conversations.

"What are you surprised about?" Ryan was fighting to stay present, but her eyes kept shifting. *Please no,* I thought, *no more weirdness, no more red flags.*

In my mind, I was being clear: Tell me your true motivations for contacting me! But instead, somehow, we got onto the topic of the book, the movie, and Ryan was telling me some story about when she first read it, repeatedly glancing over at the bar as she spoke. I followed her eyes. Our server was whispering to the bartender.

No, no, no.

When our drinks arrived, Ryan barely looked up. Were the two of them in cahoots? Was I being set up, just as Sidney had warned? Then she reached her hands across the table, hoping for mine. But I was already gone.

Escape was my default setting. I needed to get myself some breathing room. Space to think.

Beneath the table, I texted Sidney: *Jack's, 2030 Hillhurst Ave.* Then I heard myself saying things with an edge, getting up and leaving the restaurant, Ryan following me.

The photographers didn't surprise me, but the energy of the interaction did. I'd always imagined the paparazzi as sexy, exciting. Instead, it felt like that moment someone pushes open the bathroom door that you've forgotten to lock — an invasion.

I hustled down the street.

If I'd climbed into that Escalade at any other moment of my life, I'd probably have been awed by it. In the cup holder was bottled water, the seats were a rich black leather, and a music video was playing on a small drop-down screen. A glass divider separated me from the driver. He slid it open to speak with me. "LAX, right?"

I nodded.

I glanced around the back seat — floor vacuumed to within an inch of its life, not a speck of dust to be found. My dream car, quintessential Hollywood. And yet everything was wrong. The fanciest cars, the nicest wine, all the accolades in the world were no match for what was hurting me. I wished I was in my broken Civic because at least then the outside would match my insides.

And isn't that what Amanda always wanted for me?

I let my head fall back and tried to calm myself. Making decisions with my heart thrashing like a caged animal was a terrible habit I couldn't seem to break. I interlaced my hands in my lap, closed my eyes, and took three deep, full breaths.

What did my insides want? What were they telling me?

I replayed the final moments at the table with Ryan. She was reaching for my hands, but what was she saying — with her words and her eyes? I pressed my eyelids tighter and concentrated.

Love?

I pictured Ryan in that moment — deeply confused, seemingly hurt by my behavior.

I replayed the last weeks, imagined that Ryan had hatched some sinister plan to bring me out to Los Angeles, to woo and expose me. I couldn't find a motive. But also, how to explain the sequence of events? I mention Amanda one day; a reporter is calling the next.

I thought of Sidney, of the day the *Vanity Fair* piece came out a few months before when the book was first released, when everyone was losing their minds. We were sitting at the kitchen table in our Harlem apartment, and she closed the magazine and said, "You know, being the gatekeeper to a cultural secret — it's kind of fun." Sidney rarely vocalized her inner monologue, and there were so few things she seemed to enjoy, so, no — no way Sidney would willingly abdicate her throne.

Another few deep breaths. What if the truth was this: I'd been reckless, introduced room for human error. I'd expanded the circle of who knew the truth about my pseudonym and was paying the price. Maybe Ryan had nothing to do with the reporter or the paparazzi. It could have been Janie or Ryan's agent or some greasy publicist working on promotion for *Moon*.

I leaned forward, muted the music video. The back seat went silent. I glanced out at the palm trees and stoplights and endless brake lights. If what was happening was out of my control anyway, then maybe I should let the universe choose.

And into my mind slipped a thought: If the driver knew Ry Channing, I'd stay; if he didn't, I'd take that flight. Already I was knocking on the glass. The divider opened.

"Do you know Ry Channing?"

He looked at me in the rearview mirror, trying to read me, then said, "Yeah, yeah, the one from that new movie, uh, damn, I can never remember the name. It's like, *Howling at the Moon,* or something."

I smiled, said, *"Beneath the Same Moon."*

He snapped his fingers, pointed at me in the mirror. "That's the one."

"Change of plans," I said. We were waiting at one of those uniquely LA stoplights that let one car at a time onto the highway. For a split second I worried that Sidney might have told him to take me to the airport and nowhere else, but his response was so blasé I was disappointed. He was craning his neck over his shoulder looking for cars, then back at the upcoming merge, as he said, "Where we going?"

He clearly didn't understand the life-altering decisions being contemplated in his back seat. I gave him the address of Ryan's bungalow and relaxed into the soft leather. What should I say to Ryan? Maybe just start at the beginning — "I met Amanda when I was nine years old . . ." — and tell her everything? She could help me figure out what to do: kill the story or step out of hiding. I mean, if anyone understood the variables in my decision, it was her.

For the next few minutes, every yellow light he stopped for, every slower lane he chose, stole a piece of my soul. Each second seemed vital — like the universe had me on a clock. Finally, he was slowing in front of Ryan's house and my door was open before he stopped.

"Need me to wait?" he asked.

"Give me a minute," I called to him over my shoulder. My heart was pulling me forward, the rest of me catching up. I jogged toward the back door, making sure each footfall landed on the center of each stone in the walkway. (Again, good universe juju.)

But then, hearing something, I abruptly stopped. Held my breath. Voices drifted from the backyard. Quietly, I stepped forward and peered between the slats. A silky yellow blouse was the first thing I saw. Unmistakably Ryan. She had her back to me, sitting at her outdoor table, facing a striking woman I didn't recognize. The woman was smiling, uncorking a bottle of wine, the definition of her arms so impressive I had a twinge of jealousy. Then she reached over and touched Ryan's hand, which struck me as devastatingly intimate. I loved Ryan's hands.

I stepped backward. I was suddenly out of breath. No air. Just woosh, gone. My focus now was returning to the car without anyone noticing me. I hurried back, climbed inside, and quickly pulled the door closed.

My second thought was: I guess Ryan really is a wonderful actor; she made me believe in our love.

My first was: Alone, again.

"Sorry about that," I said to my driver, pretending everything was a-okay. "Back to LAX."

CHAPTER 44

RYAN

February 2007
Los Angeles

I staggered home from Jack's in a haze of emptiness. Heat behind my eyes, my throat with a fist in it. All the symptoms of brokenheartedness that I'd only played in scenes came on like a fever. The actor part of me was taking notes, in pure observation mode, while the rest of me wanted the feeling gone and needed Cass back so fucking badly. Thank God I had no way of reaching her. No doubt I would have made a fool of myself. Dozens of phone calls, banging on her door if only I'd known which one was hers.

Instead, as soon as I reached home, I called Janie and told her what had happened. My most pressing concern was the photographers. She assured me she had a friend at *Vanity Fair* — *you did that Q&A with her?* — who she was certain would buy up the photos at a premium in exchange for some future favor.

"Fine, yes, anything, of course, thank you," I mumbled into the receiver. The rest of it, Janie said, we could deal with tomorrow. Then she said, "But more importantly, Ryan, are you — okay? I've never heard you like this."

"No, I'm crushed," I said. As I used that word, I realized that's precisely how I felt, having flopped onto my bed. Like some invisible medic was attempting to give me CPR — pressing on my ribs so hard they might break.

Janie started to say something that she no doubt hoped would be reassuring. But right then I heard a knock at my back gate, where Cass had first shown up weeks before. "I'll call you back, I gotta go," I said as I scrambled off the bed and to my backyard. Hope was rising inside me for the happy ending. The final scene of the movie where the music swells and the miscommunication is ironed out and the love story continues.

I yanked open the door and standing there, holding a bottle of red wine, was . . . Sarah. The surprise appearance of this other woman, who just a month earlier I'd been so excited about, was disorienting. How quickly the brain rewires itself. "My friend who works the bar at Jack's called," she said. "I've been wanting to talk. Can I come in?"

"I'm not sure that's a great idea," I was saying and annoyed at myself as the words were coming out. *Not sure?* What was wrong with me? In a city of uncertainties, where everything was in a constant state of falling apart until it miraculously didn't, the one thing I was sure of was that she was the wrong woman at my gate.

"Just five minutes, please," she said. "Hear me out."

Pure habit, a lifetime of yes, caused me to step aside. And then she was walking into my backyard.

CHAPTER 45

AMANDA

February 2007
Bolton Landing

The Bolton Community Church billed itself as nondenominational. In high school, Annie and I had been curious about the place, so we went to a Sunday service but left at halftime, which is what we called it when they stopped preaching and asked us to line up to consume the body and blood of Jesus Christ. The pastor had made clear they believed both the Old and New Testaments were the "infallible and inerrant word of God," and sitting next to each other in the pew we exchanged a glance like, *mmmkay.* After we slipped out, we walked down to the local veterans' memorial and Annie goes, "Okay, Amanda, if in five hundred years people are worshiping at the Church of Amanda, what would you be serving as the body and blood of Amanda?"

She was standing and reading, for probably the thousandth time, the plaque near the gilded war cannon, and without looking up she said, "Everyone is in the aisle with their hands cupped and the head of your church goes, 'The body of Amanda' — and what is it, what's your body made of?"

"Probably chicken nuggets," I said.

She grinned because she loved it when I understood the game, then she said, "And the blood of Amanda?"

"Honey mustard dipping sauce to complete the experience."

"Oh my god, you'd be the most popular church in history!"

"People would make pilgrimages from the ends of the earth," I said, and we both started laughing at the absurdity of it, and I asked if our conversation was blasphemous and she said, "Borderline," and then we were off on another tangent about Madonna.

The night after my bottle smashing, I found myself wheeling into that same church. My dad had, soon after the accident, ripped the passenger seat out of a van abandoned at his garage and jerry-rigged a mobility vehicle, which we'd used ever since. He dropped me at the church entrance and said he was proud of me, and I told him not to be — I hadn't done anything yet. And I wasn't sure I would.

Crossing into the church, with its faded red carpet, wood paneling, and general blahness, I was already imagining the tequila I would pour myself after. The AA meeting was in a bonus room with cheap linoleum flooring and metal folding chairs. If I had known she was going to be there, or if I had seen her before she saw me, I would never have entered that room. And I think about that all the time: about how so many of our instincts as humans are toward self-sabotage. They say moving toward the discomfort is the way to progress, but when you've already had so much of it — the discomfort, not the progress — why seek more?

Patricia Callahan (or Annie's mom, as I'd always known her) was chatting in a small group, and the moment I appeared in the doorway she looked over at me like she'd been expecting my arrival. She even waved, at first with assurance, and then as her hand moved, she seemed to piece everything together and she began leaking confidence, slowly dropping her hand, then excusing herself from the group.

She was still beautiful. Even prettier than I remembered, I was disappointed to acknowledge. She'd cut her hair short, so it curled around her ears, and the look was good on her, really made her cheekbones the star of the show. Wearing a sweater and blue jeans, she looked at ease in a deep sense, and I realized that in all the years I'd seen her while growing up, I never once registered her as truly present — she was always somewhere else. In fact, whenever she had said my name it had startled me, like hearing it from a stranger.

Idling in that doorway, I felt trapped. Trapped and with the mother of my ex-best friend walking toward me like some chitchat was going to fix the disaster zone in which her daughter had abandoned me. A situation that Patricia Callahan wasn't blameless in, either. I knew how absent she was with Annie, how desperate Annie was to prove herself to the world, but secretly and above all to her mother.

But there she was, coming closer and closer until she was bending down and wrapping me in a hug, her gold necklace smacking into my lips. I pictured my hardcover copy of *The Very Last,* still sitting on my bedside table, and a surge of adrenaline hit — this piece of knowledge I possessed, that I could wield like a weapon if necessary.

"Hi," she said. "I'm so happy you're here," she added, holding on to me for longer than

I would have liked, but then, I would have preferred no hug at all.

"I'm just here *tonight*," I said. And as I said it, I was certain I would not be coming back. In the years since the accident, even though we lived in the same small town, I'd never seen Patricia Callahan. Not all that surprising considering I'd barely seen her when Annie was around. What I didn't need, and didn't believe myself capable of, was avoiding alcohol *while also* healing my relationship with a Callahan. One or the other maybe, but not both.

"Just tonight sounds great to me," she said and kept her hand on my shoulder, and it was all I could do not to shrug it off. I snuck a glance at Patricia, tried to scan her face, her body — did this woman know that her long-lost daughter had written one of the most famous books in the world?

I sat at the back during the meeting. Thankfully the chairs all faced forward instead of in a circle. Easier to get lost, in thought or otherwise. Plus, absorbing direct eye contact with everyone while listening to testimonials might have been too much for me that first night. Patricia sat in the second row, a few seats in, her legs crossed. She nodded at the right times, twice whispered softly to her neighbor, the pair sharing a knowing laugh. She even once placed her hand on the woman's leg when a story got intense.

The actor in me wanted to address the group, to feel the thrill of their attention, but that felt dysfunctional. The only words I had were those I'd heard others speak in movies. None were mine. I kept my eyes down each time there was a lull, the group waiting to see if anyone else wanted to share. During one such stretch, toward what felt like the end, I was staring at the black canvas toes of my Converse when I heard Patricia's voice.

"Hi, everyone," she said, tucking her short hair behind her ears, a gesture that lodged a golf ball in my throat; there was so much Annie in the movement. "Thanks for being here. I'm Patricia, four years sober." Everyone clapped and she lowered her eyes, endured their attention.

"But I'm not actually up here for me tonight," she said and now she seemed to be looking at me, a soft tilt to her head, her eyes welcoming and kind. *What the fuck.* Wasn't this supposed to be anonymous? I was unaware my body could ignite that fast. From dormant to radiating in an instant. I held eye contact with her and shook my head, as vehement as possible while maintaining subtlety. She looked confused but continued speaking, and I didn't wait to find out what she had to say. I pushed myself out of that room within seconds, a personal land-speed record.*

*****Note from Cate:** I understand my old best friend's paranoia. Trust was not something my mom had earned. (But she was not speaking about Amanda.)

CHAPTER 46

SIDNEY

February 2007
New York

When Cass returned from Los Angeles, she was shaken. I'd never seen her so upended. Which was saying something. I reassured her that the story had been killed. That seemed to relieve her, but only momentarily.

I hadn't foreseen this response from her — crestfallen — so I was slow to react, distracted by how satisfied I was to have won, to have her out of LA and back with me. Now we could go back to normal. I'd taken care of everything, including changing her cell number. When I told her this last piece, she seemed pissed.

"Without asking me?"

"There was no other choice," I said. "It was compromised."

I guess I'd miscalculated — Cass packed her bags and left the following day. She told me she didn't know where she was going, but that she'd send a forwarding address. When she was walking out of the apartment, and we both knew it was for good, she hugged me and said, "Thank you, for all of it. But we both know this is broken."

It was probably the most honest thing she'd ever said to me.

I thought about following her into the hallway, telling her she was making a mistake, but I couldn't muster the passion. That's when I knew she was probably right — we were done. Nothing I did would make her love me. And I was done trying.

I did take pleasure in having pried Cass out of Ry Channing's hands at least. People in Hollywood think the whole world is theirs. That all they need is to care enough to want something and they can have it. Cass deserved better than to be some movie star's prize, to be just more proof of Ry Channing's world-class charm and lovability.

Plus, SoulCycle had me digging deep, doing the work. And I'd started wondering if maybe my favorite part of our relationship wasn't Cass, anyway — but Cate Kay.

CHAPTER 47

Ryan

February 2007
Los Angeles–Charleston

Janie collected me the next morning for the trip to Charleston. A pile of bones inside a hooded sweatshirt would be the best way to describe me. I was unwieldy, unsteady. Janie gathered me up and half carried me to her car like I was an injured athlete being helped off the field. And that's how I felt: like I'd been maimed playing the game of life.

I spent the next however many hours staring silently out windows. First the one in her car, then on a plane. Janie tried to talk to me, softly plying me with questions, even offering me a small pack of cookies that she said could be our little secret. Turning those away was its own kind of torture, but I needed her to understand how vicious my strain of lovesickness was.

Charleston was beautiful, it pained me to

acknowledge. I peeked out from beneath my hooded sweatshirt at the gas lamps and Spanish moss and dusty pastels. The city was exactly as I'd hoped, which made Cass not being there with me even more brutal. I so badly wanted to share this perfect place with her. That first night we had a welcome dinner in the back room of some dark steakhouse. My detached mood fit perfectly. Sitting around a table not eating and feigning interest in others is an art form that movie folks have perfected. Janie carried the conversational weight. I sat next to her looking no more despondent than the other actors. The next night began three months of overnight filming, so we were all in mourning.

When we got back to the house, which was tucked away in the French Quarter and had this picturesque courtyard, Janie asked me to sit with her for a minute. I lowered myself into one of the four wrought iron chairs encircling a concrete firepit. Bistro lights hung over the space. She figured out how to turn them on, then sat across from me.

"Can you lower that hood now?" she asked.

Dramatically, I said, "No . . . I cannot."

In response she tilted her head, fixed me with a stare, said, "Exactly what will happen if you lower the hood?"

"I'll have to feel things," I said. I knew she

thought I was being silly, and maybe I was, but the hood was protecting me. If I lowered it, I'd immediately sense the broader world around me. My thoughts would fly outward like sonar, hoping to locate Cass in the vastness. The purpose of keeping my hoodie up seemed obvious.

"But isn't your job to feel things?" Janie was tinkering with the knob on the firepit, which I wasn't happy to see. How long did she think we were staying out here? Turning on the lights was already more ambiance than we needed for what was going to be a brief interaction on my way to bed.

"No, it's my job to make *other people* feel things," I said, pleased with myself at this turn of phrase. Though I knew it was bullshit. Even back then I understood the audience never felt an emotion unless I was wracked with it first.

"Okay," she said. I could sense she wasn't a fan of this version of me. The feeling of not being liked made me squirm. I rearranged myself in the chair once, then again. Janie watched me, said nothing. Finally, I yanked down the hood and said, "Happy now?" And the feeling of the hood being off was exactly as bad as I'd imagined. The world, its sounds and atmosphere, was no longer muffled. Reality came into crisp focus. It was a reckoning. I brought my hands to my face and sobbed. Janie moved to the chair next to me, edged it closer until the arms were touching, then rubbed my back.

"What do you want to do about it?" she asked gently. I didn't respond. Knowing what to do was her job. Mine was to take my shiny, lovely self wherever she told me to. What I needed was for her to tell me how to fix this. I waited for her to recognize that. She kept rubbing my back even after I stopped crying, then said, "What if . . ." and paused. I sat up, revealing my blotchy face. She leaned forward and tried to wipe a tear from my cheek. (When people wonder what managing actors is like, do they imagine dealing with bodily functions? Because that's really 90 percent of the job.)

I lovingly batted away her hand, which she landed softly on my knee to keep us connected. She was a full-service manager and I'll love her for my whole life, but right then I only cared about *Cass, Cass, Cass.* "What if what?" I said, prompting her.

"What if what, what?" she said. Upon hearing this foolishness, I rolled my eyes and gave her the small laugh I knew she was hoping for. "There she is!" Janie leaned back and clasped her hands together. She raised them overhead like a conquering hero.

"Stop, you're so ridiculous," I said, pawing at her arms to get them lowered. She instantly complied. She wasn't much of a showman. I had one of her hands in both of mine and I squeezed hard, looked her dead in the eye, and asked, "Seriously, Janie, what do I do?"

"What if you write her a note, tell her how you feel?"

What I'd been hoping for was the sudden introduction of a time-travel device. Or Cass hiding in the extra bedroom as the final reveal in an elaborate ruse. My sweet spot was a full redemption arc in about two hours.

Janie, though, looked hopeful. Like maybe this note-writing could be just the thing. "RyRy," she was saying, "you should just put it all down, how you feel, and I'll do everything I can to get it to her. I promise."

I let go of her hand and awkwardly slid down in my chair until I looked like a stoner melting into the couch. I tilted my head back and stared into the night sky. "A note," I said. I was hoping Janie would recognize how inadequate her suggestion was. Two measly syllables. When she didn't respond, I let my head roll toward her, saw that she was also staring at the sky.

"Find anything good up there?" I asked, and for a few seconds it felt like she was onto something. Some brilliant cosmic message was downloading into her consciousness. But then she just slowly shook her head without looking over.

We sat like this for a while, then finally I said, "Okay — a note." And I went inside, ripped half a page from a script, and found a pen in Janie's purse. I wrote frantically, unselfconsciously. Then I folded it in half and went back outside. She still had her head tilted back. When she sensed me, she sat up straight and accepted the note with proper reverence: two open palms.

After she looked down, she said, "This looks like a charades clue." When I glanced at her hands, I had to admit she was right.

Even when my alarm clock went off at 2 a.m., I was grateful for *The Very Last* shoot. Not only did it keep my brain occupied, but it made me feel close to Cass. Once I was settled in my trailer, my routine, Janie flew to New York to hand-deliver my note. I'm not sure how long I thought such an errand would take, but she was back unexpectedly soon. I was in the courtyard drinking a terrible cup of black coffee made from a can of Folgers roasted before I was born. It was not the best part of waking up. I grimaced with each sip.

A clatter came from the gate, then Janie was walking toward me. At first, I couldn't read her body language. I realized I'd been holding out hope that she'd bring Cass back with her, but she was alone. When she saw me, she twisted her lips into a bad shape and readjusted the bag on her shoulder. *Fuck.* I pulled the hood up on my sweatshirt and tied the drawstrings as tight as possible so that I looked like Kenny from *South Park.*

Janie's hand was on my head. Then she was kneeling in front of me, gently undoing the knot I'd made and tugging the hood back down. I let her. The bag dropped from her shoulder. She looked like she was about to propose to me. I was worried about her knee on the damp ground, but then she started talking and the words were adding up to something not good, so I shifted from actively listening to passively hearing, which is a good little trick I've used a thousand times since.

The quick synopsis: *Cass is gone, and she doesn't want to be found.* Janie reached into her coat pocket and produced the note I had written. She pressed it into my hands. I looked down and said, "What am I going to do with this?"

"Keep it," she said. "Maybe it can remind

you what real love feels like? Maybe it'll fuel a performance, win you that Oscar."

(I ignored this last part.)

Did I want to be reminded of this feeling? Tears seem to have varying density. The ones currently forming were the robust kind. I unfolded the note and read it back:

> *Cass, this is real. We are real. I know because, somehow, you're in all my memories — even the ones from before we met. When I think of my first high school dance, you're next to me, grabbing my hand as "The Lady in Red" comes on so we can point at each other and dramatically swoon to it. Or that trip to Rome before my freshman year of college, when I got lost for an hour in those ancient streets, except now in my memory, I'm not worried anymore because we're lost together and that feels better than being found alone. Apparently, Cass, my brain has built a life with you without me even knowing. I love you.*

I folded the note and stuffed it in my pocket. How many times did I read it over the years? Enough that it now looks like what a prop department would call vintage. Like a scrap from some long-ago war.

CHAPTER 48

JANIE

February 2007
Charleston to New York

On my way to the Charleston airport, I read the note that Ryan had written to Cass. I had a ticket booked to Los Angeles, for a meeting about a film I wanted for Ryan. I unfolded her small note, out of curiosity mostly, and after reading it, I knew I needed to actually deliver it. I flew to New York and tried to fix what I'd done by calling the paparazzi. I didn't know how big Ryan's feelings for Cass actually were. Not often, but occasionally, I put Ryan's quality of life above all else.

I rerouted myself to LaGuardia and took a cab to the law firm at which Sidney Collins worked. The woman kept me waiting for three hours, then ushered me into a conference room, where we sat unusually far apart from each other. I tried every angle I could, but she was adamant: Cass had left the city and didn't want to be found.

For a moment, I thought about leaving Ryan's note with Sidney — no doubt she'd have more opportunity to reach Cass than I would. But I sensed that Sidney wasn't a neutral party, and at the last second, I tucked it away to give back to Ryan.

CHAPTER 49

Cass

February 2007
New York to Charleston

When Amanda and I debated whether we'd rather die of heat or cold, I always picked cold. And in everyday life, I'd rather be too cold than too hot. "If you're cold," I explained to her, "you can always add more layers, but there's nothing you can do if you're too hot."

She thought my logic was absurd. She said, "Dying of cold feels lonely, whereas dying of heat is sexy." Then I laughed because her explanation didn't just contain less logic than mine; it contained no logic at all. Soon she also started laughing, because us laughing together was her favorite thing.

Charleston was the hottest place I'd ever been. Which I liked, because then moving there wasn't just about Ryan, about the movie — it also felt, just a little bit, like a punishment. I lived in a small home on Sullivan's Island, two bridges and ten miles from downtown. I never went on set locations, or into the city, while they filmed the movie, but I visited those areas the day after they wrapped, tried to absorb the leftover scraps of Ryan and her thrilling life.

Soon after filming for the first movie ended, I started writing the second book in the trilogy. I wrote with a sense of urgency. Ryan could only keep playing Persephone — a role that connected her to me, however invisibly — if I kept writing her story.

That first year in the South, I would take long walks in hundred-degree heat, crazy humidity, sweating so much my eyes stung. I was always looking for ways to wring myself out, hoping I could sweat out the guilt and pain of what I'd done to Amanda.

Some days, I believed I had.

CHAPTER 50

AMANDA

October 2007
Bolton Landing

True to my word, I didn't go back to AA the next night. Or the night after. But one Friday eight months later, about the time I thought Kerri would be coming home for the weekend, I heard a rap at our door then the creak of it opening. I was in the den watching the afternoon talk shows, and I called out, "Hello?" A second later, Patricia Callahan appeared, and she said, "We missed you, so I thought I'd come check on you," and I could hear in her voice that she understood the risk she was taking coming to see me, that I might demand she get out of my house. It was this small quiver of doubt — along with my secret weapon: the truth about *The Very Last* — that kept me from yelling at her to get the fuck out and never come back.

Instead, I said nothing, which was the best I could do.

"I rented a van — would you like to go for a drive with me?"

Before I could say anything, she shook her head and said, "Let me rephrase that: even if you don't want to, would you *consider* going for a drive with me?"

This version of Patricia Callahan was disarming. She was clear-eyed and warm, and as had been happening more lately, my heart hurt for Annie. Standing before me was the mom she had longed for, but who she wasn't here to experience — it made me sad. But still, I reminded myself, that was her own damn fault.

"I would just love to spend some time with you," Patricia was saying, readjusting the strap of her purse on her shoulder. Right then Kerri came home, flying through the front door, calling out "Amanda!" as if she was worried. She stopped abruptly when she saw Patricia, though I wasn't sure if they'd ever met before. Kerri ignored her, turned her attention to me, "Whose van is in the driveway?" Patricia lifted her hand and said, "That would be mine" and after years of feeling isolated, visits from friends petering out quickly, I felt a surge of adrenaline at having two people vying for my attention.

My blood started rushing like I was in a performance again.

"What's going on here?" Kerri asked me.

"Patricia, this is my younger sister, Kerri," I said, and I noticed how good it felt to act like a normal person, the kind who remembers to introduce two people who haven't met before. Civilized and mature is how it made me feel. Then I added, "She's taken care of me," so that Patricia would remember who *hadn't* taken care of me and whose karmic scale was imbalanced.

She extended her hand. "Kerri, it's so wonderful to meet you, although I do believe we've met once, when you were much smaller, at one of Amanda and Anne Marie's plays."

Kerri's eyes flew to mine, and she seemed to be searching for confirmation, which came a few seconds later when Patricia said, "I'm Anne Marie's mom."

Brave of her, I thought. Walking into our house, right into the belly of the beast, and claiming ownership over Annie in a way she had never done when Annie was here and worth claiming ownership of. Sometimes Annie had even wondered aloud if her mom, when out at the bar or with a new guy, pretended she was childless.

Kerri was the nicest girl in the world, so

she turned to me and said, "Are you okay?" and I told her that I was. What I was feeling, for the first time in a long time, was curiosity — as to what Patricia had to say, as to what had changed. And before I could filter it out, another thought: I needed to do some reconnaissance work on Annie's behalf.

"We're going to take a ride," I said.

Patricia drove us around the lake. What I'd allowed myself to hope for was that she'd heard directly from Annie. But she told me right away that she hadn't. My disappointment surprised me. Tears, actually. And I prayed that Patricia wouldn't notice, kept my head turned toward the window, but she reached over and covered my hand with hers, squeezed once. I wondered if she blamed herself for Annie, but I couldn't bring myself to ask. A question I'd asked myself a thousand times: What exactly did Annie owe me? Because we were best friends, because we had plans together, because she was there when I fell, did all of that mean that her life was forever tethered to mine? When my life suddenly became profoundly stationary, did she have to clip her own wings in solidarity? No, of course not. But also yes, a little bit. Why was I mad at Annie when what she did — leave — was what I would have asked her to do? No matter if she'd stayed and left later, or left when she did, my life right now would be exactly as it was. And yet.

"Are you mad at Annie?" I eventually asked. Patricia had already told me her story, how she didn't realize Annie was missing for two full weeks. She had known nothing about my accident, was shacked up at a cabin a few towns over, until a police officer stopped by the Chateau during one of her shifts. That night, she went home and started digging through Annie's things and came across this old T-shirt with Tom and Jerry on it that apparently Annie wore nonstop when she was a kid. She laid the shirt on Annie's bed and stared at it, remembering how angry it had made her but not remembering why. She said that at first that shirt was her kryptonite, but eventually became her talisman.

She was gripping the wheel with her right hand, then brought her left to her chest and fiddled with a necklace. She tried to show it to me, but it wasn't long enough to see, so she explained that it was a present Annie had given her for Mother's Day long ago — fifth grade, maybe? A chintzy little thing with enamel renderings of the cartoon characters from that favorite shirt. Patricia had never worn it, but now refused to take it off.

"No, I'm not mad at Anne Marie," she said.

I had intended to hurt Patricia with *The Very Last*. Another item on the list of things she didn't know about her daughter. Really dig the knife in and twist. But I realized on that car ride that Patricia Callahan wasn't a monster; she was just a broken woman piecing herself back together.

She parked in front of my house and cut the engine. She dropped her hands from the wheel and looked at me. "This has been so nice, Amanda," she said, raising her hands to her heart as if it had been soothed. As cheesy as Annie would have thought the gesture, and it was a little cheesy, it made me feel good. Then she reached over and put her warm open palm on my cheek, looked me right in the eyes, smiled. The intimacy comforted me. I wish it hadn't. It felt traitorous, but it seemed that I also craved Patty Callahan's love.

"I wasn't sure I was going to say this, but . . ." I paused.

I suddenly had the desire to set aside my weapon, my trump card: knowing about *The Very Last*. My intimacy with the book and how it captured our memories still made me feel close to Annie, and in this moment, I wanted to give a piece of that to her mother, too.

I turned my head toward the window, looked at the chaos of our side yard, where my dad tinkered with old engines and car parts, and asked, "Did you ever read *The Very Last*?"

"*The Very Last*?"

"The book," I said. "It's going to be a trilogy, they've already announced the second book. I think there's a film coming for Christmas, too." I looked down. Her hand was covering the gear shift, and I admired its delicateness, its loveliness.

"No, I haven't," she said.

"Well, maybe go get a copy," I said. "Go get it — please."

That night, I stared at *The Very Last* on my bedside table. Without my consent, the book began morphing. Becoming less the embodiment of my anger, more a lifeline to my best friend, and I couldn't stop myself, I cracked it open again. This second read was an entirely different experience.

Cate Kay.
Cate with a Kay.
Cate with a K.
Cate with a motherfucking K.

CHAPTER 51

Cass

2011
Charleston

The day I finished copyedits for the last book of *The Very Last* trilogy, I joined a book club for young moms. No, I was not a mom, nor did I consider myself young anymore,* though age is a peculiar dysmorphia afflicting all.

The story of how I joined this book club involved an interaction during which I behaved so out of character that I remember

*__Note from Cate:__ I remember when Amanda and I were seniors, a former student came to rehearsals, and when we were talking with her afterward, she mentioned that she'd just turned thirty. Amanda and I nearly fell over. We grabbed at each other to stay upright. Partly we were doing a bit, partly her age was inconceivable to us. Now I was that age; I was thirty years old.

wondering if the two women involved could sense that I was stretching myself and took pity on me. I was wandering Charleston's old streets — a favorite activity of mine. I would sometimes try to find the house that Ryan rented for the first movie shoot, years before. There'd been a paparazzi item showing the corner of a salmon-colored building; I would walk around and imagine her here or there or there, mentally build out scenes of those long-ago months. It made me briefly feel closer to her. Then I remembered that I was a cliché: pining after a movie star who clearly didn't want me.

On this particular afternoon, I settled with a book on a park bench. A few minutes later two women with strollers approached. I was purposefully sitting in the middle to deter exactly this moment but could sense that one of the women really needed to sit. I moved over and she looked at me gratefully, tucked herself onto the edge with a relieved sigh, and lowered her shirt to begin breastfeeding. Her friend nodded at me, smiled.

I looked down at my open book but focused on their conversation. At some point I worried they would notice I hadn't turned the page, so I turned one. Then another. Listening to people's conversations both tempered my loneliness and informed my writing. I think the dialogue in the last installment of *The Very Last* was sharper, the beneficiary of this voyeurism.

My ears perked when they started talking about their book club, which was meeting that night. I don't remember what that month's pick had been, but it was one I had liked. The image of them in some warm living room eating freshly baked cookies, drinking wine, chatting about books felt so domestic and comforting that I contorted my body to face them and awkwardly asked, "Do you take new members for your book club?"

They looked taken aback. Not only had I been eavesdropping, but now I was inviting myself inside their homes? But they were good Southern women and quickly fixed their faces. The one standing was softly rocking her stroller and she said, as if this would gently disqualify me, "It's actually for new moms."

Me asking to join a club of moms! What was this world? I pictured Amanda staring at me, mouth agape. The two of us had always scoffed at anything even remotely domestic. Once, the mother of one of our theater camp castmates had baked chocolate chip cookies for everyone, and Amanda and I glanced at each other from across the folding table backstage and rolled our eyes. We never acknowledged the deep-seated truth underlying these moments, which was that we wholeheartedly, so much so that it would make us want to cry, wanted moms to bake us cookies. But also, I know we would have soon faced the truth of that, together.

I wished, as I did a dozen times a day, that I could talk to her.

Thankfully, the women didn't bring their children to book club meetings, so I wasn't forced to rent a baby. I did feel bad about lying that I had a kid. Sincerely, it wasn't one of my finest moments. But I was desperately in need of some stress-free companionship, and what better place to hide than in a group of moms? I fielded a personal question here and there, but mostly I deflected, then easily turned the spotlight back onto the new organic baby toothpaste or other trendy products. (I did research.) Worked like a charm.

I really liked it. I liked what they had to say about the books we read. They often noticed things I hadn't and articulated these observations with warmth and intelligence.

Which is why I was terrified when they chose my first book. One of them tossed it out at the end of that month's meeting — *hey, you know what would be fun?* — and they all loved the idea. My take was that they thought of themselves as more literary — like National Book Award stuff — and *The Very Last* was a marshmallow. That didn't offend me; it just made me worry they were going to take their sharp literary teeth and tear into my soft underbelly.

When the day came, I wasn't planning to go. Why do that to myself? But that evening, I was too curious to stay away. I'd never had an opportunity like this, to hear readers talking about my books in a personal, intimate setting. The thought of it was intoxicating.

I went.

To my significant relief the conversation was going well. My book was holding its own in their eyes, which was satisfying to hear. Then when we seemed to be wrapping up, one of the women jumped in, said, "But one thing I can't get over is how Samantha just walks away from Jeremiah? Just leaves him — her best friend? I just couldn't understand, and I don't know why the world still celebrates her afterward. It's always bothered me. And nobody even mentions it."

Everyone turned their heads and considered this. Then another woman asked, "Do you not like that in the world of the book nobody criticizes her, or that in *this* world — like here in our book club — nobody criticizes the characters who make up the world inside the book?" She mimicked her head exploding, then took a dainty bite of cookie. We all had whiplash yet leaned in to hear the answer.

The woman who made the first observation took a beat then said, "Both."

I was sitting on the couch and leaned back, recrossed my legs. My foot was bouncing at the end of my leg, and I couldn't make it stop. I looked around at the group and allowed myself a moment of awe amid the bubbling panic: Nobody gets to hear people's honest appraisal of their work. These next few minutes would either be a gift or a descent into the depths of hell — it was hard to tell.

"I get that," said another. "But it couldn't be about their one single relationship in that moment. The world needed her to make the choice she did. For the greater good."

Another woman pounced, like she'd been thinking about this topic all her life: "But isn't it possible the author is trying to show us the most extreme example of the false binary the world presents us — that it's either ambition or relationships?"

Let's unpack that one, folks.

"Huh," responded the woman, her head tilting dramatically, like she was looking at life from a new angle. "That's really interesting."

"I just think," continued the woman who had pounced, "that the world — and maybe more accurately, society — is always trying to convince us that work will make us happy, that our ambition is healthy, pursuing it satisfying. That's the great capitalist brainwashing, isn't it?"

"Okay, that's partially true, yes," said the woman who had started this tangent. "Our society, in particular, seems to want us to believe that work will be a direct path to happiness, but we can't pretend that work doesn't matter. And also, Samantha leaves Jeremiah because she needs to help everyone in New York, to get them information — she saved thousands of lives. Whether her ambition drove that decision more than altruism, does it really matter?"

Now they were giving me far too much credit. I'd just wanted to soothe myself, while also winning the world's praise and adulation . . . although, possibly, I'd just described every writer's motivation since the beginning of time.

"But let's get back to the key question," said the woman in whose living room we sat.

"Who thinks Samantha is a see-you-next-Tuesday for leaving Jeremiah to die? Let's get an actual show of hands."

Oh, goodness — a vote? I wanted to lean forward but stopped myself. Nine women present, including me. They laughed, a few of them awkwardly. The word *cunt,* even in euphemistic form, was a little subversive for these proper Southern ladies who drove golf carts to the dog park.

"Actual show of hands," our host prompted again. "Who thinks Samantha is the worst — put 'em up."

Four women raised their hands.

"And who thinks Samantha's choice was . . . heroic?"

Four different hands.

I was aware that I needed to vote, but I couldn't distill the question to its essence — at least, not fast enough to meet this deadline. Was I voting on Samantha being a terrible person, or me? Finally, I leaned forward and clasped my hands together, started rocking back and forth.

"We've got a lone holdout," said our host, enjoying her time as emcee. "Cass, what say you? The deciding vote!"

The good news was that the other women thought my obvious discomfort was a performance.

"Yes, take your time," one of them joked. "Choose wisely."

I lifted my eyes, "Can I vote for . . . neither?"

A round of boos went up from a few of the women; it was quickly quieted by the others. The whole thing would have been fascinating if I'd been an impartial observer.

"I just can't make a decision about her based on this one action — we're all so much more, and less, than our best, or worst, moment," I said. It sounded like a ridiculous cliché, but diving any deeper was out of the question. I'm not sure I would have resurfaced.

"She's neither," I added. "Final answer."

"Ah, nuanced," said our host, whose role had shifted suddenly to peacemaker. I flung myself back against the couch, feigned exhaustion.

Everyone laughed and then abruptly, book club was over.

CHAPTER 52

RYAN

2011
Los Angeles

Over the years, *People* has twice printed that I was engaged — "a source close to the couple said" — and that "the couple" planned on keeping the wedding intimate. In fact, me and the named person weren't even dating. Blame for those stories can't fall entirely on the magazine, though, since mostly they were planted by my team, or his team, or a PR firm. And yet, there was always a part of me that was disappointed when I saw those items in print. I was hoping the journalist would do better.

There's this thing I once read about called the Gell-Mann Amnesia Effect. It's basically how when you read something on which you're an expert, you're keenly aware of the errors in reporting and understanding. But then you turn the page and assume veracity on another topic you're less familiar with. The fucked-up thing about this effect, for me, was realizing I'm not even an expert on myself. Imagine me reading some tidbit in a magazine then calling Janie to vent, only to have her tell me the rhyme and reason behind its placement and me feeling woozy at how blurry the line is between real me and fake me. Such a thing has an eroding effect on one's sense of self.

Dating fellow actors, of which I've done plenty, is satisfying only if you like getting lost inside a house of mirrors.

I was doing about two movies a year then, across genres, though I felt most comfortable playing gritty characters like Persephone, desperate to prove themselves. Janie persuaded me to do a couple rom-coms — "to show your range," she said — but I hated filming those. Every scene was about me looking tasty for the camera.

One morning when I was home between movie shoots, I called Janie. I asked her to meet me at the Los Feliz house. I waited for her in the backyard, walking the tiled edge of the pool. Eight steps long, three steps wide. I had watched Cass do it many afternoons. "It calms me," she said when I asked why she was essentially walking in a circle.

But she was right. It was like a form of meditation.

In the years since, I'd spent hours pacing this backyard, wondering if I possessed the courage for what I was finally about to do. Janie was still on the phone when she arrived. She gave me a little wave, held up a finger. I continued walking the edge of the pool. Head down, mind churning. Would I be making my life harder or easier? I couldn't say.

"All yours," Janie said. I paused. I was on the far side of the pool.

"I think it's time," I said. "I'm coming out."

Janie raised her eyebrows, held them like that.

"Call *Vanity Fair*," I continued. "I know who I want reporting it."

CHAPTER 53

AMANDA

2011
Bolton Landing

Annie was always setting up these games with the universe. Like this one time we were waiting for an elevator during a school trip to the Egg, this strange theater in Albany that really did look like the bottom half of a Cadbury Creme Egg. The teacher called the elevator, and Annie leaned into me and said, "If the elevator comes within ten seconds, then we're going to be safe." My eyes darted toward her. "Um, no thank you to *that* little game," I whispered.

She didn't say anything, but when the elevator took a long time, long enough that the teacher pressed the button again, she finally said under her breath, "Yeah, that was crazy."

Another time this happened was when she was pulling open the door at the local pizza place, and she said, "The guy behind the register, if his first word is 'hi' we get cheese; but if his first word is anything else, we get pepperoni, okay?" I went along with this one because I had no preference. But when we sat down with our slices — pepperoni; the guy had said *How can I help you?* — I took a deep sip of my fountain soda, then said, "All right, can I ask you a question?"

She was midbite, so she just nodded.

"I don't understand these games you play," I said, gesturing toward the counter.

She brought her elbows to the table and propped her chin on closed fists, exhaled long and slow. "It's like these things just pop into my brain," she said. "And I can't get them out. I try to spare you — most of the time."

"It's just weird," I said.

"Weird how?" she asked, taking another bite and chewing slowly, watching me. My thoughts were only half-baked, so it took a little while, and Annie kept eating as she waited. My pizza went untouched.

"Okay," I said, finally landing on an explanation. "I think it's just . . . odd, seeing you surrender to the universe. It's so unlike you in every way."

She didn't seem upset — she seemed to

really be considering this. "Huh," she said, starting in on her crust. "It's funny you say that because to me it feels like a relief — like my brain's way of saving me from obsessing endlessly about every single decision."

Then she stuffed the rest of the crust in her mouth, could barely get her jaw to move. She glanced at my soda, mumbled, "You gonna share?"

These strange games with the universe that Annie played must have made more of an impression than I realized, because once she was gone, I found myself playing them, too. A few years after I got sober, I started working the front desk at my dad's garage. Did he really need my help, probably not, but he wanted me to find purpose, and he thought showing up somewhere three times a week was a start.

Mostly I read books. Or stared at the clock above the door. Then one afternoon, out of nowhere, a little voice inside my head introduced an idea: if the next person who walks through the door smiles, your life is going to get better. And I swear, not a second later, Mr. Riley walked in. He didn't notice me at first, had his head down looking for something in his wallet, but when he got to the counter he looked up. He shook his head, smiled softly. "Amanda, I can't even tell you how good it is to see you." He walked around the counter, leaned down, and gave me a long, warm hug. And as he did, I was thinking how quickly the universe had delivered: my life was already better.

"I was just thinking of you this morning," he said, shaking his head in disbelief. "Seriously — I was. We're doing *Twelfth Night* again. Today was the first day of rehearsals. So, of course, it made me think of —" He hesitated slightly, almost imperceptibly, before quickly finishing the sentence, "you." Then there was this pause during which we were both thinking, but absolutely not talking, about Annie.

A second later he slapped his wallet against his open palm and said, "You know what — why don't you come by, help us out? Nobody knows this play like you do. I'd love your help."

I was honestly stunned by how quickly this moment had come upon me. Maybe Annie had been onto something with this universe stuff. I stuttered for a second, which was unlike me. Then I stopped, took a quick, deep breath and looked at Mr. Riley like, *Allow me to gather myself.* A beat later:

"Yes. I would love that."

He nodded once, sealing the agreement, then handed me his credit card. I'd almost forgotten that he'd come in for his car. When he left a few minutes later, I couldn't understand why my joy was presenting as burning-hot tears. Then I covered my eyes and sobbed into my hands, pausing only to fling a stapler at the wall.

I think my anger was about realizing that even now, even after everything, Annie was still involved in all the good moments of my life.*

CATE KAY

The Very Last

The city was asleep when Persephone Park, the only daughter of Samantha Park, left it for good. Persephone, still just a young woman, had grown up in the public eye, as she was the only child of one of the world's most revered figures. She was American royalty.

Born three years after the blast, Persephone was called a miracle baby, but growing up she felt like an afterthought. She harbored no ill will toward her mom, only profound disappointment, and sadness. She'd been raised by a dying woman

***Note from Cate:** And she in mine.

whose energy and attention were consumed with the business of staying alive.

And Samantha Park had succeeded, had lived for nearly ten years after that legendary broadcast, dying when Persephone was seven years old. The funeral was broadcast to billions.

Persephone commanded the devotion of the world and yet she felt empty. And emptiness, she had learned, created hunger — hunger for what, she didn't know.

Possessing things wasn't what she wanted; she wanted the feeling that came with striving and making and building something never seen before. And to do that, she believed she had to start at zero.

And so, Persephone had decided to leave this version of her life in pursuit of another. She would go to The Core. To the deserted island formerly called Manhattan where, according to media reports, a community had been established completely off-line and outside government control.

The blast that destroyed Manhattan had taken seventeen years to clean up. At first, scientists hoped the city could be rebuilt, but the cost, the rising water levels, the areas with still dangerously high radiation levels — they determined it shouldn't be done. A decision was made to give Manhattan back to nature.

But in the final days of cleanup, a small band of native New Yorkers vowed to return, to build something new. An unspoken agreement existed between these re-settlers and the last workers to leave the island. And when the government officially left the island for the final time, a dozen containers filled with scrap metal and found items were left behind.

It was from these artifacts that The Core was built — from the scraps of the city that had once been the most famous in the world. The Core was a society built off the grid, with its own laws and rules and customs, and Persephone was joining them because she needed to prove herself — if only to herself.

She left on a summer night, the week after college graduation. Her best friend, Kelly, was asleep in the guest room of her penthouse apartment, and Persephone peeked in on the way out — she hated the pain she would cause her, but she had to go.

It was just after midnight, the best time to avoid the patrols guarding the river. Nobody was allowed to cross, as if it were a border, which struck Persephone as counterproductive — people always want to go where they're told they can't.

Persephone was carrying two items: a backpack on her right shoulder, a red sleeping bag on her left. She walked past two NO ENTRY barricades and a warning about nuclear fallout, then she slipped through a tear in one part of the fence. She was amazed with her herself, with how boldly she was taking action, while also, if she dug deeper, she worried that she'd come to regret this night, this radical decision.

But mostly, she felt unstoppable, which she noticed was a double-edged sword. She felt both powerful and out of control.

Persephone could feel the river before she could see it, the way the sky above seemed more open, the breeze unencumbered. She spotted the rowboat that had been promised by her contact. It had been dragged onto the riverbed just where they said it would be.

Persephone looked up and down the bank. Nothing but overgrowth. Nothing amiss. She had a small window to row herself across before the patrol circled back. She moved quickly, dropping her backpack and sleeping bag on the central wooden slat, then wading into the water with the wooden boat.

She couldn't believe she was doing it. She looked up into the dark night sky — this was a moment she'd remember the rest of her life — then she began rowing across the Hudson River toward the only place she believed she could truly discover who she was.

* * *

Weeks later, Persephone was asleep on her red sleeping bag in the corner of the one-room structure she had built from scavenged wood and sheet metal. In The Core she had become consumed by the work of building a new life. Walls, a roof, food, water. Starting from scratch was taxing — emotionally and physically.

On this morning, Persephone was awoken by a wet tongue on her exposed hand. The sensation startled her at first, and she recoiled, but then she remembered and placed her hand on the smooth head of Puck, the gray-and-white pit bull mix who had made life in The Core a million times better.

Puck had been a surprise; Persephone still didn't know who she belonged to and was terrified that eventually someone might come claim her. Puck made her feel like they were a duo on an epic adventure

— and Persephone liked how cinematic that made her life feel.

She rubbed Puck's head then pressed herself to standing and walked over to her backpack, pulled out her favorite sweatshirt — light gray with the cartoon characters Tom and Jerry lounging against palm trees, the word *California* written in cursive above them. *The bane of my existence,* her grandma had said about the sweatshirt whenever Persephone wore it, which was every day, always — it reminded her of the last time she had felt safe and whole and loved.

"C'mon girl," Persephone called to Puck as she walked toward the old shower curtain that currently served as her front door. She drew the curtain back and peered outside.

Persephone marveled at the world she now inhabited. She took in the patches of dry land grown high with weeds and young trees and wild vegetation, shallow rivers slicing through. The sea had risen. The water from the rivers, from the ocean, had crept higher and made the southern chunk of the island swamp-like in many areas. The tiny population of The Core — last count was ninety-one — used rowboats to navigate the arteries and passages, and

Persephone watched as in the distance a woman rowed a peeling silver boat from her shed.

Persephone took a deep breath, exhaled. She had almost gone back across, then home to Newark, a dozen times. Was always one second away from going back.

But she wouldn't go home. She couldn't. She knew what that life felt like. And it wasn't enough.

CHAPTER 54

Cass

2011
Charleston

Star, Us Weekly, Variety, In Touch, People, Vanity Fair — I had subscriptions to every celebrity magazine. Neatly formed stacks would grow on side tables and counters until the yearly purge when I tossed every issue except the ones in which Ryan appeared. Those went in a box, and every so often I'd drink too much wine — a big and bold cabernet, always — and spend the night rereading each item, reassessing every picture: Ryan walking in her LA neighborhood in a beanie and Jordans; talking on the phone outside a hot restaurant; walking with her new boyfriend — really, Ryan, really? — along the beach. I'd look closely at each image, searching for clues, pretending she'd been thinking of me the moment the photo was snapped.

But also, I worried that love just wasn't for me. How much love do you get to run away from in this life before you're cut off for good? First Amanda, then Ryan, and finally Sidney. Although Sidney? That was different. That was an arrangement — we'd used each other. Me, to get out of the painful limbo of Plattsburgh; Sidney, to find the perfect person to exert control over.

One afternoon, a couple months before they started filming the final installment of *The Very Last* trilogy, I'd just come back from a run — my latest method for quieting my brain. It was hot and muggy, per usual. I stopped by my mailbox, which was covered in jasmine. I did love how lush and exotic Charleston was compared to the austerity of the Adirondacks. I grabbed the bundle — mostly junk mail — and was shuffling through when I stopped dead.

There, staring back at me, on the cover of *Vanity Fair,* was Ryan. I didn't move. She was walking away from the camera, a jean jacket tossed over her shoulder, glancing back at the lens. Her hair was pulled back, and the image seemed to capture her quality of movement, midstride, a pair of black-and-white Nike Dunks on her feet. I admired how she kept a little candle burning for the sporty kid inside her.

The headline read: "Ry Channing Has Something to Tell You." The phrasing promised intimacy. An actual profile, not a paparazzi shot with a caption.

I hustled inside, chilled instantly by the high-powered air-conditioning. I tossed the other mail onto the entryway table and walked my sweaty self to the staircase, sitting on the third step, placing the *Vanity Fair* by my side. For a moment, I stared into space and wondered if reading this story was a good idea. Was it a healthy choice? Maybe the universe was sending me a sign — that now was the time to detach from Ryan, from my obsession with what could have been.

And yet, I knew with 100 percent certainty that I would read the article. But pausing made me feel in control, mature. Here I was, calm and collected, considering other options. Once enough time had passed — two to three minutes, approximately — I opened to the article.

Ry Channing Has Something to Tell You
Jake Fischer

Ry Channing is unhappy. Not in life — although we'll get to that — but at this moment. She's in Lawrence, Kansas, at her favorite local bakery, and they have run out of croissants. She is standing at the counter, craning to see into the kitchen as if a new batch might magically appear. Her reaction is half performance, half genuine, which later Channing will say pretty much sums up her life so far. (And something she wants to change.) The cashier pitches Channing on a palmier, which the woman describes as "basically a flattened croissant crusted with sugar."

"Say no more," Channing responds. "A palmier and a mocha with whole milk."

Breakfast in hand, she tucks herself into a corner seat. She's dressed casually in FREECITY sweatpants, and nobody bothers her. One reason, she says, why she loves coming home. She takes a huge bite of her pastry and washes it down with a gulp of mocha — the food appears to ground her.

"It's my ritual," she says, lifting the cup. "I'm done starving myself. Who is that for, even? As best I can tell it's . . ." She pauses and it seems like she's thinking, then she continues.

"Okay, so there's this scene in the movie *Notting Hill* where Alec Baldwin, who plays Julia Roberts's boyfriend — they're both playing movie stars — orders her like a salad or something from room service, and when she protests, he slaps her on the butt and goes, 'I don't want people saying, "There goes that famous actor with the big, fat girlfriend."' I actually think about that scene a lot. Like, that's who I'm starving myself for — that's why? So that guys like Alec Baldwin can feel better about themselves? And that's not about Hollywood, by the way. I mean that in general — that's why women all over the world make themselves smaller, so men can feel better about themselves?"

"Yeah, no thanks," she says before taking another bite.

After she finishes her pastry, we chat for a few minutes about The Very Last. She's leaving soon for Charleston. Then she pauses, takes a deep breath, looks at me. She's ready to get to the heart of the matter; the real reason she's invited me to Kansas for this chat.

"It's funny I brought up Notting Hill," she says. "Funny that it was on my mind today, I mean. It's actually my favorite movie. For lots of reasons, but mainly because it's while watching that movie that I realized I'm gay."

Below is our conversation, edited for clarity.

Jake: Um, why Notting Hill? That wasn't a particularly gay movie.

Ry: Okay, so, I've thought about this a lot. The thing with that movie is that the story is framed from this point of view of, here is this everyday person smitten with this singularly beautiful woman. It's a movie about fascination with a woman. It doesn't matter that Hugh Grant was a guy, really. He was just a character I could project myself onto.

Jake: If it's all right with you, I'm just going to ask questions that follow my interest, jump right into things — have you ever been in love?

Ry: He's just going right for the jugular.

Jake: I serve at the pleasure of our readers. So . . . ?

Ry: Once.

Jake: That's all you'll give me?

Ry: I'd rather talk about bigger-picture issues. You know, the why of it — why I'm coming out. My love life is only so interesting.

Jake: Your love life is why people will read this article.

Ry: Do you believe that, for real?

Jake: Yes, they're thinking right now: Get to the good stuff already.

Ry: Why did I pick you again?

Jake: I was going to ask you that question.

Ry: I liked your previous work. You've written great stuff since coming out, getting engaged to your husband — and then also your coverage of The Very Last by Cate Kay. You could say I'm a fan.

Jake: I'm flattered. So, what happened . . . that "one time" you were in love?

Ry: It didn't work out.

Jake: You or her?

Ry: I wrote her a note, professing my love, a whole big thing — but no, it was her, she wasn't into it.

Jake: So, why — why are you going public now?

Ry: I just couldn't be the person who surrendered the joy of openly loving someone *in exchange for, like, an uptick in popularity. Seriously, think about how sick that is. It's unsettling. The savagery of what I was doing: taking a cleaver to my own heart. I just couldn't keep doing that. That's not what I want for my life.*

I read the whole piece, including the photo captions. Then I read it again. My heart had leapt at seeing Cate Kay mentioned, and I read the rest of the article hoping for some coded message from Ryan. But nothing. And even worse: She'd admitted to being in love with some other woman, to pouring her heart out in some love letter. I carefully placed the magazine by my side. Ryan had come out. Such a bold move. If possible, she was even sexier to me now. I was happy for her, I was. But, also, selfishly, I'd just lost something: the intimacy of being one of the only people in the world who knew the real her. She'd just gone from my personal gay icon to the world's.

It was time, I realized. Time to save me from myself. Extinguish the torch I'd been carrying for her.

The only hat I owned was this hideous army-green safari thing with a pull cord under the chin, a necessary purchase for a hike two years prior. On the coolness scale it was a zero. But it provided two layers of protection: the hat itself was a disguise, and its ugliness provided additional motivation to keep myself hidden from Ryan while wearing it. Imagine the story we'd have to tell people: "The reeds were blowing in the breeze when I saw her across the water wearing a bucket hat . . ."

Not that I thought Ryan and I could still be a thing. That was done. This excursion to watch filming of the final scene in *The Very Last* trilogy was for closure — for the three books, Ryan, Sidney, the whole era. My goal: When I woke the following morning, the next chapter of my life would begin. I had no clue what that would look or feel like, but I told myself I felt ready for it.

They were shooting at this place called Gold Bug Island, which was not exactly an island, tucked away down a small slope just before a low bridge about twenty minutes from downtown Charleston. No houses for a mile in either direction, but thankfully the island itself was filled with palm trees that I could hide myself behind. I parked a half mile away, on the side of the road. Because they used public land, often filming on waterways, the sets couldn't be closed to the public. They did their best to keep locations a secret, though word always got out. I had a granola bar in my pocket and a book in my hand — I was prepared.

As I walked along the side of the road, I kept my head down. Thoughts and images of Ryan, of those weeks in Los Angeles, played in my mind, and I kept ushering them out, only for them to reappear. I'd put the celebrity magazines in the attic, but I'd never really succeeded in moving on from Ryan. Eventually, to keep my brain occupied, I started counting my steps.

There was water on both sides of the two-lane road, wending itself through greenery and marsh. An egret was flying low, nearly skimming the surface. It was approaching dusk on one of those beautiful Charleston nights. Light pinks and golds blended with one another and with the sky, and the temperature was so perfectly suited to the human body that the fact of weather disappeared entirely. No doubt the director and cinematographer were in a mad rush to capitalize on such perfection.

The turnoff for the island was up ahead, and I jogged lightly toward it, eager to get lost in the trees and vegetation. Just then, a gray Mercedes Sprinter van rumbled past on my left, a little close for comfort. Instinctively, my eyes darted upward, and my heart jumped — Janie Johnson was sitting in the back window seat, a cell phone pressed to her ear. She hadn't seen me; my lovely bucket hat had done its job. I tugged it lower and cut across the road toward the tree line.

Wherever went Janie, went Ryan — she was absolutely inside that van, which had already disappeared around the corner. I stopped and waited for a feeling to come over me. Even reached out and touched a tree to ground myself. But no feeling came. I couldn't tell if I was pleased or disappointed, but I think the latter. I began walking the long way around the island and found a palm tree, sat beneath it, opened my book. Over the years I'd consumed a lot of Ryan Channing content — maybe I'd inoculated myself.

But then I actually saw her, and my heart started hammering. She was walking with the director, away from the trailers of basecamp and toward a short dock. She was wearing the *Tom and Jerry* sweatshirt that features prominently in Persephone's story. I knew it was Ryan for many reasons, but mostly by the way she touched the ends of her hair, with this kind of absentminded curiosity. She was doing that now as they walked, the tips of her fingers assessing her hair's texture. A moment later she stopped, gathered it, and spun it into a messy bun. This, from afar, seemed to relax her, make her sink into herself. She was always more comfortable when casual. A second later, she and the director shared a laugh.

My body started humming, a low-level tingle. It felt good, and I tried not to think about later when I'd walk back to my car alone, drive home to an empty house — the painful comedown. For now, there she was, my magazine spread come to life. She and the director walked to the dock, pointed here and there, really took in the approaching sunset, its orange and purple, then the director glanced at his watch — it was go-time.

Less than an hour later, everything was set. A skeleton crew. The director was on the dock with one other person and the camera. Behind them was a small group, including Janie, who stood with her arms crossed, cell phone gripped in her right hand. She was chatting happily with a woman who must be makeup, a large fanny pack around her waist. A rowboat was in the water just off the dock. Right when the director must have been asking after Ryan — his assistant was lifting a walkie-talkie to his mouth — she appeared from behind a trailer and began walking toward them.

But this wasn't Ryan; it was Persephone. The way she carried herself, the tilt of her chin — she now embodied a woman who'd faced hardship and grown stronger because of it. And that was the purpose of this final scene: to show Persephone Park, shedding the final connection to her former life, to the world that was offering her everything, yet nothing she valued.

Ryan walked to the dock without speaking to anyone. An assistant brought the boat in, and she stepped onto it, staring out at the water, hands in cargo pants.

The director was looking toward basecamp, impatient, and I wondered who else he was waiting on. Then I saw Puck. How could I have forgotten? She was trotting happily alongside a handler, and she gracefully jumped into the boat. Ryan knelt to greet her, scratching behind her ears, grabbing her muzzle, kissing her wet nose.

The interaction made my insides hurt. I wished they were my family, the two of them. I wished we could curl up on the couch together, that Ryan and I could take her on walks and watch her play and glance at each other, smiling. *What a simple, perfect life* the smile would say.

The director clapped, snapping me back. And then it was happening. The boat pushed from the dock, Ryan and Puck drifting together on the calm water. The sun was just kissing the horizon, and no doubt the cinematographer was in a state of anxious bliss. Everyone turned their attention toward the boat; a hush fell.

A few moments later the director said "Action," his voice urgent.

Ryan was standing with her back to the camera, her hand resting on Puck's head. The boat was moving slightly, a gentle turn that the cameraman was adjusting for on the dock. I was sitting against the palm tree, and I let my head tip back gently until it was resting against the trunk. The low-level tingle had escalated to goose bumps, and I closed my eyes, just for a moment, to see what else I could feel. My heart, a golden circle, throbbing inside my rib cage. I pictured Amanda, the first love of my life, saw the bold and rich colors of the mountain lake at her back, her skipping and jumping, her arm around my shoulders. And then I saw Ryan, squinting into the soft light of the West Coast, pictured her unique beauty, her lips a whisper from mine. The two of them, my heart's electricity.

My eyes snapped open just in time to watch Ryan remove the sweatshirt. Her movements were assured but graceful, infused with melancholy. Once it was off, she lifted the fabric to her face and inhaled deeply, then she released the sweatshirt and it dropped out of sight. The sun was only embers on the horizon, and the night was ashy pink, and depending on your perspective, Persephone Park was either watching the last sunset of her old life or the first of her new one. Me, I think she was living in both, one last time.

The two of them drifted like this for a long time, long enough that I began wondering when the director would yell "cut." When he finally did, everyone started clapping, but I stood up and turned my back, began the walk to my car.

When I got home, I fell into bed with my clothes on. I'd been right earlier: the comedown was vicious.

The next morning I woke up ravenous. Like I hadn't eaten in days. I ate toast, then eggs, then granola; the feeling wouldn't abate. A peppermint tea was steeping on the corner of my desk as I turned the cover on one of my cheap spiral notebooks. This emptiness, it was deeper than Ryan. I'd passed that floor and headed south, to the basement. I looked around and recognized it as the Amanda-shaped hole inside me. I'd been here before. But I couldn't keep writing from loss, begging for forgiveness, hoping she'd sense me, wherever she was. What I needed was joy — to write us back to life, together.

I pressed the tip of my pen to the blank page and wrote "The Road Trip," underlining it, skipping past the leg of the *p*. A few seconds later I crossed out what I'd written and replaced it with "The Rain Check." I liked that none of the letters dipped below the line — their uniformity satisfied me.

What the next line would be, I wasn't sure. I spent a few minutes staring off into space, assessing each thought as it entered my mind, escorting out the mediocre ones. Then a memory appeared, and my arm landed purposefully on the desk. The writing began.

CHAPTER 55

RYAN

2011
Los Angeles to Charleston

Janie and I were sitting in the living room of my fancy Hollywood Hills home. It had five bedrooms, six baths, walls of glass, and low-slung couches. Real A-list movie-star energy. An interior decorator had chosen the artwork. I hated it. She and I had a fling, and for a few weeks I thought she might be more. But one night cooking dinner she told me she wasn't into books. Magazines, she liked those fine. I paused while sautéing the onions and said, "It's just a 'no' for you on books, across the board?"

She shrugged like it was neither here nor there. Not even worth the seconds we were spending discussing it. Reading had always made me feel closer to the world, and everything in it. I guess it's no surprise that the art she hung felt violent.

Sipping tea with Janie, comfy in my sweatpants, I thought, once again, that I needed to change the decor. But that house in the Hills was never going to be what I wanted. My heart was in my Los Feliz bungalow.

"Like I'm going to a funeral," I replied when Janie asked how I was feeling about shooting the final scene of *The Very Last* trilogy that weekend. After six years playing Persephone, immersed in Cass's words, her creation, this felt like the final goodbye. Janie frowned, said she would love to join. But pointless, she said, when we were filming just one scene, and not even any dialogue.

When she said *pointless,* I popped off the couch. I went to the bookcase, scanned the rows until I found my original hardcover copy of *The Very Last.* The one Matt had couriered to my trailer all those years before. I held the spine in my right hand, let it fall open like it was the Bible and I was a revivalist. I'd pressed the note to Cass between the pages and gently removed it.

The note was wrinkled and worn and with an unfortunate coffee spill on it, but still legible. I walked over to Janie and held it out as evidence of my broken heart, of my need for hand-holding on this final day of filming. She was texting, but when she looked up, she dropped the phone and raised her hands like she didn't want the note coming any closer. Warding off bad spirits or something. Over the years I'd noticed that Janie, who usually seemed to relish telling me no, bent easily to my will whenever Cass was involved. I suppose unrequited love is a terribly sad thing to everyone, even a ruthless Hollywood manager.

"I get it, I get it," she said, already back on her phone. "You know, though," she added without looking up from the screen, "I'll have to reschedule some key meetings about that script you want for your directorial debut."

My directorial debut. My hopes were pinned on directing. That it would satisfy something deep within me. By that point, acting and Hollywood were pure emptiness to me. A nagging inner voice wondered if I'd been sold a rotten bill of goods. No pot of gold existed at the end of this Hollywood rainbow.

But who knew? Maybe my love of acting had run its course, but directing would fulfill me. I hoped so. I was about six months from selling everything, shaving my head, and disappearing into the wilderness. (Wilderness = a well-appointed camper with a Chemex and almond milk about fifteen to twenty minutes from a major city.)

"Janie, I need you in Charleston," I said.

She didn't miss a beat. "Then I'll be there, RyRy."

A Mercedes Sprinter van collected us from our downtown Charleston hotel. Janie spent the drive on her phone. She was now my manager, agent (I fired Matt), and head of my production company, so I couldn't complain when she slacked on her duties as best friend and confidante. Though she was those things as well.

I had the note to Cass in my pocket. I kept closing my eyes and attempting to meditate. But each time, I was hijacked by a fantasy: Cass appearing after we shoot the final scene. The director calls "cut" and then I see her, walking toward me. The light is stunning because of course it is. Nothing beats the sunsets in Charleston.* Then I remembered I was supposed to be meditating. I wasn't mad; it was a lovely daydream to step into.

Finally, the van was zipping across Gold Bug Island. Named after the short story Edgar Allan Poe wrote after living there, I'd been told. (And told and told and told . . . they were proud of him down South.) Then

*__Note from Cate:__ The Great Sunset Debate: New York City vs. Charleston.

we were pulling into basecamp. The driver parked the van and disembarked. Janie pocketed her phone. Outside, waiting for me, was an ending that I wasn't quite ready for, but that was coming anyway.

"Tell me how you're feeling," Janie said.

I pulled the note out of my pocket, went to unfold it, but Janie covered my hand.

"Forget that for a second," she said.

"It's like I want this day to feel, I don't know, profound somehow," I said, enjoying the warmth of her hand on mine. "But I'm worried it'll just feel empty."

She patted my hand, said, "It'll feel how it feels."

I inspected her words, looking for wisdom. Had she given me her best or put her brain on autopilot? I gave her my one-eyebrow look, said, "Is that from Yogi Berra?"

She laughed. "And if it is?"

"He does have some excellent observations," I offered.

"Exactly," Janie said, then I watched her turn serious again. I loved that we could do serious-funny-serious in such rapid succession. I remembered that I'd loved that about Cass, too, though that wasn't a helpful thought right then.

Janie released my hand, turned to face me. "I once spent an entire train ride from

Milan to Rome imagining the Coliseum and how transported I'd feel when I stepped inside. But when I got there, it felt like an overrun tourist trap, empty of whatever I'd hoped would fill it, and I'd never been so disappointed. It might still be the most disappointed I've ever felt. And I crashed. I felt so lonely I changed my flight to leave a day earlier than planned because I was so miserable. And who wants to be lonely and sad in Rome, with all those people eating pizza and gelato? So, I fly home early and I'm sad and wondering what the point of life is. I mean, if I can't even find meaning in a place like that?"

She paused and I waited for her to continue. When she didn't, I asked, "Does this story take a turn toward relevant at some point?"

She fixed me with a look. "And that flight home, that's the flight I met Nick."

Nick was her husband of sixteen years.

"What's the moral of the story?"

She grabbed my forearm, shook it lightly. "You just never fucking know what's going to happen next in this life — okay?"

CHAPTER 56

AMANDA

2012
Bolton Landing

What surprised me about Mr. Riley — I'm sorry, *Richard* — is how earnest he was. I didn't have much experience with earnestness. Our first few months working together, I tried to read second and third meanings into everything he said, only to realize none existed. If he invited me for coffee the following morning, I'd immediately respond, "Is everything all right?" And when he looked at me curiously, I'd say, "Rehearsals not going well enough?" He'd chuckle, put a hand on my shoulder, say, "I'd just really love to buy you a coffee."

When he asked to take me to a Broadway play, I resisted the urge to ask if what he meant was *let me show you how "real actors" do things*. Instead, I said, "Yes, please," and I was even more enthusiastic when he told me that we were seeing the play he had picked for us this coming spring: *Twelve Angry Men*. I was relieved because Annie and I had never done that one. (I tended to compare everyone in a role to my memory of Annie's performance. It was exhausting — for the kids especially.)

"Mind if I DJ?" I asked when he settled behind the wheel of my van. I was already opening my iTunes app.

"Please do," he said. "Teach me the ways."

I scrolled through my iPhone and felt the old gravitational pull toward my "Merry Go Freedom" mixtape, which over the years I'd re-created, first on CD, then on MP3, and now in a playlist. Something about those songs — in that order — was pure magic. I surrendered to it, hit Play, and tucked my phone into the cup holder.

As always happened, I tumbled back through time to that spring night, to 1998. Annie rescuing me from the floor of Tommy's bathroom, driving us home, the songs she selected filling the cab of my dad's truck. That night, I was trapped inside the fuzzy bubble of too much alcohol, but still listening intently. I knew the third song was the one that mattered, because I knew Annie. And when that one began, Sarah McLachlan's voice, sexy and smooth like wet paint, my body began tingling, the lyrics stinging me — little electric shocks. When the song ended, I resurfaced briefly — a struggle to do so — and said, "It's about us."

I wanted her to know she wasn't alone in her feelings.

"You remember when you did *Twelfth Night*?" Richard asked when we were an hour outside the city. I found the question odd, as it was the play that he'd first asked me to help him with and also one I'd performed in, so, not one I'd ever forget. But when he brought it up, I felt that familiar pang. I never understood why he had chosen that play, a play I blamed for driving a wedge between me and Annie. The choice never made sense — I thought he loved watching us together onstage.

"Why did you do that?"

He could sense something in my tone and glanced over. "Do what?" he asked, squinting, drawing out both words.

"Pick that play," I said. "I never understood it."

He looked bewildered. Like we were having two different conversations. And then a moment later, a realization dawned, and his expression softened. "Oh," he said. "You didn't know?"

"Didn't know what?"

"That Annie asked me to pick *Twelfth Night*. Came into my office one afternoon certain it was just the thing."

Wait . . . *what?* I tested the potential veracity of that, laid it next to what I knew about Annie back then. Gut reaction — it was true. I started to respond a few times but couldn't produce words. What could I possibly say to this? Admit that I didn't know, laugh it off like no big deal? Or maybe lie to him, say I had known, that I'd just forgotten for a sec? Nothing seemed right.

And while I sputtered, this revelation was speeding back through time, a virus threatening to corrupt all my favorite memories. Shutting it down was paramount; suddenly nothing else mattered. Which is how, far too quickly, I found myself saying, "Did you know Cate Kay is Annie? I mean, Annie, she's Cate Kay. The author — Annie wrote those books."

Mr. Riley reached his other hand to the wheel and gripped both tightly. "Wow," he said. He stared out at the road for a moment. "We just covered *a lot* of ground." He shook his head once, quickly, added another "Wow."

"Yeah," was all I managed.

"Aren't you worried I'll tell someone?"

Was I worried? I searched my body for concern, found none.

"No," I said finally. "I mean, it's not my secret."

"So why have you kept it?"

Huh. Odd that it had never crossed my mind to not keep it for her. We were in this thing together, she and I. Even though we weren't, we still were. That will make sense if you've had a friend who could look at you from across the room and make you laugh.

"Because I love her," I said, then looked at him, and we held eye contact for a second. Then I shrugged like, *Maybe that makes me a fool, I don't care.*

We talked for the next hour about everything: how I realized it was her, how I felt about it, what it was like in the years after the accident, how I was doing now.

It's a strange feeling when you break old alliances and form new ones. The only word I can find for it is, ironically, *dystopian.* High school me would be baffled by the social order, the rules of this future society in which I found myself. But, like everything in life, you'd be amazed at what you can get used to.

A few hours later, on the drive back home, Richard was listening to Bruce Springsteen and trying to sing, but mostly stumbling over the lyrics. (Springsteen sing-alongs aren't for the faint of heart.) My eyes were closed, had been for a while, but I wasn't sleeping. I was listening to him hit every third word, mumbling through the others. Then suddenly, a memory — how he'd once, when Annie and I were seniors, messed up an idiom so badly that we used his wrong version for the rest of the school year. I pried the memory open and stepped inside with Annie, smiled into the night.

When he dropped me off a short time later, I went right to the kitchen drawer and pulled out a sheet of paper and wrote what I knew would be my final letter. I gave it everything I had. Left it all on the field. As I licked the envelope, I wondered if Annie read her fan mail, or if someone did that for her. Either way, if what I'd just written didn't bring her back to me, no words ever could.

Chapter 57

Patricia Callahan

2012
Bolton Landing

The longest stretch I was sober during Anne Marie's childhood was almost seven months. I'd go a few days here and there, sometimes a week, but I couldn't make it stick. Then I started cleaning rooms at the Chateau with a woman named Christie. She was in town for the summer season. She drank too much, like me, and she had a young daughter, also like me. Plus, she wanted to change. So did I.

We worked together and held each other accountable until she got a phone call that her mom had fallen down the stairs and she needed to come home. Home was Watertown, three hours away.

From June 2, Annie's birthday, to Christmas Eve 1988 not a drop of alcohol passed my lips. Anne Marie was six at the time.

The memories from those months sit on the front shelf of my mind. One is clearer than the rest:

It's from late summer. I'm finally getting around to spring cleaning. A day late and a dollar short, like everything I did back then. But I'm doing it, that's what counts. I'm cleaning out the closet. It's not big — a short rod to hang clothes on, shelf above. A cardboard box is up there, tucked into the corner. I'm on my tiptoes, tips of my fingers brushing the cardboard, but finally I scoot the box over and bring it down.

Inside are my old clothes. Most of them from high school. Some even earlier. I unfold each item, hold it before me, reminisce. The last piece in the box is a soft white T-shirt. I'm lifting it up — oh, my *Tom and Jerry* shirt! How I had loved that thing. To think I'd forgotten all about it. My heart warms with the joy of finding a cherished item.

I hear Anne Marie giggle at the TV from the living room. The sound makes me smile. There's so much I've failed to notice about my daughter before these months. I look again at my old shirt, poke my head into the living room, trying to gauge whether the shirt might fit her. A little too big. But that's all right.

"Anne Marie," I call out. She turns off the

TV immediately. I've noticed that whenever I want her attention, I have it.

"Hi, Mommy."

"I have something special for you," I say, walking toward her. She's facing away from me, and I admire her little head that barely clears the back of the couch. Now she cranes her neck and watches me walk over. I sit on the coffee table facing her. She's swinging her feet, excited.

"Okay, honey, what I'm about to give you is very, very special." I'm holding the shirt behind my back. Anne Marie pretends to peek around, but only half-heartedly. It's obvious that for her I'm the star of the show.

"When I was your age I loved — I mean loved, loved, *loved* — this cartoon about a cat and mouse called *Tom and Jerry*. I loved it so much that I even had this cool shirt with the characters on it — it was my favorite thing to wear."

I bring the shirt around and present it to Anne Marie, holding it out like a bullfighter. We both look at the shirt. Her eyebrows are raised, and her eyes are big like this is the best thing that's ever happened to her. I want to squeeze her for this. Some small part of me had been worried she'd think the shirt was lame.

I jump back in: "Obviously I can't give

this shirt to just anyone. I need to give it to someone who can carry on its legacy. Someone who is kind and funny and smart. And guess what?"

"What?" Anne Marie asks, her voice rising with hope. She is already allowing herself to believe that maybe *she* is that someone.

"It's you," I say, confirming her suspicions. She throws both arms in the air, and I lean forward and wrap her in the tightest, longest hug I can manage, letting go only when I sense she's about to pull away.

I've never let myself fully relive this memory before. It's always been front and center but cordoned off behind yellow caution tape. No doubt my brain's way of protecting me from feeling as I do right now, which is like a bomb of regret has exploded all over me and no amount of scrubbing could ever remove the stain.

CHAPTER 58

JAKE

2013
Cabo

My husband, Danny, is one of those do-gooders; a recovering alcoholic who believes in the karmic energy of the world and the obligation all of us have to try, as best we can, to keep our ledgers balanced. How we came to fall in love is another story for another day, but being with Danny meant my days in the closet were over, and now that I was on the other side — well, good-fucking-riddance to all that lying. Being closeted can make you angry. Without even knowing why, you're acting like humanity is rotten at the core because how could a world denying love be any good at all? And forget about empathy; that's just something people discuss on afternoon talk shows.

We went to Cabo for our honeymoon. In the middle of that week, we were sitting side by side on lounge chairs; he was sipping an herbal tea and me a black coffee with cream. The crazy thing about that day is that I was already thinking about Sidney Collins, which was never a welcome or pleasant thought. But anytime a restaurant or coffee shop had a particular type of pourer — porcelain white with silver accents — for their cream, I thought of that years-ago interview with Sidney at the Blue Star.

I was dreading having to tell Danny what I'd done. But I knew I needed to.

The *New York Times* was folded under my arm, and I leaned back and cracked it open in front of me, one of those small joys I'd come to notice and appreciate thanks to Danny. Right there, right in the middle of the Arts section, was the headline THE VERY LAST COMING TO BROADWAY — FINALLY. Each day I didn't tell Danny was a day I'd have to explain why I'd taken so long. Our honeymoon was at least pretty damn early on the timeline of 'til death do us part.

I read the accompanying article and learned that *The Very Last* would be debuting on Broadway the following year, seven years after the original book had published, and after many delays because no director was willing to compromise on their vision for what The Core would look like. Creating the illusion of lowlands and rowboats in a postapocalyptic New York City was, apparently, always more expensive than even the shrewdest pencil pushers could budget. But, according to the article, they'd finally found a producer willing to foot the bill, and it was estimated that it would be the most expensive Broadway play in history. Nobody had yet been attached, but the ever-elusive Cate Kay was said to have — from her cave in the wild or shed atop a mountain or outpost in the stars — given her blessing to the stage adaptation.

I read the article twice. Then a third time. Finally, I folded the paper in half, then again, and laid it on my lap. My legs were extended in front of me and crossed at the ankles. Danny was to my right looking at his phone. I'd taught him well: the day couldn't begin until the crossword puzzle was done. He sensed my attention and looked up, asking, "We ready to rumble?"

"Almost," I said. "Just one small thing first — if you have a minute?"

He tossed his phone onto the chair and said, "All the minutes for you, whatcha got?" His hair was buzzed short all the way around because he was insecure about his hairline, and he had this tic of running his hand over his head like he was making sure it was all still there, which he was doing just then.

"I know this probably isn't the perfect time to tell you this," I said. "But it's come up twice for me today and you know how you're always saying 'the power of now'?"

"I mean, yes," he chimed in, "but technically that's the title of a book, not my own personal saying."

The man didn't even want to plagiarize during an interpersonal conversation, that's the level of integrity I was dealing with, and realizing that did not make me feel better about what I was about to say. I reached over and took a sip of my coffee.

"All right, so," I said, exhaling sharply on "so" as a way of indicating I was going to dive into the deep end on this.

"I did this thing a few years back. I wasn't in a good place back then, which isn't an excuse, but I'm just telling you for context. And I said yes to this offer that came my way, to do something that wasn't illegal — nothing like that — but certainly wasn't what you might consider *moral*. It kinda haunts me still and, well, I wanted you to know, I guess because we're . . ." I paused for the briefest of moments.

"Married," he jumped in before I could finish.

"Married is what I was going to say." I gave him a look like *Patience, please.* This micro interaction distracted me, but only for a second, from the much bigger thing I was trying to say.

"Thank you for sharing," he said slowly. "But that was incredibly vague. Let's pretend this is an elevator pitch, or the caption on a photo, and your job is to convey as much information as possible in as few words as possible."

I really did love him.

"Okay," I said, then I did a couple rapid rounds of breathing like I was a weightlifter preparing for a world record attempt.

"Seven years ago, a woman named Sidney Collins called and asked me to make one semi-threatening phone call that I believe was to the actual Cate Kay, then this Sidney Collins paid me a bunch of money to never publish anything else about Cate Kay. The whole thing was — yeah, suspicious."

After a long moment, he leaned back and batted his hands at the air like something terrible was attacking him. (He had been a theater major at the University of Virginia.)

I said, "That bad?," which was of course rhetorical. I knew it was *that bad,* otherwise it wouldn't have haunted me this whole time.

"Jake, what the fuck? What in the actual fuck?"

"Please, and I say this earnestly, be more eloquent than that so I can know what you're really thinking and if I need to do something about this?"

He looked deeply into his tea, took a sip, then met my eyes and raised his eyebrows as he inhaled. Later that night, we'd do the dirty work of how this would affect our relationship, but right then he wanted action — from me.

"What did you say to her, to Cate Kay?"

The man was detail oriented. These weren't memories I necessarily wanted to plumb, but the only way out was through.

"I told her I knew that her anonymity was because she was involved in a death in her hometown," I said. "Those were the exact words — 'death in your hometown.'"

"And was that true?"

"I mean, she hung up the phone," I said. "Clearly something about it was real."

He cocked his head, which is what he did when I tried to sell him some bullshit.

"I don't know if it was true," I said. "Part of the deal was signing an NDA, walking away from the story."

"Call this Sidney Collins and tell her to make it right, or else you'll break your NDA and go public."

"Impossible."

"Call her." He glanced at my iPhone, which was on the table next to my coffee. "Call her and tell her if she doesn't make it right, you'll write a story about the whole thing. And after you do that, we're going to write a letter to Cate Kay apologizing."

"And if this powerful lawyer threatens to sue me?"

He dramatically pressed his hands into his legs and went to stand up, but I reached over and touched his arm, gently pushing him back down.

"Okay," I said. "Okay. Just give me a minute."

It was late morning in New York. Sidney Collins answered on the first ring.

CHAPTER 59

SIDNEY

2013
New York

I'd been married twice since my relationship with Cass. The first — a whirlwind affair with Astrid, my SoulCycle instructor. That one hit Page Six because she'd been married to some up-and-coming Broadway producer. He planted a few items, trying to paint me as some high-powered womanizer. Total backfire — flattered, is how I felt. But Astrid and I only lasted a year. I was high on the SoulCycle endorphins, focused on getting over Cass. It wasn't a solid foundation for long-term partnership.

But my second marriage — the real deal. Helene. She worked in politics. Chief of staff for the mayor. We were on equal footing — no strange power dynamics — a healthy relationship. In stark contrast to what I'd experienced with Cass. Cass had used me. And since I couldn't have her love, I had forced her dependency. Great sex, but dysfunctional at its core. I told Helene about the things I'd done in that relationship, culminating in the stunt with Jake Fischer, prying Cass away from Ryan. Helene understood. She wasn't above such tactics — no one who succeeds in politics is. We'd both gotten our hands dirty over the years, and likely would again, but also, we donated monthly to six different nonprofits and sat on the board of three others — morality is a delicate ecosystem.

I got Jake Fischer's call late on a Monday morning. I'd gone for a nice long run before work, best one in years, and I was sitting in my corner office, looking at the sweeping view of New York thinking about how I had it all. The job, the apartment — elevator opening directly into our living room — and most importantly, the woman — finally. Then my cell rang and I saw Jake's name. On any other day, I'd have ignored the call and sent him a notice of intent to sue for breach of NDA. He was supposed to have lost my number. But, lucky him, I was feeling generous. I answered on the third ring.*

***Note from Cate:** Did Sidney answer on the first ring (as Jake says) or third ring (as she says)? On one hand, the answer is utterly trivial; on the other,

"Mr. Fischer," I said by way of hello.

He told me he was making amends. His exact words were "righting past wrongs," and I was curious — the bad-boy reporter, smoothing out his rocky past. To what did we owe that turnaround? He said he would write a letter to Cass Ford ("Cate Kay"), and that he wanted me to deliver it to her, to "come clean" about what had happened all those years ago. Jake was smart enough not to threaten me with an article, but I knew he'd done well at *Vanity Fair* — I closely followed his career.

The truth was: It was time. Time to relinquish Cate Kay, return her to Cass. I'd been a faithful custodian, always done right by her — protected all assets, created a behemoth. Even after she left, I managed the business as if it were mine. And now the trilogy was finished — the movies made — and my work was done.

I pictured Cass the first day we met, in that classroom. How young and brazen we both were, how hungry — it was all forgivable, all of it. As a gesture of goodwill, I included with the binders a note of my own, explaining what had happened in Los Angeles.

---

it is vital in understanding each and how they view themselves.

CHAPTER 60

Cass

April 2013
Charleston

My go-to coffee shop was about a half mile from my home, which I walked to most mornings. Not because their coffee was good, but because if I didn't, I might not see anybody at all during the day. We had a rapport, me and one of the baristas, and I share this because whenever I made a connection with someone, I began imagining what it would be like to tell them I was the author of the famous trilogy. What would they think of me?

To the outside world, I was just an average woman living in an average house in Charleston, who worked as a remote customer service representative for Delta Airlines. It was the ideal make-believe job — who could prove I *wasn't* a remote airline agent? A fake mundane life is what I was living, the kind I would have dreaded as a kid when I caught the sickness of wanting to eat the world.

"She's early," said my barista as I pushed through the door. The chime jingled. My favorite thing about the kid was that even though he was in college, he was a morning person, which gave me a deep and abiding sense that the future was in good hands. He also reminded me of Amanda — she'd loved mornings, too, and had the same carefree energy. His floppy hair was always in his eyes, and he did this little flip of his head to get it out of his vision when he steamed milk.

"Am I first in the door?" I asked. He shook his head in response, then nodded toward a table in the back corner. Which is when I saw it: the cover of *The Very Last*. A woman sat at the table, looking at her phone, and my book was unopened next to her. To an author, the cover of their book is unmistakable — we can identify our book just by glimpsing a corner of it even when we're a million miles away. But that one is recognizable to everyone, everywhere. The half-black, half-tan design with the crumbling CITY HALL subway sign. When I first saw the cover design, I thought of that beer that's half stout, half ale, and I still think of that drink every time I see it. My mom ordered it one too many times.

"Can you see what she's reading?" I asked, taking a step toward him while peering back. *Did he know my book?* Presented with the opportunity to find out, I couldn't resist.

"Looks like the first *Very Last*." His voice conveyed such familiarity that I tried to soak it up and let the feeling satisfy me. "The mysterious Cate Kay," he added absentmindedly while pressing down on a shot of espresso. Then he looked at me — "The usual?"

I nodded. I tried to take my mind off the woman in the back corner, off my book sitting on the table like a beacon, an opportunity. A hundred times, if not more, I had been in the presence of a copy of one of my books. Many times, at coffee shops or on subways. Once, at a Kansas Jayhawks* game where I saw a preteen girl with thick glasses reading a copy. She'd clearly been dragged to the game as a family outing.

In all the times I'd been in the presence of my book out in the wild, I never felt drawn to it. Occasionally, when I was procrastinating from writing, I stared at the cover of one magazine I had framed, the one with

***Note from Cate:** I wanted to see Ryan's hometown, to find James Naismith's house, to see her world. A self-indulgence for the brokenhearted. I highly recommend it.

the headline "WHO IS CATE KAY?" above the nine *Brady Bunch* boxes, each filled with a different rendering of what I might look like. I always thought the one in the bottom right-hand corner looked most like me: brown hair, strong cheekbones.

Sometimes, like a kid pressing her nose to the glass, I would live inside my alter ego's life for entire days: I would rewatch the movies and read all the gossip magazines and the exhaustive profile pieces attempting to discover my identity.

What a life I wasn't living!

I've even imagined the opening paragraph of a real profile on me, including details a writer might spot. Something like:

> The mug of steeping peppermint tea rests on Cate Kay's desk. Yes, that Cate Kay. She is sitting in her lime-green Herman Miller chair and showing me her writing studio — a tiny, well-appointed "shed" (her word) in the backyard of her modest Charleston home. The room is the only place in the world where the woman in front of me and the mythological figure that has become "Cate Kay" are made one.

As a soothing exercise, a kind of catharsis, I've imagined myself through someone else's eyes. In turn I've been flattering and brutal ("her cheekbones cut a cruel line," I once wrote in a mock profile). Best to get these sharp thoughts out of my brain. I've often wondered if I was harsher on myself than others would be.

I leaned against the wall while my barista was grinding coffee beans. I pulled my phone out of my back pocket and opened the Notes app and typed a few sentences I wanted to remember for later. I had finally turned the corner on my fourth book. Then my latte was ready for me on the counter. I paid and turned to go.

"Until next time," he said, and I was sideswiped with the knowledge that maybe he didn't know my name. Had I never said it, or did he not think it important enough to remember? Behind me, the copy of my book loomed. I veered away from the door, headed toward the woman.

She was wearing yoga pants and sneakers, and I vaguely wished for a less cliché scenario for what I was about to do. As I got closer the woman registered my presence and glanced up, her face warm and open, but also a bit bewildered, and I rested my hand on the cover of the book and I heard myself saying, "This is my book." She was confused, glancing between me and the book and processing a million other variables, maybe I meant that the book was my possession, a lost item.

Her mouth opened and she managed, "It's . . . nice to meet you?"

A small step toward my future, that's all it was.

"Hope you enjoy the book," I said, then the shop's quaint little chime announced my departure. It's crazy that on that same day, when I got back to my house, the FedEx package was waiting on my porch.

CHAPTER 61

CASS

April 2013
Charleston

I carried the box — quite heavy, actually — to my backyard writing studio and placed it on my desk. With a pair of scissors, I sliced through the tape, folding back the cardboard flaps, revealing a stack of blue binders. Resting atop was a handwritten note. It was clearly from Sidney. I would recognize her handwriting anywhere — tiny slanted block letters. Nothing graceful about them. I found a second note beneath the binders — its author was at first a mystery to me. I picked up Sidney's letter, to get it out of the way. I'd heard nothing directly from her in six years — all business correspondence went through her assistant — and the truth was I didn't think about her much.

I was speed-reading, glancing ahead for keywords, trying to find what the point was. She was explaining the binders, what they contained, the documentation, bank info, fan mail P.O. box, key correspondence. All well organized, efficient — trademark Sidney.

I was anxious for the why; why she was forwarding me all of Cate Kay's correspondence. Knowing Sidney, she probably wouldn't give me the satisfaction of an explanation. Then, finally, the last paragraph:

Cass, I know we took turns hurting each other — I'm sorry for that. Some of it was inconsequential, some wasn't. When you were in Los Angeles I was the one who had the reporter call you. His name was Jake Fischer — he's written a note I've included. I was hurt, angry, jealous. Ryan had nothing to do with it.

Be well. I'll think of you — fondly. xo, Sidney

Jake Fischer. The name didn't ring a bell. I quickly scanned the guy's note. He was nothing to me — just Sidney's tool. I instantly forgave him, a small payment against my gigantic cosmic debt. And sustained anger for Sidney I just couldn't do. The reason I couldn't rage at her was because I pitied her. I once heard a story — a parable, no doubt

— about how fish balance their relationships and environment by alternating which fish chases, which fish gets chased. All I could do was picture Sidney, who doesn't understand this delicate balance, who only chases, and who everywhere she goes spins up a maelstrom with her obsessiveness. It's punishment enough being her. Also, honestly, most of my brainpower was being spent conjuring memories from Los Angeles, rebuilding that last night with Ryan. I squeezed my eyes shut and replayed those final minutes, Ryan frozen on the sidewalk as I climbed into the Escalade, the confusion in her eyes, apparently 100 percent authentic.

What had I done?

I leaned back in my chair and tried to remember the chain of events from all those years ago. I could see now what role Jake Fischer played, with Sidney pulling the strings from New York, but not everything clicked into place. What about the photographers outside the restaurant? And Ryan, later that night, with another woman — neither Sidney's doing. But even so, maybe this was a justification for calling her? *Hey, just found out this thing, maybe that changes how you feel? If not, totally cool.* At the very least, I could tell her I read her *Vanity Fair* interview. She didn't need to know how many times.

Then, before I could stop it, my brain was jumping the tracks, and I was engaging with far-flung scenarios such as whether I should sell my house in Charleston and move to Los Angeles, just in case — a question I spent a full minute pondering before realizing its absurdity. I physically shook my head, told myself to slow down. One thing at a time.

First, the blue binders. I spent an hour with them. Two items stood out: the note from my agent, Melody Huber, pitching me on writing a memoir. (Maybe someday.) But most exciting was the P.O. box info for Cate Kay/*The Very Last* fan mail. How had I never thought to inquire about fan mail? I imagined the bags of letters, the fan fic, the artwork. For nearly a decade, I'd subsisted on message board comments. Now I imagined feeling the paper between my fingers, smiling at a crossed-out line or misspelled word — such intimacy with readers.

The mailbox was in New York. I would drive there the next day — a road trip. Road trips always made me think of Amanda.

That was one thing settled. I leaned back in my chair, staring at the cell phone on my desk: Should I, shouldn't I?

I'd deleted Ryan's number two years prior — the morning after watching her film the final scene of *The Very Last*. Janie, though, I still had her number. I picked up my phone, went to Contacts, brought her up. I stared at the digits until they went fuzzy and my mind emptied. After a few minutes, I pulled myself back and glanced at the time, watched it change from 11:10 to 11:11.

Do it, I told myself, and I called Janie Johnson.

CHAPTER 62

RYAN

April 2013
Los Angeles

Long-haul flights had become sacred to me. No phone, no internet. Hoodie up, headphones on. A level of anonymity and quiet I was rarely afforded in public spaces. But this return flight from Australia was neverending. I used the bathroom every hour, just to kill a few minutes. And when the plane finally touched down in Los Angeles, I was delirious. The brightness of the day felt rude.

Normally I'd have a driver, but Janie texted to say she'd collect me. She was waiting curbside in her Range Rover. That car never looked right on her. I thought of her as a Volvo: reliable, safe, a dash of curb appeal. I put my bags in the trunk, climbed into the front seat.

"Bed, please," I said, closing my eyes and leaning my head back. Janie was good at empathy, and I was craving some. I had just finished three months of overnight shoots outside Perth. Another failed fling with a closeted costar. I needed Janie's tender touch. But she was silent. And why weren't we moving? After a few seconds, I opened my eyes, looked over. She was turned slightly toward me.

"Ryan," she said. "I have something to tell you."

I'd been slouching. I sat up straighter — "You're scaring me."

"No, it's not bad," she said. "I don't think it's bad."

"What is it?"

She searched my eyes, transmitting something. Priming me, maybe.

"Cass called me," she said. "She explained what happened."

"Cass called you," I repeated.

"Yes, two weeks ago," she said. "She said she just received some information about that last night she was in LA, and she said it changed everything and she wanted me to tell you — if I thought it would matter to you. And I do think that it would. Matter to you, that is."

I gave my head a quick shake. One thing at a time. "Two weeks ago!?" This was something I would have wanted to hear, preferably the second after it happened. And she knew that.

"I didn't tell you because what could you have done? You were in your final days of filming, then a long flight home, it made no sense."

It wasn't a point worth arguing, given all the other delicious information on the menu.

"What did she say about Los Angeles?"

"She said, well, the takeaway was that she was wrong to leave like she did — that she had thought one thing had happened and she just learned the truth."

"Okay," I said. I leaned against the door, stared out the window. Cass. My ghost. She'd haunted all my relationships. No one had made me feel like she had. What was there to think about?

"So, what's my play?" I said, clapping my hands.

Janie smiled at me. "Well, I told her you were in Australia and that I'd pass this along when you got home. Why don't you call her and talk to her?"

I looked at her like she'd lost her mind. I pictured calling Cass, felt the intimacy of it. The pauses and stops and starts. I was out of practice with awkwardness. Being a movie star can really mess with your human-being abilities.

"Yeah, let's workshop some other ideas," I said.

"Or," Janie said, "you could hop on a plane. A grand-gesture moment."

I gave her the *say more* look. I'd regretted not taking bolder action all those years ago, relying on something as delicate as a handwritten note.

"Well, we've talked a couple times," Janie said. "She told me where she's going to be. She said, 'just in case.'"

I raised my eyebrows, "Just in case?"

"Yes, 'just in case.'"

CHAPTER 63

CASS

April 2013
New Jersey

I spent the drive north picturing canvas sacks filled with fan mail, bursting with readers' letters. So many bags, in fact, that once I loaded them in my car, I wouldn't be able to see out the back window. A hazardous amount of fan mail is what I pictured.

My first stop was the branch that housed Cate Kay's actual P.O. box. The postmaster told me all unclaimed mail was sent to the warehouse across the river, and he did not seem optimistic about my chances. I told him that I understood, but I was happy to see what they had, and he handed over a card with the address.

An hour later, as I walked through the front door of the warehouse and saw the vastness of the space, which looked as if it could house a fleet of jumbo jets, I realized what I really needed was a miracle.

"Can I help you?" came a voice from behind me. I spun around and there was an older woman with a raspy voice who looked like she subsisted on cigarettes.

"Yes, hi," I said. "I've had a P.O. box since 2006 or so, and was told that possibly the uncollected mail from over the years might be stored here?"

She chuckled — again, not reassuring — then said, "So you're looking for the clerical office then, hon?" The "hon" was a nice touch. "See that big sign?" I followed the direction of her bony hand.

"You're gonna find the office right below that sign there," she said. "And make sure you get Carl. If anyone knows about your mail, it'll be him."

Carl, my man, had on a John Deere trucker hat that seemed a size too small — he wasn't so much wearing it as it was perched atop his head. I knew it was him because of his name tag and the unlikeliness that another Carl worked in an office the size of a walk-in freezer. "Hello young lady," he said without looking up, pecking away at a tan computer that might have been one of IBM's first models.

"Hi," I said, then waited. On the remote

chance Cate Kay's mail still existed somewhere inside this building, I knew I was only going to find it if Carl decided I should. He hunt-and-pecked on that computer for a few more minutes, then hit a button with a final flourish and looked at me with his narrow face and lively eyes.

"You're up," he said, and I stepped closer, put my elbow on the counter and said in my best spy voice, "I have a mission for you." Thankfully, this made him grin.

"My life's a series of missions," he said, which struck me as some astute everyman philosophy.

"So," I said, leaning in conspiratorially, "somewhere in this massive building there are a few bags of overflow mail from a P.O. box, and I'm desperate to find them."

He was already typing on his computer again, eyes down, as he said, "We can do this. What's the name on the box?"

(I loved the "we.")

Right before I said it, I did have a moment during which I wondered how he'd react, but then I went ahead, "Cate Kay."

"Cate Kay," he repeated back to me as he typed it in, then he slowed down and looked at me. "Cate Kay, you say? From *The Very Last?*"

"That's right," I said, and I'd be lying if

I said I wasn't pleased that Carl — post-office-working, John Deere–trucker-hat-wearing Carl — knew me and my books. He reminded me of Amanda's dad. Carl looked at me and said, "And you're Cate Kay." Like really looked at me, and I swear my eyes welled, Carl became blurry, and my throat closed for a second.

Then I said, "Yes, I'm Cate Kay," and he grinned big and wide like the universe had just impressed him.

"Well, I'll be damned."

CHAPTER 64

CARL KOSAKOWSKI

2013
New Jersey

My wife's name was Charlene. She died of breast cancer the year the final book in *The Very Last* trilogy was released. I read it to her. I was thankful for its existence because she looked forward to it each day — one of the only things she did at the time. We had been childhood sweethearts, me and Charlene. Small-town New Jersey. Yes, there is such a thing. I always worried she regretted marrying me, but I never regretted marrying her, not for one second. My tastes were simple. I ate the same lunch — bologna and pickle on rye — for forty years. But she was adventurous, always wanting to try new things. I didn't know how to change to make her happier.

But I loved her so, and I hope I showed her that. Our last years together were good ones, and getting better and better. Then the cancer. I took a leave of absence and never left her side, nor did I want to. I was steadfast and loyal. Maybe not qualities she had pined for as a younger woman, but good ones at the end.

The third book of *The Very Last* was the only one I read. Charlene was the book person in the family. She read every night until she got sick, then I read to her. It took me three weeks to read that book aloud, and when I finished the last page, I closed it and placed it on my lap. I didn't want it to end. Finality scared me. I avoided endings of any kind during those months. Still don't like them much.

That night I looked tenderly at Charlene, brought her hand to my lips and kissed it, placed it gently back beside her. I could see she was thinking. It was easy to tell when she was. A far-off stare, a soft squint to her eyes. Whenever I noticed this look, I'd say, "Penny for your thoughts," which had charmed her when we were young, but less so as we aged. She liked to keep some things for herself. We were different like that. I didn't mind her knowing everything I was thinking.

I stopped myself from asking after her that night. Let her be, I told myself. But a minute or so later, she said, not really to me, but aloud, "I think the person who wrote those books is young — it's like she's trying to work something out about the world."

"Yeah?" I said, 'cause I sure didn't have anything else to say.

"Those main characters — Samantha and Persephone — they remind me of me when I was younger. They want so much from the world. Seems they haven't learned the most important lesson yet."

My ears perked up. Oh man. Did I want to know? Yes — I wanted to know everything Charlene thought about life or anything else.

"And what's that, my love?"

"The trick of life," she said. Then she got caught in a coughing fit. I offered her the glass of water by the bed, but she waved me off, continued.

"The trick of life, as I see it now, is to make what's around you beautiful. It'll grow from there. Took me a long time to see that."

I sat back. I hoped, I hoped so dearly, that she meant that even though our love hadn't been perfect, that it had been beautiful in its own way. Broken things are beautiful. More beautiful in the end than perfect things, which are usually an illusion of some sort. I hoped I had given her a beautiful life.

Slowly, she turned her head and met my eyes, and I don't know what she was thinking in that moment, but she did reach for my hand and held it without letting go, and that was enough for me.

She died a few weeks later.

That winter, I was transferred to the warehouse and put in charge of the P.O. boxes. When I saw Cate Kay/*The Very Last* on my list, I took it as a sign from Charlene. I think I even glanced upward and shook my head.

And when that striking young woman came asking after it, I knew. Right when she walked into my little office, I was reminded of Charlene, who was also always impatient for what might come next. I just knew, with a deep certainty, that she was the young woman my wife had predicted, trying so hard to work something out about the world.

CHAPTER 65

Cass

April 2013
New York

My home for the night was a four-room suite at the Mandarin Oriental overlooking Central Park. An extravagant purchase for what I hoped would be an extravagant evening. The valet delivered my many bags of mail. I tipped him $100, extending the single bill between us and making eye contact. I silently implored him to understand that I wasn't one of those same-old rich people; I was salt of the earth. Then I wondered if that was the story all wealthy people told themselves. Once the door closed behind him, I pushed aside the coffee table and dumped the letters on the carpet, one bag after the other.

I sat on the couch, the city twinkling at my back, and stared at my paper mountain. How to begin? A prayer, like before a big meal? A glass of champagne to commemorate the moment? Or, I could just lean forward and randomly grab a letter, start reading, which is what I did. I snagged one whose corner was jutting out, held it in my hands — thick and rectangular like a birthday card. I looked at where it was from: Minneapolis, Minnesota. The handwriting was loopy — probably a woman's. I opened it, inhaled its message: *I loved the book, you're amazing, the ride at Universal Studios was rad!*

I placed the letter on the carpet, separate, then reached for another.

This went on for many hours, until the second pile was the same size as the first — a mini mountain range at my feet. I stood and stretched my arms overhead, forced a yawn. My phone told me it was 3:53 in the morning, but I was wide-awake.

My favorite items so far had been the artwork of Puck. In crayon, from little kids; in oil paint, from old men. I dropped onto the couch, twisted left, twisted right, loosening up my lower back. Age, coming for us all.

I leaned forward and plucked another piece from the pile. A business envelope, words on the other side. I spun it in my hands, noticing first the stamp, affixed with precision in the top right corner, then my eyes drifted to the return address and the air left my body, an electric shock hit my chest.

AK
Bolton Landing, NY

But, it couldn't be. I caught myself before my heart exploded. The handwriting bore no resemblance to Amanda's, which had been flamboyant. *I'm channeling Marilyn Monroe,* she'd explained — I hadn't thought of that in years. It's not — it's not her. It's another person with her initials. Plenty of A first names, K last names. And yet my heart had swelled to double its size, was choking off air.

Amanda is dead, I reminded myself. Adrenaline flooded my body. Not a good feeling.

I carefully opened the envelope. Inside was a piece of loose-leaf folded precisely in thirds and goose bumps ran across my arms. I quickly unfolded the letter:

Dear "Cate Kay,"
FUCK YOU.
–A

Something about the quote marks rocked me. I launched myself onto the pile of unopened mail, flinging aside letters, digging, and separating, my eyes flying across return addresses and then — I found one. Same business envelope, same handwriting, same return address. I touched it, reverent. Then I placed it carefully on the couch and dove back into the heap.

When I was done, I had found five envelopes.

Around me was a sea of paper. I crawled to the couch, sat next to my treasure. Calm down, I told myself. Amanda is dead, this is just some terrible coincidence. The universe playing games with me. I arranged the letters in chronological order, by postmark. Then I closed my eyes, bowed my head.

Dear universe, I whispered, *if there's any chance that this is real, that she's — I'll give anything. Anything to make it real. All the money, anything, everything — whatever I have. I don't need any of it. I promise.*

I opened my eyes, reached for the letter from 2008, opened it. Same loose-leaf paper, same precise folding, same heat waves coming from my chest. This one wasn't much longer than the first:

Dear "Cate Kay,"
Who inspired the name Samantha?
–A

My heart, a big, deep thud. Amanda had always wished her name was Samantha; I'd wanted mine to be Kelly. I tore open the next letter (*and Puck?*), then the next (*New York sunsets?*). All were cryptic in the same way, and I became frantic, going faster and faster. Then, the penultimate letter: *I'm alive again now, really living, and I wish I knew you were, too.*

I sucked in the deepest breath possible, sucked in a little more, and opened the final letter, dated 2012, unfolded it. A sea of blue ink:

Dear Cate with a K,

Do you remember during rehearsals for Twelfth Night when Mr. Riley was trying to show us the blocking for that one scene, but we just couldn't get it? He was so stressed, and you and I slowly inched toward each other on the stage until we were pressing our shoulders together, just watching his meltdown. They were rare, those meltdowns, but when they happened — oof, right?

Anyway, then Eric asked some dumb question, and Mr. Riley just lost it, yelling out: "Ladies and gentlemen, we have got to get on top of our ducks!" And you and I slowly looked at each other and just doubled over laughing? (Those ducks, we had to get on top of them... and stay there!) We couldn't stop, and Mr. Riley came over to us and was like, "Is something funny, ladies?" Then for the next year, or however long it was, we'd tell people struggling with anything — big, or small — to get on top of their ducks, then just walk away straight-faced.

I know you remember. I know everything we shared is threaded through you as it is me.

In the last dozen years, anytime someone says the phrase "get your ducks in a row" it feels like my heart catches a splinter. If that was the only time my heart felt that way, it would be okay, I could handle it. But it's also anytime I see a crack in a mirror or a chicken nugget or a red car or a Honda of any color or a romantic comedy or a boat or a sunset on any night, ever.

You're everywhere, always — in all my conversations. A student told me last week that we speak five thousand words a day. Instantly you appeared next to me, giddy over this factoid, trying to do the math: okay, so let's say half our words are to each other, that's 2,500 multiplied by 365 days multiplied by — how many years have we *been friends? I pictured you calculating the many millions of words between us.*

However many, they were hardly enough.

My life is nothing like what I imagined. And not because of the accident, but because you're not in it.

Come home, Annie. I still love you.

Amanda.

An earthquake rumbled through me. I pictured it rippling through the hotel floor, the surrounding skyscrapers, the miles beyond. Amanda, alive.

I sat upright, rigid, staring straight ahead. My throat began closing. An act of self-preservation. *Nothing else inside,* my body was saying, *not even air.* Then, finally, a gasp, and the rapid rise and fall of my chest. I dropped the letter, brought my hands to my face, silently sobbing into them until even sitting upright felt like too much and I let myself fall to the right. A pillow was tucked under me, and I wrenched it out and curled into it like I was back in the womb, pressing my face into the purple velvet.

Images of Amanda appeared — her

gunning the boat engine, hopping while tying a shoe, fighting to keep her eyes open while I told a story — and I was sobbing and laughing and sobbing. I didn't want to open my eyes, didn't want the Amanda movie in my mind to end, but I had to get moving. I needed to shower, pack my bag, call the valet for my car.

Amanda was waiting for me.

CHAPTER 66

ANNIE

April 2013
Bolton Landing

The highway was a blur of pavement out my window, and something about being on the Northway again had my brain picturing Sidney, that covert trip to my hometown that ended with her sitting in my car, telling me Amanda was dead. I let that scene run again and again, searched for the lie that I now know I should have spotted. Was it in her eyes? No, couldn't find it there. In her words? Not there either.

Fucking Sidney — she was good. I ran my left hand through my hair. I'd underestimated her. I'd known she was needy, of course I'd known that, but I'd thought it was garden-variety need. Like, blocked-number after breakup, worst case. What a profound miscalculation. Sabotaging my relationship with Ryan felt quaint compared to this new revelation. I tightened my hands on the wheel. But my anger at Sidney was quickly morphing into something much more potent: regret. I could feel it roping around my heart.

I had never loved Sidney. I had never even *liked* Sidney! So then why was she there in the first place, inside my car, and why had I let her kiss me, and why had I kissed her back, and why had I done any of it when every moment with Sidney made me sad, my whole self wishing she was Amanda.

I rolled down the windows and let the air mess my hair. Then I put my hand, balled into a fist, outside and let the wind slowly pry my fingers apart.

As I drove the last stretch into Bolton Landing, I felt — well, fuck, there's no single English word for it. Amanda used to love learning words from other languages that captured meanings ours never could. It started with *schadenfreude,* which Mr. Riley said at some point, talking about what it's like to be an understudy, and all of us gave him some side-eye, so he slowed down and explained the definition.

"But, like, 'malicious joy' or 'gloat' doesn't even begin to capture that meaning," Amanda was saying, absolutely amped about this word and the thing it named. "It's like knowing the word unlocked the feeling. It's crazy."

"It's cool," I said, and in response she shoved me playfully.

"Um, it's *more* than cool."

After this, whenever she heard a word that did this for her, she'd bring it to me and explain. Always the same energy, too: hands moving, talking a mile a minute. One time she brought up the Japanese word *boketto*. A clumsy translation might be zoning out, but that's not quite right; it's more like non-doing or cultivating stillness by staring into the vastness.

I was staring into the vastness now. Both hands on the wheel, straight ahead, *boketto*. Landmarks passed outside the window, and deep in my mind they sparked memories but they turned to dust as soon as they formed.

My old building was on my left, those same green plastic Adirondack chairs. My eyes were not on the road, but past it and through it, *boketto*. The library, the coffee shop, the high school. Then I turned left. I parked outside Amanda's old house. I cut the engine, and when I did, I cut off whatever invisible thread was tethering me to the alternate universe, and that was fine with me. It was this universe I wanted to be in, anyway, because now I knew this was the one with Amanda still in it.

After knocking a few times and waiting long enough to be certain, I walked down the street to the diner that looked exactly as it did when I left. I wondered if they'd think the same of me. It was lunchtime, and the place was empty except for two construction workers sitting at the counter halfway through their burgers and fries.

 A middle-aged woman carrying a plastic menu came to seat me, gesturing for me to follow. I reached for her, gently touching her arm, and said, "Do you know Amanda Kent?" She turned and the way she looked at me reminded me of the feeling I would have, all those years ago, about outsiders who came in expecting things. My car keys were in my hand, and I glanced down and wondered if I was holding them like they were a sexy prop, wondered if to this woman I seemed like city money and carelessness. "I used to live here," I said, surprising myself with how much pride I felt in that fact.

 Her shoulders softened. "Well, hon, best I can say is that Amanda would be over at the school. Now, can I get ya anything?"

 "No, thank y—" I began, but then a flash

of memory. "Actually, yes — a slice of key lime to go, please."

Auditorium doors are oddly noisy. Amanda and I used to wonder why. Each time they opened, especially when you needed silence, they sounded possessed, like the entire energy of the room went rushing toward them along with the audience's attention. Bad engineering, maybe. Keeping this in mind, it took me many seconds to turn the brass handle of the heavy door — I did it slowly as if sneaking out for a party. Finally, I turned sideways and slipped inside, and nobody on the faraway stage was the wiser.

I suddenly realized that all I'd ever really wanted was the universe's permission to come home. And maybe I wrote *The Very Last* as a way of asking for it. I think. I don't know. Maybe that's all bullshit.

Then I saw Amanda onstage, her movements still so generous and assured, just as they had always been. I could have spotted Amanda from any distance. Right then, she was showing a student the precise spot at which she needed him to stop, and she rolled herself there in one quick motion then spun herself out toward the imaginary audience with a dramatic flourish.

And it was then that she saw me. Maybe

she also knew *my* body's movements from any distance, had looked out at the woman leaning against the back wall holding a slice of key lime pie, one knee bent, foot propped against the wall. Maybe to Amanda that silhouette screamed *Annie.* How sublime the feeling, to be known again.

She stopped midsentence and stared at me, and it was like her vision created an energy. I felt it on my arms first, the hairs standing on end, tingling. The feeling was pleasantly terrifying, as if my soul was warming itself by a wildfire.

Then she turned her head slightly toward the students waiting patiently behind her and said, "Start again at the top of the scene." That sent the kids into a flurry of movement, and they were the backdrop as I watched Amanda wheel herself off the stage to the front row so she could assess them as an audience member might. Mr. Riley used to do the same thing.

For a moment, I wondered if maybe she hadn't seen me, maybe I'd misread the moment, but then I closed my eyes and I swear the energy had an actual heartbeat, it could make flowers bloom, light bulbs pop. Amanda had seen me, was waiting for me, and I shouldn't keep her a moment longer.

I pressed myself off the back wall, carefully

walking down the aisle as if I'd arrived late for opening night. When I reached the front row, I made myself small and shifted across the many seats so as not to block the view of the make-believe audience behind. Amanda kept her eyes fixed on the stage the whole time, even as my left hand silently pressed down the seat next to her, even as I eased into it, settling, the little box of key lime pie on my lap. We were now inches apart. She was staring at the students, who looked prepared to restart the scene.

"Ready when you are," she called to them, and I seized the moment for myself, turned to her and opened my mouth to say her name. But as I did, she lifted her right hand and silenced me. The glow of the stage lighting was glancing delicately off her lovely features, and at least this soothed me. No matter what else had changed, no matter how brutal whatever had been, and whatever was about to come next, this remained: Amanda, beautiful in every setting, at every stage.

The students began the scene, and my mind started running through what to say when they were done. I took one long, deep breath and tried to tune in to what was happening onstage. Perhaps I could figure out what play they were doing. But my mind was too crowded with thoughts — *had I read this all wrong? did Amanda actually hate me? and what will I do if she does?*

We sat like this for minute after minute, Amanda's attention laser-focused on the stage. Finally, she leaned slightly into me, her eyes still on her students, and instinctively my body responded, leaning into hers. She tilted her head toward me a few degrees, now closer to my ear, and the moment was like a thousand others we'd had growing up — whispering so only the other could hear.

She paused and held us like this, still watching the stage. Then I spotted it. And I watched as the young man strode confidently, hit his mark, and spun to face out, his eyes gleaming. Beside me, I heard Amanda's satisfied exhale as the boy's classmates hooted and hollered, the imaginary curtain dropping on Act I.

"So," Amanda said, turning to me and nodding at my lap. "We gonna eat that or what?"

CHAPTER 67

AMANDA

April 2013
Bolton Landing

I hadn't had a slice of key lime pie since Annie left. It was even better than I remembered, and we shared a piece every night that first week.

CHAPTER 68

RYAN

April 2013
Los Angeles to Bolton Landing

I went home for a quick shower and a costume change, then Janie brought me back to the airport. I layered up on disguises: big glasses, Jayhawks hat, hooded sweatshirt. To my fellow travelers I would be someone to avoid. A cranky and hungover woman, coming home from some bachelorette party, maybe. This felt like maturity to me: caring less what people thought.

Except Cass. I spent the flight reading the latest *New Yorker* in hopes of impressing her with my intellect and worldliness. I needed a crash course. I'd spent the last seven years on a conveyer belt: one movie after another. Chunks of my life in trailers. Entire months lost inside production bubbles. The biggest change I'd made was coming out. Which I had hoped would reconnect me to the world.

(Okay, yes, and maybe also to Cass.) An insane thought, in retrospect, that a *Vanity Fair* cover would make me relatable. What it did was tilt my career on its axis, spin it off in a different direction — edgier parts, a new legion of rabid fans. I hadn't become any more real to people, just a different kind of icon.

As the pilot announced our descent into Albany, I thought about all my actor friends who dated other actors. Their explanation was always the same: We understand each other. That rare work-life compatibility. I did believe that if two good people found each other, they could cling to one another and stay afloat. But all I'd experienced was people grabbing my hand and plunging us deeper into the abyss.

I just — I hoped I was still normal. Was it possible for me to still be normal?

Landing in tiny Albany International was about as far away from LA as I could get while remaining in the country. Years had passed since the last time I'd done things like stand in line for a rental car, which I did, behind a businessman in khakis who kept stealing glances at me. For a little while, I reveled in my independence, this exotic experience. But, wow, rental car lines are slow-moving. After about half an hour, I texted Janie, "Being a real person is both exhilarating and time-consuming." She responded with, "You *are* a real person."

My destination was a hotel called the Chateau. Janie had repeatedly asked if she could organize a meetup, but I said no. That I needed it to be a surprise. That I needed to find Cass on my own. I didn't want a coordinated reunion; I wanted to know if she still loved me. I needed to see her eyes the moment she saw me: they would hold the truth.

The Chateau's lobby was dated opulence. Flower-printed couches, lace doilies, oak credenzas. But the view of the lake and mountains beyond was timeless. Now that I was in the same small town as Cass, I felt my whole body flood with awareness. The feeling was familiar to me. It happened occasionally when shooting deeply emotional scenes. Or before a speech or public appearance when I had no character to wear. Anytime I felt exposed, really. I'd feel cold, start shivering.

Janie had always tried to fix this response in me, pitching me on benzos. But I didn't want that. Even though it was uncomfortable, my body was cueing me: pay attention, something important is happening. Next to the front desk was a silver urn, and I fixed myself a tea. Hot water was the only natural remedy I'd found. I held the paper cup in both hands, brought the steam to my face. I took a small sip, then walked to the front desk.

"Hi, there," I said.

"How may I help you?" said the young woman. Stylish black glasses, admirable posture.

Janie had given me a name, and I gave it to this woman, added, "Could you try her room?"

My teeth started to chatter, and I leaned into the shiver, brought the tea to my lips. The woman smiled as she lifted the phone. We each stared off in separate directions for a few seconds.

"Sorry, ma'am," she said, placing the receiver down. "Try back again later?"

As I was walking toward the elevators, resigned to go to my room for now, I heard someone say "Excuse me" and gently touch my shoulder. I flinched — habit. A bellboy was leaning toward me, and obviously he had recognized me. His eyes were wide, and he seemed nervous. He whispered, "She went for a walk a little while ago, the woman you're looking for? I saw her heading toward town, not sure where, of course, but maybe that helps? Also, I *love* your work."

Interactions like this were usually loathsome

to me. I wanted to match the person's excitement and openness, but any response — *thank you, that's so kind of you to say, I appreciate that so much* — felt practiced, tired. No matter what I said, I walked away feeling like I lived inside a glass case.

But this was different. He had a gleam in his eye. I gave him a fist bump, which seemed to thrill him.

I had been looking forward to a hot bath, but instead I asked the valet for my car. A minute later, I was behind the wheel of my Nissan Altima rental and driving into town.

I drove as slowly as possible through downtown Bolton Landing. I was sizing up everybody I saw on the sidewalks. Glancing through the windows of stores. The whole thing started to feel like a fool's errand. What I needed to do was get Cass's number from Janie, give up this fantasy of surprising her. And yet, and yet, *and yet* . . . maybe just one more spin around town?

Thankfully, my nervous system had calibrated itself somewhere near normal. Perhaps I simply didn't believe I'd find her. I was taking easy, full breaths, enjoying the feeling of calm. I was just coming up to the edge of town when I looked to my right at an apartment complex. The building was brown with faded yellow doors. I spotted a figure sitting outside in a green Adirondack chair. A pang of recognition. The woman was in the shape of Cass. Her legs pulled into her, facing across toward the lake.

I slowed down, tried to whip the car around, but the Altima's steering radius had other plans. A three-point turn was not as suave as I wanted, and the car behind me tapped their horn. My reaction was *Shhh, don't blow the surprise*. But Cass was not on the lookout for a Nissan Altima with me inside.

I can report that the sun was setting as I pulled the car off the road and got out. That was one thing in my favor. Plus, the sounds of the lake — the frogs and crickets — was another. I looked in both directions, then jogged across the street, very much aware that after all these years there was suddenly absolutely nothing standing between us.

CHAPTER 69

ANNIE

November 2013
New York

My first-ever book event was eight months later. By then I'd sold something like seventy-one million books worldwide and twice been named to the TIME100 list of most influential people. These facts worried me. I didn't have the polish of someone with that bio. Would people be disappointed?

So, when the staff at the Strand offered me a back room, I declined. I needed to watch the audience file in — not for my ego, but for my sanity. My anxiety was simmering on medium heat, threatening to boil, and watching people arrive helped me acclimate to the moment. Plus, the alternative was alone in a back room with my brain. No thanks.

It was thirty minutes before showtime, the place half-filled, when I felt someone slide next to me. I glanced over: a man, trimmed beard, chocolate eyes.

"Jake," I said formally, nodding once.

"Hello there," he said, leaning back against the wall.

"Thanks for doing this."

"Are you kidding?" he said. "Thanks for asking."

No doubt he was hoping for a longer moment between us, but right then I saw Amanda roll in, a young woman holding the door for her. Amanda said something and the two shared a laugh, her smirk suggesting that she'd just deployed her trademark wit. She was wearing a black leather jacket with the collar turned up, gold hoop earrings, crisp white blouse beneath — just effortlessly cool. For the thousandth time since our reunion, I was reminded of how deeply I'd underestimated her all those years ago. Nothing could keep her from herself.

I thanked Jake again and walked over, catching Amanda's eye halfway there. She'd tucked herself just out of the way, nestled in front of a bookcase. Someday the fact of Amanda's existence wouldn't make me giddy. The high would wear off. But it hadn't yet, and I savored the feeling as I bent over and wrapped her in a hug. I held her for an extra beat, breathed her in.

"How was your day?" I asked. She was coming from the theater; they were a month from opening *The Very Last* on Broadway. Ryan was directing, Amanda was playing Samantha in the third act. I had wanted to produce, but Ryan said absolutely not, with Amanda adding *hell no*. They both believed I needed to move forward.

It was the right decision, obviously. But I admit I felt a little left out.

"They're doing final fittings right now," Amanda said. "Ryan told me to say good luck and that she'll try to make it later."

Amanda, though, wouldn't be missing a second of it. This event had been her idea.

"It would be *so* poetic," she had said. "The full circle of it is too irresistible!"

"But an event — it's not enough time to explain everything. And what if they hate me? Maybe let's just wait for the book?"

"Nobody could hate you," she had said. "Trust me — I tried."

And now, the night was upon us.

"I'm so nervous," I said, kneeling beside her as people streamed past. She patted my hand like, *there, there,* and I asked her if that was all the support she could muster for my pivotal life moment.

"Annie-baby," she said. "Don't let that

brain of yours trick you: you're not nervous, you're *excited*."

"Wow," I said.

She shrugged, turned up her palms — "I know, I know. I'm a fountain of wisdom."

"No, not that," I said, putting both hands on my bent knee, grimacing. "It's my knees, I can't sit like this anymore. Oh my god, we're getting old."

"Indeed we are. But any thoughts on my wisdom?"

"Yes, obviously," I said. "The depths of it are stunning."

"Thank you," she said, then paused and caught my eye, steadying me. "And also — it would be an honor."

I loved when she did this, took a buried layer of our conversation and surfaced it. My curiosity was piqued. How bored I'd been all those years, with no Amanda to talk to.

"What would be an honor?" I asked.

"Oh," she said. "You know — getting old together."

We looked at each other for a few seconds — earnestly, seriously — then she started gesturing for me to turn around: the event coordinator was walking toward us, apologizing, saying that I was needed in the back.

■ ■ ■ ■

The event was standing room only. I walked out with Jake — *in conversation with,* as they like to say. Within seconds, I remembered how good it felt to be onstage, my mind crystallized by the audience's attention. (Amanda, as always, had been right: I was excited.)

As we settled in our comfy chairs, I noticed the door open slightly, and watched Ryan step inside. Her head was down as she unwrapped her scarf. A minor miracle, such moments — seeing your person before they see you.

In the months since, I often wished I could have been Ryan, on the night she found me outside my childhood apartment. But I couldn't be greedy; we each get our moments.

That night in Bolton Landing had this fuzzy, ethereal quality. I was back home, Amanda was alive, and I felt connected to the world again. My life had been restored to me. I was sitting in that green Adirondack chair and the sun was hitting my eyes just right and so when I opened them, the light refracted and Ryan appeared, a dozen of her, like I was seeing her through a kaleidoscope. My eyes felt like love beams.

"Hi," I had said dreamily.

Now here Ryan was, appearing again. Jake was welcoming the audience as she stealthily crossed the back of the room and carved out a space next to Amanda, then dropped her hand to Amanda's shoulder and left it there. With her other hand, she gave me a little wave.

Be still my heart.

Over the next hour, Jake asked every question, from every angle: take us back to what happened, why you ran away, why "Cate Kay," and what about this, and then what?

This was my first time telling the story. Some things were off-limits, of course — this book you now hold was only half-written at the time.

After an hour of questions, Jake closed his notebook and placed it on the little table next to him, said, "Okay, last one before we open it up to the audience: If you could tell younger Annie —"

"Jake, no," I interrupted. "Please."

"What?"

"It's just that, I should probably never give anyone advice."

"But it's not advice for them" — he gestured at the audience — "it's advice *for you*."

I threw him a look. "What's the difference?"

He put up his hands.

"Okay, okay, I got this," I said, smoothing over the awkwardness I'd introduced. Everyone laughed. They were a generous audience, and I was grateful for their warmth. When I'd explained what happened on that island so many years ago — my heart galloping in my chest — there'd been a few sharp inhales, noises of disapproval. I had willed myself to look at Amanda as I finished our story, and she gave me a nod of encouragement. Miraculously, the audience had kept listening. And now I wanted to give them my most honest answer to Jake's final question.

I dropped my head in thought, imagined my childhood: a blur of colors and movement and smells, and I thought about everything, flying through moments and memories, trying to distill it all down — sifting my life for a golden nugget of wisdom.

Then, I had it.

I looked at Jake.

"I'd tell her that only love will fill the black hole — that it's the only thing worth chasing."

He considered this for a moment, said, "Sounds like there's a backstory, maybe?"

I laughed and said, "Always — there's always a backstory."

"I bet it's going to be in the book," he said.

"It will be," I said, winking. I debated the

wink in the microsecond before it happened, then regretted it immediately. (Two-time TIME100 here, folks.) Jake then turned to the audience. "She's all yours now," he said, leaning back.

A bunch of hands shot up. A microphone was brought to a woman near the back. She stood to receive it with shaking hands.

"Hi, I'm Violet," she said softly, clearly outside her comfort zone.

"Hi, I'm Annie," I said, and it felt good saying my real name.

Violet continued, "Okay, so, um, my question is, why did you name the book *The Very Last*?" She immediately returned the mic, relieved, and sat down; the book-event equivalent of *I'll hang up and listen*.

"I didn't name it actually," I said. "That was the publisher's choice. I had no say."

Violet didn't have the mic anymore, which seemed to upset her — now she had a follow-up! She was gesturing for it back, then gave up and called out, "Will you tell us what your original title was?"

The title popped into my mind. In the years since, I'd realized that the publisher had been right to rename the book. My title had been too personal, too specific.

"Sure," I said, then paused. I looked out at Ryan, at Amanda next to her; I thought of my mom, waiting patiently for me at home, doing her best to repair things between us — these women who were my world.

"You know," I said. "Actually, I think I'm going to keep that one for myself."

ACKNOWLEDGMENTS

My deep gratitude to Laura Brown and Darcy Nicholson, who loved this story from the beginning, then worked tirelessly to make it better with each draft. I wasn't sure I'd ever find true teamwork after sports, but we got damn close, and I think this book reflects that rare blend of joy, dedication, and cohesion. It's an experience I won't soon forget.

Katie Greenstreet, my agent at Paper Literary, is a superstar and a dream. She saw the potential — in a much rougher version — and guided and advised Cate Kay toward greener pastures. (All of this goodness even though the first thing I learned about her is that she's a Duke basketball fan.) Many thanks also to the rest of Paper Literary, including Catherine Cho and story whisperer Melissa Pimentel.

To everyone at Atria: it's been my good fortune to work with an imprint that so clearly has its finger on the pulse of the industry. Thank you to Lindsay Sagnette, to Holly Rice (publicist extraordinaire!), to Zakiya Jamal, and to Morgan Pager. Leora Bernstein championed this book from the start. My thanks to her as well as the rest of the Atria team across sales, production, and copyediting.

To everyone at Bloomsbury: thank you for your unbridled enthusiasm from day one.

Lauren McBrayer, your early and detailed notes were a godsend. I aim to pay that generosity forward. A few early readers also gave me confidence or helped shape the story (or both!). They are Kelly Wild, Marion Nelson, Caroline Shea, Rachel Zoller, Shawna Hawes, Jess Vande Werken, Kristen LeQuire, Meg Younger, Brit Liegl, Tess Carver, Sweet Lu, and many others within the beautiful community of Inky Phoenix Press. A big shoutout to Kate Scott (my b!) for providing the ongoing, evolving soundtrack for the writing of this book — first Janelle then Carlie then Maggie then Chappell — as well as for reading multiple versions and believing in the whole thing from the start. (Please thank Nicole and Piper/Puck for me, too.)

My mom has been with this book every step of the way. Actually, let's rewind and rewind . . . ever since my first step! That's how lucky I am. Mom, I know you know how important you are to me. My sister, Ryan, read an early draft and her enthusiasm made me believe I was onto something. I love you both. (Dad, I love you, too. The 11:11 was for you; I miss you.)

Kathryn, it's not surprising that it's your name at the start and end of this book. You're the most important thing in my world (+Ragnar, of course). We're the best story of all.

ABOUT THE AUTHOR

Kate Fagan is an Emmy Award–winning journalist and the #1 *New York Times* bestselling author of *What Made Maddy Run,* which was a semifinalist for the PEN/ESPN Award for literary sports writing. She is also the author of three additional nonfiction titles, a former professional basketball player, and spent seven years as a journalist at ESPN. Kate currently lives in Charleston with her wife, Kathryn Budig, and their dog, Ragnar.

The employees of Thorndike Press hope you have enjoyed this Large Print book. All our Thorndike Large Print titles are designed for easy reading, and all our books are made to last. Other Thorndike Press Large Print books are available at your library, through selected bookstores, or directly from us.

For information about titles, please visit our website at:

http://gale.cengage.com/thorndike